THE SHUTTLE BAY DOORS
REMAINED SEALED . . .

. . . but Morgan Lefler, mother to Lieutenant Robin Lefler, did not see that as being a problem for much longer.

From the shuttle's control panel, she targeted the bay doors and opened fire. The phasers blasted outward, pounding into the doors and easily smashing through them, sending large pieces of the triple-layered duranium doors tumbling into space.

She prepared to lift off . . . and that was when something ricocheted off the front of the shuttle, tumbling away. Then she heard something much fainter, a bump against the lower section of the ship.

"I don't believe it," she said.

Ambassador Si Cwan, former prince of the Thallonian Empire, was clutching the right warp nacelle of the shuttle, with bare seconds to live before the howling vacuum of space dragged him to his death. . . .

STAR TREK®
NEW FRONTIER

BOOK SIX

FIRE ON HIGH

PETER DAVID

New Frontier concept by
John J. Ordover and Peter David

POCKET BOOKS
New York   London   Toronto   Sydney   Tokyo   Singapore

An *Original* Publication of POCKET BOOKS

POCKET BOOKS, a division of Simon & Schuster Inc.
1230 Avenue of the Americas, New York, NY 10020

STAR TREK is a Registered Trademark of Paramount Pictures.

A VIACOM COMPANY

This book is published by Pocket Books, a division of Simon & Schuster Inc., under exclusive license from Paramount Pictures.

ISBN: 0-671-02037-4

First Pocket Books printing April 1998

10 9 8 7 6 5 4 3 2 1

POCKET and colophon are registered trademarks of Simon & Schuster Inc.

Printed in the U.S.A.

FIRE ON HIGH

ELSEWHERE . . .

THE ONLY SOUND ON THE PLANET Ahmista is the sound of a woman singing.

Oh, there are a few other sounds as well, but they are merely the sounds of the planet itself. The gentle breeze glides across the plains, moving the ashes through the air with subtle urging. (The ashes have been there for quite some time, but they dwindle in quantity with every passing day and every vagrant breeze, to say nothing of the cleansing provided by the occasional storm or downpour.)

There are also the normal grindings of tectonic plates, and a continent away there's an island of volcanoes that can raise a particularly impressive racket. Birds flap their wings against the wind; waves lap against shores, occasionally leaving a film of ash decorating the beaches.

But other than that . . . nothing.

The noise is rather conspicuous in its absence. No noise of a living, breathing population. There are none of the sounds of industry. Nor are there the sounds of people laughing or talking, or children crying out to be tended to. There are no sounds as subtle as lovers whispering in the dark, or as officious as bombs whistling through the air.

Nothing but her singing.

It is an odd song in that the tune seems to vary from one moment to the next. She lilts her way through it, never stopping except at those times when her fatigued mind and body require sleep. She does not like to give in to those urges, because it interferes with her vigilance, but every so often her head simply droops forward of its own accord and sleep steals into her head. Hours can pass with her in that condition, but then she snaps awake and is neither conscious nor caring of how much time has genuinely passed.

Even if there were sounds of any living beings on Ahmista, it is unlikely that she would hear them. She lives upon a mountain, if such a term as "lives" can be applied to her existence. It is not the highest mountain on Ahmista, but it is a fairly nice one, as mountains go. She is not quite at such an altitude as to feel a significant chill . . . not that she would even if it were subzero temperatures, because her lover keeps her warm.

In fact, her lover does more than that. Her lover keeps her company, her lover keeps her close. Her lover is the be-all and end-all of her existence on the planet, of her existence in the universe. She feels her lover in her mind, and she is content.

Her lover is sleek and gray, vaguely cylindrical in

2

shape but with a variety of sections branching off in an assortment of directions. Its sections are inserted directly into her nervous system at a dozen points. In a way, her lover looks like a great thorny bush with limbs trailing off and intertwining with one another. And ultimately, all the branches come back to her, and she comes back to it, for together they are one. Together they are a whole. They complete one another.

She is singing to her lover more than she is to herself.

Her lover never tells her what it thinks of her songs. That's okay, really. She doesn't need to hear her lover's approval, because she knows she already has that. How could she not? After all, she has given her life over to her lover. She neither needs, nor wants, anything else. Her lover gives her so much. Gives her nutrients, gives her life and the ability to live. And all she need do is make her lover her entire reason for living. That she has managed to do.

It suddenly pulses in a different manner beneath her fingers. She has been drifting slightly, but the alert manner of her lover snaps her back to full focus. She reaches out with her mind, reaches out through her lover.

There is a creature.

It has just hatched from an egg, approximately twenty miles away, deep in a forest that is otherwise devoid of life. It is small, covered with fur, and looking for a mother who is long since dead. It has no claws, not yet. It's fairly helpless, really, at this point. Without its mother, it might very likely die on its own. However, it might be resourceful enough to survive, to grow and thrive. And possibly someday be a threat. Birds . . . birds have never been a threat, and for some reason she has always considered the sounds of their wings comforting. This, though, she cannot chance. She knows that. Her lover knows that. Or at least, she knows it now that her lover has told her, but she is—of course—in complete agreement.

At her urging, her lover reaches out with a crackle of energy, shudders slightly in her grip, and belches out an energy ball. It's nothing particularly large, because none such is needed. The energy that her lover is capable of disgorging is directly proportionate to whatever job is required. In this instance, it's fairly insignificant.

The energy ball covers the intervening distance in no time at all. The newborn creature senses something coming, looks up, and feels a source of light and heat. Its little eyes are still blind and so it cannot see what is approaching, but nonetheless makes the false—if understandable—assumption that it's about to meet its mother. It opens its mouth wide and makes a small *yeep* sound.

A second later, it's enveloped by the energy. The creature didn't really have time to have a full sense of its own existence before it didn't have an existence anymore. Instead it is reduced, in no time at all, to little more than a pile of ash. There is a hint of a tiny claw in there, and a few stray tufts of fur flutter away, caught in the breeze that quickly stirs the ashes into nothingness. Otherwise, though, there's no sign that the creature was ever there.

Back on the mountaintop, she begins to tremble. She wraps herself more tightly around her lover than before, for she knows that it has acted to protect her.

The knowledge is exciting to her, stimulates her, and she begins to tremble.

She runs her hands along the surface of her lover. She has stopped singing. Instead she is beginning to quiver in anticipation, for this is how she always feels when her lover shows its strength on her behalf. And her lover knows that it has pleased her, and that knowledge excites it in kind.

She gasps out a name . . . a name known only to her and her lover. A name that has never even been spoken aloud, but is instead something communicated without need of clumsy speech. It is something deep within their mutual soul, for her lover was soulless until she had joined with it.

It had been so long since she felt the fire within her, that for the briefest of moments she entertains the notion that her lover had sought out something to kill for her. Something to obliterate, because that was the only way that it could possibly find sufficient stimulation to give her, and itself, what it needed.

But then she quickly dismisses the idea from her mind. Her lover would never do that, would have no need to do that. Her lover is not the embodiment of destruction. No. Her lover is the giver of light, the provider of joy.

The heat fill her mind, radiates from throughout her lover, and she can feel her heart speeding up, thudding against her chest with such abandon and power that it threatens to burst through her rib cage. If that were to happen, of course, then she would die, but she is not concerned. She trusts her lover implicitly. She knows it would not hurt her.

Her lover, though, is not mortal. She realizes that on some sort of base level. Her lover is something else, something special. Something beyond anything that she has ever known before.

And she comes to the realization, even as its love floods through her, that she can never return to anything that once was.

Her lover prefers the silence, for it makes it that much easier for it to hear her as she starts to sob with the pure joy she derives from their bonding.

It used to come much more frequently, back when there was more life on the planet. As each thing threatened her, her lover dispensed with it, and each demise would fill her with orgasmic pleasure. Such encounters now are few and far between, but that is all right with her. She has her memories, and she has her lover to keep her warm, safe, loved.

Slowly, so slowly, she tries to steady the pounding of her heart. She sags against her lover, clutching it even as her fingers open and close spasmodically. Deep in her chest she laughs softly to herself, enjoying the warmth her lover has given her and the sense of security and safety.

"Thank you," she whispers, which are the first words spoken on the planet in some time. "Thank you . . . for that. Thank you for being mine. Thank you . . . for choosing me."

Her lover does not reply, nor does it need to. It simply continues to pulse against her, and if it is pleased that it has given her pleasure, or displeased at her reactions, or completely uncaring, it's really impossible to say. It just sits quietly, unchanged, unreacting. She strokes it once more and she feels her consciousness drifting. She wants to stay awake, unwilling to surrender to a hazy sensation of bliss that threatens to carry her away to slumber. "Not . . .

tired," she moans like a petulant child being shunted away for a nap, and she does her best to resist.

Ultimately, however, she fails. Her eyes flutter closed, her head sags forward and thumps gently against the metal sheath that is the exterior of her lover. Moments later, still warm from the gentle pleasures of her lovemaking, she falls into a peaceful sleep. She does not snore, does not make any extraneous noise. And so, for a time at least, there is no vaguely humanoid sound on the planet Ahmista aside from her soft breathing as she sleeps. Sooner or later, though, she will awaken once more. At that point, she will begin singing again in that odd, aimless way she has, remembering what her previous lovemaking was like and wondering when the next opportunity will come along. . . .

I.

COMMANDER ELIZABETH SHELBY ran the video log of the bridge of the *Excalibur,* not quite able to believe what she was seeing.

Nearby Dr. Maxwell was watching her with an apologetic expression on his face. Behind him, sickbay personnel were going on about their business as Shelby sat in the private office usually used by Dr. Selar, studying the last moments of consciousness she had known before keeling over several days ago. She had been certain that she was fully recovered but now, watching the video log with a growing sense of doom, she was wondering if perhaps she should take a permanent sick leave.

Through her off-the-cuff strategy, she had just managed to dispatch a warship belonging to the dreaded Redeemers by using, literally, the power of a sun to do so. But she had come on to the bridge still suffering from head injuries sustained during a disastrous landing expedition to the planet Zondar. All she remembered was that she had passed out right after saving the *Excalibur* from destruction, but now she was watching the immediate aftermath.

She watched herself leap to her feet, her fists exuberantly pumping the air over her head. She called out triumphantly, "Hah! Spectacular! Engineering, great job! You too, McHenry! Excellent all around! Oh! Look!" She pointed into midair.

"Look at what, sir?" McHenry was asking.

"Colors!" Shelby called out excitedly—and then she pitched forward, Si Cwan just barely catching her before she hit the floor.

But that wasn't the worst of it.

She wasn't unconscious, oh no. No, that would've been too merciful. Instead she had stared up into the air as Si Cwan had said with concern, "Are you all right, Commander?"

"They're all different colors!" Shelby had said. "Blue, green, pink . . ."

Si Cwan looked with confusion at the others on the bridge, who seemed equally perplexed. "What are, Commander?"

"The colors!" Shelby had said again, joyously. And then she had passed out.

In sickbay, separated from the event by several days, Shelby clicked off the video record and tried not to display the pain she was feeling. She was not especially successful, unfortunately.

"You said you wanted to see it, Commander," Maxwell reminded her as if concerned she was going to be angry with him. "I advised against it, remember."

"I remember," she sighed.

"It's not important, Commander. It was just a . . . a stream of consciousness comment. Dreaming with your eyes awake. I guarantee you, no one's going to think about it or even remember it by now. And I'm certain that absolutely no one is going to kid you about it."

She looked up at him bleakly. "On *this* ship? No way are they going to let it go," she said as if she were awaiting her turn to step into the cart that would bring her to the guillotine. She put her face in her hands. "Face it, Doctor—I'm a dead woman."

"She looks rather healthy for a dead woman."

Mackenzie Calhoun, captain of the *Excalibur,* scratched his chin thoughtfully as he studied the picture that was staring back out at him from the computer screen. On either side of the table, Ambassador Si Cwan—former head of the Thallonian ruling class—and Lieutenant Robin Lefler, the ship's Ops officer and part-time assistant to Cwan, had just heard him make this pronouncement. Although Lefler generally had a very ready smile, it wasn't on display at that particular moment. Si Cwan, who customarily had something of a deadpan, didn't look any different than he usually did.

Calhoun leaned forward thoughtfully as if closer examination might yield some bit of information that he'd previously missed. The picture on the screen was of a woman with long, dark hair, a square chin, narrow nose, and a steady gaze that appeared to have a piercing, intensely intelligent air to it. Not an easy thing to project over a mere photograph made for computer identification, but somehow she had managed it. He could only wonder what she was like in person, if that was how she came across in a simple photo.

"So let's see if I've got this straight," he said after a moment, meeting Lefler's gaze. "The Momidiums, out in the Gamma Hydrinae system, claim that this woman was rooting around on their planet about five years ago. This would have made her a trespasser as far as both the Momidiums and the overseers of the Thallonian Empire"—and he gestured suavely to Si Cwan—"were concerned."

"That is correct."

"If the Momidiums had turned her over to the Thallonians, they likely would have executed her."

"I dislike the term 'execute,'" Si Cwan said. "It sounds distasteful to me. Cruel and most impersonal."

"Your pardon, Ambassador," said Calhoun. "How about 'killed'?"

"Much better."

"As you wish. They likely would have killed her." He watched Si Cwan nod his head in agreement and continued, "However, they had no desire to overlook the crimes of trespass and perhaps spying, so they imprisoned her. Have they given any indication as to precisely what they have to hide that they thought was subject for a spy's interest?"

Si Cwan glanced at Lefler, to whom the question seemed addressed, but she made no reply and he came to the realization that she was barely listening. He lightly tapped her shin under the table while stepping in himself to say, "No indication at all,

Captain. They have been fairly circumspect in that regard. As with most sentient beings, they like to have their secrets."

"Fine. We nccdn't dwell on that at the moment. But now," he said thoughtfully as he drummed his fingers, "they want to make nice to us, so they offer to turn this female over to us. One Morgan Primus by name." Even though he knew the name he nonetheless glanced at the computer screen for reaffirmation, much as someone who has just looked at his watch will look at it once more if someone asks him the time even a second later. "They offer her in exchange for certain promises which you, *Lieutenant Lefler,* feel are not unreasonable."

He said her name with sufficient emphasis that it appeared to jolt her from her slightly dreamy and distracted state. "I'm sorry . . . ?" she said as she realized she wasn't focused on the question.

"The Momidiums," Si Cwan gently cued her. "About their demands . . ."

"Oh. Not unreasonable at all, sir," she said quickly. "They are a fairly simple people, actually. They desire some advice from any agricultural specialists on designs for a new irrigation system they've developed for their farmland. Oh, and they have a flu epidemic in one of their outlying provinces. They believe that they've managed to synthesize a cure, but it will take them approximately two weeks to finish running tests on it, and they want to know if our facilities could possibly cut that time down."

"And—?"

"I've already run it past Dr. Maxwell, sir. He assures me that our labs could test the effectiveness of the cure through cross-matching and molecular analysis within three hours of receiving it."

"Good. And if the good doctor finds flaws in the formula, I imagine it would not be overly demanding for him to correct those flaws, now, would it."

"Bordering on Prime Directive violation, isn't that, Captain?" inquired Si Cwan.

"Bordering but not over the line, Ambassador," replied Calhoun. "However, in this instance, Starfleet agreed to give us some latitude. So, Lieutenant, in exchange for these agreements, the Momidiums will present us with this human female."

"That's right, sir."

"A female whom you claim could pass for your mother's twin."

"No twin, sir," said Lefler and she tapped the screen with a knuckle. "That is my mother."

"The mother whom you said died in a shuttle accident about ten years ago."

Lefler squared her shoulders, pulling herself up straight, for Calhoun had made no effort to hide the disbelief in his voice. "That's correct, sir. Morgan Lefler. At least, that's the name I always knew her by. 'Primus' wasn't even her maiden name, so I don't know where that name came from."

"And was the shuttle accident anywhere in this vicinity?"

"No, sir. Actually, it was in New Jersey. She was on vacation, visiting family there. She was flying a private shuttle and it went out of control and crashed into the Atlantic Ocean."

"You'll excuse me if I don't seem properly sympathetic to your, uhm . . . loss," he said, leaning back in his chair, "but do you have any theories or guesses as to how your late mother managed to get all the way from a watery grave to the Gamma Hydrinae system?"

"I believe," she said promptly, for naturally she had given the matter no small amount of thought, "that she never died in the accident."

"Well, that would certainly follow."

"Her body was never recovered after the crash. They found the shattered remains of her personal transport shuttle, but it was cracked open and there was no sign of her. Since there were no traces of transporter energy or any other intelligent agency that might have rescued or abducted her, we had always assumed that some . . . some oceanic form of life had simply made off with her body and, uhm . . ."

"Eaten it?" Si Cwan supplied after she was silent for a moment.

She fired him an icy look. "Yes, thank you," she said, although she didn't sound especially appreciative. "That was the phrase I was searching for."

"You're welcome," replied Si Cwan graciously, sarcasm being totally lost on him.

"It is my belief," continued Lefler, "that she allowed us—my father and me—to believe that she had been killed."

"She could have been kidnapped."

"She had been."

"But I thought you said . . ."

"She had been, to my knowledge, abducted at least eight times in my lifetime. She was not a stay-at-home kind of mother. Each time she escaped within hours and returned within days. After the accident, my father and I held out hope for a long time. Hope that she would just walk in the front door. In the end, we had no choice but to assume she was dead."

"Were your parents getting along? Happy marriage and all?"

"To the best of my knowledge, yes, sir. Certainly nothing my father said to me indicated otherwise. He, uhm . . ." She looked down. "He . . . passed away several years later, shortly after I entered Starfleet. He was never quite the same after she was killed, and it was like he just . . . just drifted away from life, and was only waiting until my life was on track and settled before he . . ."

Si Cwan reached over and put a hand upon one of hers. The contrast could not have been greater, for his hands were large and red, while hers were small, pale, and rather delicate. Under other circumstances, the physical contact between her and Si Cwan would have sent a secret little thrill of pleasure through her, but as it was she was simply grateful for the gesture. She squeezed his hand tightly in acknowledgment and he nodded slightly as if to say that he understood.

"I'm sorry for your loss, Lieutenant," Calhoun told her. "But that still leaves us with the question of why she would vanish without a trace ten years ago only to show up in Thallonian space."

"I don't know!" Lefler cried, her voice raised, and she quickly realized that her tone was inappropriate for such a response, particularly considering that she was addressing her commanding officer. She looked at him nervously, but he simply put up a calming hand, indicating that she shouldn't get too concerned over the breach of etiquette. "I don't know," she repeated, far more calmly this time. "I suppose that's why I'm

rather eager to find out. When can we leave, sir? Our mission on Zondar is concluded, but we're still in orbit here. We could easily depart immediately for—"

"In case you haven't noticed, Lieutenant, our science officer is still not aboard."

"Yes, of course I noticed, sir," Lefler said. "She's on the Zondarian surface exploring some sort of archaeological dig. Can't that be concluded another time, sir? Or perhaps we could come back for her?"

"Lieutenant, as much as I appreciate your anxiety here, this is simply not an emergency."

"Captain!"

He shook his head, a grim smile of amusement playing across his lips. "If it's really your mother, Lieutenant, and you've believed her dead for the last ten years—and she's been stewing on Momidium for the last five—then a few more days isn't going to cause the total collapse of the galaxy as we know it."

"Then let me go on ahead."

"Negative, Lieutenant. The last time I sent any members of this crew 'on ahead' in a shuttle, it was with the best of intentions with the most cataclysmic results."

"Captain, this is hardly the same situation," Si Cwan said. "I know what you're referring to: When the science vessel *Kayven Ryin* informed us that my sister was aboard, it turned out to be a trap set for me by an old enemy. But the situations are hardly analogous, Captain. It's not as if the lieutenant has enemies in this sector."

"I'm not saying she does, Ambassador," replied Calhoun. "The point is, the moment I send any of my people away from the *Excalibur,* I'm sending them into potential danger. I won't hesitate to do so if I feel it's necessary. In this instance, I don't feel it is."

"But Captain . . ." began Lefler.

He looked at her levelly. "Lieutenant, are you under the impression that my decision is open for debate?"

She opened her mouth a moment, then closed it and looked down. "No, sir," she said quietly.

"Good. The fact is that Lieutenant Soleta's investigations are potentially very important for our ongoing mission, and I'm not going to put a phaser to her head and tell her to hurry it up. Nor am I going to abandon her on Zondar so we can head off to retrieve your alleged mother."

"Yes, sir," sighed Lefler.

Calhoun tapped his commbadge. "Calhoun to Soleta."

After a moment, the science officer's voice came back. "Soleta here."

"Lieutenant, I'm not trying to rush you, but a matter has come up that may require our attention. Can you give me a rough estimate of when you'll be completing your investigation of Ontear's cave and the surrounding vicinity?"

"Nineteen hours, twenty-seven minutes, Captain."

He blinked in surprise. "Nineteen hours, twenty-seven minutes?"

"Yes, sir."

"I'm surprised you didn't pin it down to the exact number of remaining seconds."

"You *did* say a rough estimate, Captain," she replied.

"So I did," admitted Calhoun. "All right, thank you, Lieutenant. Calhoun out." He turned to face Lefler and Si Cwan. "Ambassador, I would like you to contact the Momidium government. Let them know that their terms are acceptable if they are indeed as described. I respect the fact that there is a time pressure regarding the illness they are trying to combat, but we won't be able to set out for about a solar day. I assume they can hold on until then."

"I imagine they will have to," said Si Cwan.

"Lieutenant, follow up with Dr. Maxwell. Inform him that we will indeed be needing sickbay's assistance in this matter and that they should have some lab time set aside to accommodate us."

"Yes, sir."

He thumped his palms on the table. "Sounds like a plan," he said briskly and rose. "Unless there's anything else then . . . ?"

Si Cwan and Lefler looked at each other questioningly. "No, I think that is more or less all, Captain," Lefler said.

"Good." He rose, and then paused and added, "Lieutenant . . . for what it's worth, I truly am sorry over the personal difficulties you've had with your parents."

"Thank you, Captain."

He nodded, turned and walked out.

Lefler sat back and sighed. "That didn't go as well as I'd hoped."

"He agreed to make Momidium our next port of call," replied Si Cwan. "Considering the number of worlds that are vying for our attention, that alone is something of an accomplishment."

She sat forward, propping her chin up in her hands. "It's insane, Si Cwan. I feel like Alice."

"Alice?" His brow furrowed. "What is an 'Alice'?"

She sighed. "When I was a little girl, one of my favorite books was *Alice in Wonderland.* My mother introduced me to it, in fact."

"I can't say I'm familiar with it."

"I wouldn't imagine it made the Thallonian best-seller list," she said, speaking with an amusement she didn't really feel. "It was actually somewhat subversive in its time. It was created to be a satire of Brit— of a particular Earth government. But functioning in and of itself, it's the story of a young girl who falls down a hole burrowed by an animal called a rabbit and discovers herself in a strange and mystical realm in which no one and nothing makes any sense. It has maintained its popularity for centuries."

"I can easily understand why. Entering a realm that makes no sense? My dear Lieutenant, the technical term for that is 'birth.' Or are you under the mistaken impression that life as a whole makes sense?"

"I guess not, but damn it, Si Cwan, you'd think some things would be a given, wouldn't you?"

"A given?" He looked at her quizzically, and then he rose from his chair and slowly circled the room, never taking his eyes off her. They had that piercing quality that she found so attractive in him, but somehow at that moment, she wasn't really paying attention to them. "What things?"

"Losing my mom . . . it was . . ." She took a deep breath and then said, "Look . . . this isn't stuff we really have to discuss, okay? I mean, it's kind of personal. And you and I . . . we don't really know each other all that well, when you get down to it. I mean, we've known each other for a little while, but not enough for me to feel comfortable discussing it with you."

"Are you certain?"

He was behind her then, and he placed a hand on her shoulder. She felt the strength in it then, even more so than when he had rested his hand atop hers earlier. Part of her wanted to embrace him, to just flee from the turmoil going through her mind by disappearing into his large and powerful arms. But she was feeling vulnerable at that moment, more so than she could recall in quite some time. Her gut reaction was to keep her distance from him, and after another moment's thought, that was exactly what she decided to do.

She stood quickly, gently brushing his hand away as she did so. "I'm sorry," she said, sounding more brusque than she would have liked.

"No need to apologize," he said mildly. "This is a very difficult time for you."

"I should be glad," she told him, although it was as if she were speaking more to herself than to him. "Really, I should be glad. I mean . . . if it's her, if it's really her . . . I get a second chance. Whatever the reasons, I get a second chance with her, and that's really the important thing, isn't it?"

"Is it?"

"Yes," she said firmly. "Yes, it is, and everything's fine, and we don't have to discuss it anymore. I appreciate your help, but I'm going to be fine, okay?"

"Okay."

"And I shouldn't be looking for things to be wrong with what should be a joyous moment. Lefler's Law

Number Thirty-two: If life hands you lemonade, don't try to make lemons out of it. Do you agree?"

"If I knew what lemonade was, probably."

"Good. Good." She seemed about to say something else, but instead she quickly exited the room, leaving a more-than-puzzled Si Cwan wondering if there was something else he should have said.

II.

IN SICKBAY, ENSIGN RONNI BETH lay back on a medical table, her wavy hair surrounding her face like a corona of curls. As she did so, Dr. Karen Kurdziel checked the scanner readings and nodded approvingly. Kurdziel was a trim, blue-haired woman with an apparently endless amount of patience and a keen sense of the absurd. Both of those were serving her well at that particular moment.

"I'm gonna kill him," Beth said for what seemed the hundredth time.

"I know you are," said Kurdziel. "You've made that painfully clear." She ran her tricorder over Beth's ankle. "That's healing up nicely. Look, do me a favor and stay off the slopes, okay, Ron? Even holodeck slopes are tricky for novice skiers."

"Yeah, yeah, yeah," Ronni said impatiently. "Can I sit up?"

Kurdziel nodded and Beth sat up, pulling on her boot gingerly. "He was supposed to be with me," she fumed. "Did I tell you this?"

"Yes," Kurdziel said.

As if Kurdziel hadn't spoken, Beth continued, "Christiano was supposed to meet me on the slopes. He promised me. Then he's running late, and I figure, no problem, so I start a trial run because I figure, you know, how difficult can this be?"

"And you found out." Kurdziel was trying to remain sympathetic, but even her infinite patience was beginning to flag. Beth had been involved with Ensign Christiano, who was in Engineering same as she was. But that relationship had apparently just crashed and burned, as Beth was quick to tell anyone who was stationary for longer than five seconds.

"Yeah, but that was nothing compared to finding out he was with another woman. And after the ring I gave him!"

"Ring?" This was news to Kurdziel. "What ring?"

"Got it off a dealer on space station K-Nineteen. Picked it up just before being assigned here. I was . . . I dunno . . . I was saving it for just the right guy. And I thought sure Christiano was him."

"So ask for it back," Kurdziel told her matter-of-factly.

"I'm not going to ask for it back!" Beth said indignantly. "It was a gift."

"If an engagement is broken off, isn't it customary to ask for the ring back?"

"But this wasn't part of an engagement. I just gave

it to him because . . ." She looked down. "Because I really felt like he was the one. So I got ahead of myself and did something stupid. And now I know for next time. Live and learn."

"I'm sorry, Ensign."

"Well, it's a sorry galaxy, I guess."

She was about to say something else along those lines, but then she noticed something. She didn't want to point, because somehow it seemed rude, so instead she just angled her chin in the general direction of where she was indicating and asked, "She's up and around?"

Kurdziel looked where Beth was pointing and, by way of responding to the question, said, "Commander. You're looking fit."

Commander Shelby was striding across sickbay in her familiar confident manner. There was still some faint discoloration on her face from injuries sustained during a fairly battering excursion on the surface of Zondar, but at this point she seemed none the worse for wear from it.

"Feeling ready to get back to work?" Dr. Kurdziel asked.

"You could say that," Shelby said agreeably. She flexed her shoulder. "Still feel a little tightness, but Dr. Maxwell assures me that'll pass."

"If he says so, I'm sure it's true."

"Other than that, I've been judged fit for duty." She smiled, looking somewhat relieved. "I'm not much for sitting around and recuperating. Glad to be back in action."

"The way I heard it, you got back into action a little too . . . fast . . ." said Ronni Beth, her voice trailing off, realizing that, woozy from the painkiller she was under, she'd actually spoken aloud. Immediately she tried to figure out if there was some worse way she could have shoved her foot in her mouth. If it weren't for the painkiller . . .

Shelby, whose back was to her, slowly turned, her smile frozen on her face. "I beg your pardon?" she said with a voice that would have frosted a supernova.

"I'm sorry, I—Oh, look at the time," Beth said quickly, hopping off the table and trying not to hobble. "I'd better get go—"

"I asked you a question, Ensign," Shelby said, taking a half step that put her squarely in Beth's path, making it clear in a fairly unsubtle manner that Beth wasn't going anywhere.

"I . . ." She looked to Kurdziel for help, but Kurdziel simply shrugged in a way that said, *You're on your own.* Looking visibly pained, Beth said, "Well, word was that you went back to the bridge during a red alert, that you put us on a collision course with a sun, and that you passed out after seeing . . ."

"After seeing what?" pressed Shelby, no less icy.

Beth said something very quietly.

"I didn't catch that," prompted Shelby.

"Colors," Beth said more loudly. "Word is that you pointed into midair, said, 'Oh look! Colors!' and fainted dead away."

"And did 'word' also mention," inquired Shelby, "that my maneuver toward the Zondarian sun saved this vessel and all aboard—including, might I point out, yourself?"

"As a matter of fact, yes," Beth admitted.

"Good. Because as long as the crew is having a laugh at my expense," said Shelby, raising her voice a bit so that it carried, catching the attention of others in sickbay, "it would be nice for them to remember that particular respect is to be accorded all senior officers of a starship. Particularly those senior officers who have, through their actions, kept everyone on the *Excalibur* in one piece. Understood?"

"Understood, Commander."

"Understood?" she said again, this time directing it to the general populace of sickbay, and she got nods from everyone there. With that settled, she squared her shoulders and walked out of sickbay.

Lefler's quarters were not especially large, but she'd never been much for anything fancy. She was more of a people person, really, and so spent very little time in her quarters. A friend of hers had once speculated that Robin Lefler had only one true fear in the galaxy, and that was of being alone. That her need to be with people was so incessant that solitude was utterly anathema. When informed of her friend's appraisal, Lefler had vehemently denied it while, at the same time, wondering to herself if there wasn't just a little bit of truth to it.

At this particular point in time, however, she wanted nothing but to be alone. Even though she was on duty, even though she should have by rights been heading up to the bridge, she had bolted into her quarters, the door sliding shut behind her. She closed her eyes, leaning against a bulkhead, and slowly shook her head. "It can't be her," she whispered. "She couldn't have done that. It can't possibly be her."

She said that several more times before gathering herself and going to one of her dresser drawers. She pulled it open, rummaged around for a moment, and then removed a holotube. It was a cylinder about six inches tall, and inside was a carefully preserved hologram of her mother, the late Morgan Lefler.

She remembered the day she had gotten it. It had been the day before her mother had died.

She recalled how the irony had weighed heavily upon her. How her mother had had the hologram produced as purely a spur of the moment thing. A gift to send off to her beloved daughter, a keepsake with no particular meaning other than that her mom was thinking about her. No . . . no, there had been another meaning, Lefler now recalled. She and her mom had had a big fight the night before. Her mother had made it clear that she had matters to attend to and that she absolutely had to go off and visit relatives the next day, and so she had left her daughter—for the last time, as it turned out—with things still unsettled between them. Robin racked her brains, trying to remember what it was that she and her mother had argued about, and she couldn't for the life of her recall.

All she could remember was the guilt that she had carried with her when she'd gotten that hologram the day after her mother had died.

Not died.

Abandoned her.

With a strangled roar of humiliation, anger, and frustration, Lefler's arm drew back and she hurled the holotube with all her strength. It flew across the room and, in her mind's eye, shattered, the tiny pieces of the delicate technology littering her floor like so many precious snowflakes.

Unfortunately, or fortunately, depending upon how one looked at it, the holotube was made to last. All it did was ricochet off the wall and land on the floor with a gentle clatter. It rolled a few feet and then came to a stop.

She looked at the holotube lying there on the floor, and felt it was looking at her mockingly. Feeling anger building inside her, she moved quickly toward it and stomped down on it. But the tube shot out from under her foot, rolled up against the wall, and lay there.

Robin let out a sigh, her initial rage spent. She walked over to the holotube, picked it up and looked at it while slowly shaking her head. "You always did have a knack for bouncing back, Mom," she said ruefully before putting the tube carefully back into the drawer from which she'd removed it.

Shelby was convinced that everyone was looking at her.

Stop it! You're being paranoid! she scolded herself as she made her way down the corridors of the *Excalibur*, but she simply couldn't help herself. Looks or nods of the head that previously would have greeted her without her thinking anything of it now seemed fraught with hidden meaning. She was convinced that the entire crew was laughing at her behind her back.

Colors?

What had she been thinking? What in God's name had been going through her mind?

Try as she might, she couldn't dredge up the slightest reason why such a complete non sequitur would have popped out of her mouth. Sure, she had been a bit punchy. When they'd carted her back to sickbay, the doctors there couldn't believe that she'd been up and around at all. Even so . . .

Colors?

What could possibly have possessed her?

This was ridiculous, Shelby realized, as she headed for a turbolift. She couldn't figure out why she was being this way.

All right, that wasn't true. She did have some inklings. It had to do with the fact that, to some degree, she had felt like, and continued to feel like, an outsider on her own ship. Her style was very different from Mackenzie Calhoun's, and although they were supposed to be working in tandem, she still couldn't help but feel a streak of competitiveness with him. That was the truth of it, really. In many ways—in *all* ways—Shelby felt as if she were not only extremely qualified for command, but more qualified than Calhoun. Yet she was playing support to him, and not only that, but it seemed to her as if the crew liked him more than her.

It's not about being liked, she scolded herself. That wasn't it at all. It was about getting the job done. It was about acting in the best interests of Starfleet. It was about routine, and regulations, and procedures, and getting back in one piece. Calhoun, damn him, could afford to be flamboyant, daring, and heroic. He had Shelby to clean up the mess for him: Shelby to run interference with Starfleet, Shelby to remind him of the way things should be done as he thoughtlessly flaunted the rules. Calhoun was busy carving himself a status that could only be considered legendary, and here was Shelby, feeling like a grunt.

Besides that, she felt extremely vulnerable in that status. And matters hadn't been helped by recent developments.

But, dammit, she *had* sustained injury. That was the thing to remember. That's what she should be thinking about.

The turbolift opened and she stepped onto it. "Bridge," she said briskly.

The lift hurtled toward the bridge, and as it did so, she continued to ponder the situation. She knew the reputation she was developing around the ship. Grim, humorless, a total hard-case.

The turbolift slowed and the doors slid open. Robin Lefler was standing there, her hands draped behind her back, looking lost in thought. She glanced up and looked mildly surprised to see Shelby there. "Oh! Commander! Feeling better?"

"Just heading up to the bridge." She gestured for Lefler to join her and the lieutenant quickly did so. As the doors slid shut and the lift continued its way upward, Shelby suddenly inquired, "Lieutenant . . . you hear people talk. You get around. You know what people around here have on their minds."

"I . . . guess I do, yes," allowed Lefler. "I am in charge of Ops, so I tend to—"

"To the best of your knowledge, does the crew lampoon me? Behind my back? Do they value my contributions and qualifications?"

The questions seemed to catch Lefler completely off guard. "I beg your pardon?"

"Am I . . ." She tried to find the best way to express it, but nothing seemed to come to mind immediately. Finally, for want of a better phrase, she said, "Am I . . . 'one of the guys'?"

Lefler stared at her as if she'd grown a third eye. "Would you want to be?"

"I . . ." She'd been looking at Lefler, but now she

stared at the door. "I don't know. I don't know that fraternizing with the officers is a particularly good idea."

"But is being so rigid all the time a good idea either?"

Now she looked back at Lefler and there was a slightly pained smile on her face. "Is that what they say I am?"

The door to the bridge hissed open and Shelby strode out, brimming with new confidence. Lefler walked quickly past her and headed over to her station at Ops. Mark McHenry, at the conn, was sitting and staring dreamily at the world of Zondar turning lazily below them. He looked as if his thoughts were a million miles away, but by this point Lefler—and everyone else on the bridge—was used to him, knowing that his apparent distractedness was just that: apparent.

Calhoun was seated in the command chair, going over a report, and he glanced up when Shelby entered. It was as if he were expecting her. But she was in no hurry to walk down to his level, feeling perfectly content instead to stand on the upper deck of the bridge and look down. She found that it gave her a nice dominant feeling, like a queen on high regarding her realm. Zak Kebron, standing at the tactical station, didn't even glance her way.

The captain raised a questioning eyebrow. "It's good to see you, Commander. Planning to come down here and join us?"

"Of course, sir. It's good to be back."

She slowly walked down the ramp, and as she did so she looked over the bridge personnel. She tried to see if any of them were grinning her way, or whispering among themselves, or in any other way behaving in a disrespectful or discourteous manner that would not only have been not in keeping with Starfleet decorum, but would have been inappropriate in keeping with the respect that she was due.

Calhoun caught her eye and made a subtle "come here" gesture. She drew close to him and he said in a low voice, "Are you all right?"

"I'm fine, sir. Why?"

"You seem . . . stiff."

"I'm displaying posture and poise that is suitable for a Starfleet officer," she replied.

Calhoun had been slouching slightly in his chair, and she felt a bit of smug satisfaction as he reflexively drew himself up. Nodding slightly as if having achieved a major personal triumph, she moved around the edge of her chair and took her place in it.

"Our current situation," Calhoun informed her, "just to keep you apprised, is that we are continuing to orbit Zondar pending Science Officer Soleta's return. We will then be setting course for the planet Momidium to pick up an individual being held there under . . . unusual circumstances."

Lefler overheard the conversation and breathed a small sigh of relief to herself that the captain remained deliberately vague. She didn't especially feel like having the bizarre circumstances of her potential maternal reunion being broadcast all over the bridge.

"All the information," continued Calhoun, "is in your duty log, Commander. You can get current on it at your leisure."

"Thank you, Captain," she said formally.

And then she waited . . . waited for him to say something, to make some sort of comment on the way in which she had handled matters in his absence. It would be perfectly in character for him to make some sort of teasing comment about the "bunnies," or—more appropriately—to offer even a cursory "well done" in regard to the way she had handled the conflict with the Redeemer war vessel that had wanted to blow them out of space.

But Calhoun said nothing. Instead he went back to studying his report, his legs comfortably crossed, his left foot waving in leisurely fashion.

She made a slow visual survey of the bridge. No one was looking at her. No one seemed particularly interested in welcoming her back other than with a quick, cursory nod. Otherwise, that was pretty much it.

She should have been happy about that; relieved even. Instead it left her feeling oddly discontent for some reason that she couldn't quite isolate.

The turbolift opened and Lieutenant Commander Burgoyne 172, chief engineer of the *Excalibur,* walked out. Shelby turned and looked at the Hermat. If there was anyone who could be counted on for making an offbeat, uninhibited response, it was Burgoyne.

"Chief," Calhoun acknowledged hir entrance.

"Captain," Burgoyne replied with a tilt of hir head. "I wanted to run some cross-checks on the energy transfer problems we've been having. Thought I'd use the station up here since the main one's being tied up for research."

"Be my guest," said Calhoun.

"Afternoon, Burgy," Shelby spoke up.

"Commander," replied Burgoyne by way of greeting, and then s/he went on about hir business.

That was it. That was all.

Shelby felt utterly crestfallen.

There was no reason whatsoever that the bridge crew should make a big deal over Shelby's handling of the crisis earlier. In her heart, she knew that. At most, the captain would make a notation of it in his log and register a commendation. But that was all. Nothing further need be acknowledged, because really, when you got down to it, Shelby had simply done her job. The fact that she had done it extremely well shouldn't really have factored into it.

Except . . .

Except that the *Excalibur* was unlike any other ship she'd served on.

She couldn't help but feel that part of it was that the crew took their cue from the captain. Calhoun was a cowboy, no question, who walked with a slight swagger, wore a look of weathered amusement, operated in unexpected and unorthodox manners, and seemed to delight in having little to no regard for the standard procedures under which other ships and commanding officers operated.

As for the situation that Shelby was in, the people she was surrounded by . . .

An ambassador who had come aboard the ship as a stowaway in the science officer's luggage; a conn officer who was . . . what *was* McHenry doing now? She glanced over at him and saw that he was moving his fingers in a manner that indicated he was making a cat's cradle with imaginary string. Okay, they had a conn officer who seemed barely there, except when he was needed. And he was having an affair with a multisexual chief engineer, who was in turn (according to the latest rumors, and since the entire vessel seemed to be powered not by dilithium crystals but by innuendo, it was probably accurate) serving to sate the mating lust of the normally staid chief medical officer. The head of security was relatively normal . . . at least as normal as a walking land mass could be, but the night-side security head was different story. A large, shaggy story. It was as if Calhoun had gone out of his way to handpick a crew designed to appeal to his eclectic and rather offbeat tastes. It was less like serving on a starship than serving on a funhouse mirror version of one. The only one who seemed relatively normal was Lefler.

Shelby glanced over her duty log, which had been kept up to date by her yeoman so that she would be able to review it handily. She took one look at her, saw that the intended passenger from Momidium was Lefler's mother, who had been dead for a decade, and moaned softly to herself. *Et tu, Lefler,* she thought.

Still, with all the quirkiness, with all the oddities that seemed prevalent through the vessel, everyone seemed to be having . . . Well, fun wasn't the right word. It was a combination of professionalism mixed with camaraderie.

That was it. That was the bottom line, really. There was an air of joie de vivre on the ship. For all the craziness that went on, for all the offbeat attitudes, everyone—from the captain down to the lowest ranking technician—all seemed to be *alive* and part of a circuit of energy.

And Shelby felt as if she wasn't a part of it. She felt wedded to decorum, a living incarnation of Starfleet rules and regulations. It was as if the ship was a party, and she was the designated pooper thereof.

It was not an attitude that made her feel particularly good about herself, but dammit, she was a trained Starfleet officer. Just because Calhoun's com-

mand style was very much a shoot-from-the-hip prop-
osition didn't mean that she had to go along with it.
She was complete unto herself, confident and sure of
the rightness of her worldview.

And yet . . . she was lonely.

She hated to admit it, but there it was. She had
chosen a certain way in which she desired to be
regarded, and the fact was, her return to the bridge had
been the test of that. If they'd teased her or lampooned
her, it would have been roundly insulting, and she
would have been well within her rights to light into
anyone who treated her in such a disrespectful manner.
But instead they treated her with the esteem to which
she was entitled. It should have made her feel good
about herself, but instead she couldn't help but feel as
if it just underscored her outsider status . . . the status
that she had been boasting of to Lefler just a little
earlier.

And then she heard something: the sound of slow,
steady hands slamming together. She opened her eyes
and turned to see Calhoun, standing, slowly applauding and nodding his head in approval.

Then McHenry joined in, as did Lefler. When
Kebron tried slamming his hands together it created
an almost deafening explosion of air, so he did it
more gently. But ultimately, within seconds, everyone
on the bridge was applauding Shelby and cheering.

And Shelby, to her own astonishment, started to
laugh.

She couldn't help it. She had clearly been set up.
Calhoun had orchestrated it, of that she was positive.
He'd wanted to single her out for praise and commendation, but being the maverick and relatively bizarre
person that he was, he couldn't find it within himself

to do it in anything vaguely approaching a normal manner.

She continued to laugh, louder and with greater delight, because she felt genuinely touched and amused and even liked. An entire barrage of emotions, one tumbling over the next.

Calhoun patted her on the back and she turned to him and said, "You always have to be different, do you know that?"

"That's what my first officer keeps telling me," he replied sanguinely.

"But what about . . ." Shelby began, "you know, what I said—"

"But nothing," Calhoun cut her off. "What you said doesn't matter. It's what you did that counts."

Looking into the solemn eyes of her crewmates, Shelby suddenly felt ashamed of herself for doubting them and her place among them.

As if he sensed her discomfort, Calhoun jumped into the silence. "Let me tell you, Commander," he said, "about the colors I saw, wounded and raving, after I won the Battle of Maja on Xenex. . . ."

III.

THE SNORING OF HER SECURITY GUARD was beginning to get on Soleta's nerves.

The science officer had been probing every inch of the area known as Ontear's cave, displaying the customary patience that was a valuable part of her Vulcan heritage. Her streak of impatience, unfortunately, to say nothing of her more human reactions, could be chalked up to that part of her that was her Romulan heritage. She did not like to dwell on that, though, Instead she far preferred to focus her mind on the task at hand.

Ontear's cave was situated in a remote and rocky area of Zontar, many miles outside the main city. The ground was pebbly and slippery, and there were crevices that were almost impossible to see until one was practically stepping into them. Ontear, according to Soleta's research, was a seer and wise man who had lived five hundred years previously, and had been instrumental in shaping the direction of his world. He had died, or disappeared, depending upon one's interpretation, under most mysterious circumstances. According to legend, he'd literally been plucked up and away by the wrath of the Zondarian gods themselves. That was just a tad too mystical and over the top as far as Soleta was concerned. Far more likely there had been some sort of freak storm occurrence that had been responsible for hauling Ontear away to his "eternal reward."

But she was further intrigued by reports that Captain Calhoun had made to her, namely of seeing some sort of ghostly image in the cave while he had been a captive there. That was something that neither he nor she had been quite able to explain and, thus far, she had found no means of supporting its existence.

Calhoun had been very detailed in his description of the phantom being, which appeared, on the surface of it, to be the ghost of Ontear. But that was not an explanation that thrilled Soleta. What was even more disturbing, though, was that Burgoyne had likewise claimed to have encountered the phantasmic shade, and Soleta had absolutely no idea what to make of that. Group hallucination? Projection of some sort? Possibilities, but none that particularly thrilled her.

And then there had been the mental assaults. Some sort of telepathic being who had, insanely, seemed to be artificially generated, if such a thing were possible. It had acted as the first line of defense against intruders, driving them mad with fear, assaulting them, in one case even killing. But it seemed to have vanished altogether, as if its job was done or its time had passed. It all left Soleta seeking answers that did not seem remotely interested in being forthcoming.

Soleta had determined that she was going to explore the area until she had some sort of explanation for the events that had occurred in the area. However, the political climate of Zondar—although it was improving—was nonetheless in a state of flux, and Calhoun had not wanted her down there without an escort. It had been with the extreme glee, in Soleta's opinion, that Burgoyne 172 had eagerly urged Calhoun to assign Ensign Janos to the task. Since this would be a day-and-night exploration (thanks to Soleta's considerable stamina) the fact that Janos was primarily on the night shift did not factor in to the decision. Moreover, Janos had already been down to Zondar once and so at least had some familiarity with the territory. What Burgoyne did not bother to mention to Calhoun was that Soleta—while she'd been in command of the vessel—had gone out of her way to assign Janos as Burgoyne's backup when Burgoyne had embarked on a rescue mission of hir own, and this was a convenient means of payback as far as Burgoyne was concerned.

For Ensign Janos was something to see . . . a white-haired, ape-like being from a species that was generally more inclined to growl, snarl, and try to tear someone apart than engage someone in polite conversation. Janos, however, talked incessantly in an offhand, chatty manner with an accent that the British would refer to as "cut glass." In that respect he was unlike any other member of his species, although he did bear a strong resemblance to his father. Janos's background and history was unique to say the least, and Soleta found him intriguing in that respect. But she felt it was inappropriate for the science officer to consider a crewmember interesting from a scientific perspective. It was patronizing somehow, for no reason she could quite put a finger on.

Aside from his string of chattiness, though, Janos presented another problem as well: He tended to sleep if he was not actively engaged in eating, working, or sex (and considering the dearth of suitable mates for him in Starfleet, he had more or less adopted a permanent state of celibacy, which was a state of mind that did not weigh happily upon him).

Since time was of the essence, Soleta had not returned to the ship since she had arrived at the dig site. Instead she had worked steadily, probing and testing, searching for clues throughout the entire area. When she had felt fatigued, she had rested for a few minutes, fifteen at most. During all that time Janos had remained on duty, never flagging in his attention, and never shutting up. Soleta had requested a number of times that he find something else to do other than talk, and he had always oh-so-politely agreed to try and curb his normally loquacious nature. But within relatively short order he always slid back into his old habits, and finally Soleta had just developed the ability to screen him out completely.

At this point, however, languor had finally caught up with him, and he had suggested that he return to the *Excalibur* and have a replacement be sent down.

"That," Soleta had replied, "is a waste of manpower, Janos. The fact is that, truthfully, I do not even feel that your presence is required here. It seems foolish to engage the services of yet another security guard. Take yourself off-duty, and if there is any difficulty, I assure you I will alert you immediately."

"That, Lieutenant, is simply too, too considerate of you," Janos informed her with a grimace. A grimace was the closest he could come to changing his facial expression, since his species wasn't exactly geared for smiling, frowning, and other human-like actions. "I'll just toddle off for a quick one then, with your kind permission."

"Consider it granted."

Janos found a stone outcropping near the mouth of the cave and moments later was dangling upside down from his knees, as was his habit. Soleta found the quiet to be exceedingly peaceful, up until a few minutes later when Janos started snoring. She could have sworn that the vibrations were actually causing the rocks to shake.

She had initially explored the cave first, followed by the surrounding hills, cliffs, and crevices. She'd found no trace of any of the technology that she had been sure must be in the area. Technology that had generated holographic figures, mind-probing creatures, and shields that had interfered with the *Excalibur*'s scanning equipment to the degree that they had not been able to track down the captain while he was a prisoner there. Now, though, with the crisis having passed, it was as if the entire area had simply gone dead. She could find no energy emanation that might lead her to what she sought. Nothing. Nothing at all. There was nothing of any interest in the vicinity with the possible exception of Janos's snoring.

Soleta reentered the cave, the one where not all that long before, Captain Calhoun had been held prisoner by a Zondarian holy man who not only believed that Calhoun was the messiah, but that it was his duty to kill the aforementioned messiah for the sake of his world. For what seemed the hundredth time to her, she scanned the interior with her tricorder, trying to find something, anything, that might provide a clue or a lead. But once again, her tricorder told her nothing.

"All right," she said to no one in particular. "Then I will try it the old-fashioned way."

She unslung a satchel that she'd had looped around her shoulder, laid it down on the ground, and rummaged through it. From the satchel she removed a tool pouch. It had been given to her by her parents on her twelfth birthday, back when her interest in archaeology first surfaced. It was a superbly crafted and carefully maintained batch of tools. Of course, on her thirteenth birthday, her interest in astronomy drove her, and her fourteenth it was xenobiology, by which point her parents realized that she was looking at a potential career in general sciences since she couldn't seem to make up her mind as to a specialty.

Carefully Soleta extracted a small hammer from the pouch that looked as new and shiny as on the day that she had first gotten the set. Then, at the mouth of the cave, she got down on her hands and knees and proceeded to tap the floor with the hammer. She listened carefully, her sharp hearing strained to the utmost, her face a mask of concentration, as she sought to learn if there was anything on the cave floor that might lead her to something else, *anything* else.

That was how she proceeded for the next hour and a half, moving one square inch at a time, her carefully neutral face never betraying the least bit of impatience or weariness with her task. *Tik tik tik* the hammer continued, never wavering or letting up in its implacable rhythm.

After ninety-one minutes, she found something.

The difference in sound was ever so faint, so mild that the likelihood was that no one else would catch it. But Soleta's ears pricked up and her eyes narrowed as she studied the floor where she was certain she had detected some sort of mild differentiation. She ran her fingers carefully over the rocky surface, and then expertly the tips of her fingers began to probe.

She detected it almost immediately. There was a circular area, about six inches across, but the stone was inset as if it had slid over it to obscure something else. It was like a tiny trapdoor, and she wondered what it could possibly be hiding.

She tried chipping away at the rock, but it resisted her attempts. Reaching into the pouch, she removed a miniature laser carver and started to slice up the rock ever so delicately. As she cut up each section, she removed it and found that she was becoming more and more excited by what was being revealed beneath it.

It was some sort of disk, inset into the ground. A glittering silver disk with a small etching of something that looked vaguely like a flame. Soleta ran her fingers across it and she felt a warmth to it . . . a warmth and . . . and something else . . .

You . . .

She felt something.

It was ever so gentle, a butterfly's brush against her mind. The fluttering beginnings of something that seemed vaguely evocative of a Vulcan mindmeld.

From a disk? It seemed impossible. At most, the disk would be some sort of device, a machine. A machine wouldn't have mindmeld capacity in either direction.

But then she realized she was wrong. There was precedent in mindmeld techniques for merging with a machine. No one less than Spock had achieved such a blending, with a floating, threatening machine called "Nomad." And if Spock could do it, and if there really was some sort of device that was reaching out to her . . .

You . . .

She had reflexively removed her hand upon first making contact, but now she steeled herself and placed her hand squarely on the disk. She reached out cautiously with her mind while, at the same time, allowing the probe to brush against her mind.

You . . . hear us, you are . . . there . . . after all . . . this time . . .

She could feel the impulse, originating from . . . from wherever it was . . . trying to slip more deeply into her mind. But she was being understandably cautious, and she kept mental shields in place that let the other "mind" go only so far and no further.

"I hear you," was her reply. She had spoken out loud to help steady herself, but mentally projected the answer as well.

And it exploded into her mind.

The response was so overwhelming, so massive,

that her shields crumbled like sodden tissue. Soleta tore her hand free from the disk, but physical contact was no longer an issue, for the thing had completely invaded her. She fell backward onto her back, twisting and writhing, trying with all her might to shove the intruder out of her skull.

She rolled over, propping herself up onto her elbows and hauling herself forward using her forearms. She was trying to get to the mouth of the cave, as if sensing somehow that once she was out of the cave, she'd be out of danger altogether. But her mind was feeling heavier with every passing moment, and her body mirrored her mind as she found herself unable to make her muscles function in concert with one another. She tried to gather enough air into her lungs to shout an alert to Janos, but she couldn't manage it, couldn't get out a single word. Her desperate fingers fumbled to touch her commbadge, but she couldn't even mange the manual dexterity required for that simple feat. Instead her convulsing, palsied hand banged against the commbadge and sent it clattering to the floor of the cave. Unfortunately, it fell on its edge and rolled a couple of feet away—not far at all, but it might as well have been in Alpha Centauri for all the good it was going to do her.

Come to me . . . it has been so long, and I deserve companionship, the same as any of my kind . . .

Your . . . kind? It was a massive effort for her just to be able to frame those words.

Come to me. . . . Yes? You will . . . come to me?

Deciding that she had absolutely nothing to lose at that juncture considering that whatever had grabbed

46

her was perfectly capable of frying her brain into cinders, she managed to get out the single word: "Yes."

Then come to me . . . now. . . .

For no reason that she could quite discern, Soleta lunged for her satchel. It was as if she regarded it, however illogically, as the equivalent of a lifeline or life preserver. It took everything she had, every ounce of willpower, and total refusal to accept the concept that she simply could not move. Her fingers fell barely inches short, and then an additional push forward allowed her to snag the strap with the tips of her fingers. She pulled it towards her . . .

Suddenly she felt the ground opening up beneath her.

It was the most outlandish sensation. It wasn't as if the ground had gone soft beneath her, like quicksand. Nor was there some sort of trapdoor that was tilting and spilling her down to some subterranean area. It was as if the ground was just . . . just melting around her, phasing into nonexistence below her and then resealing above her. And it was pulling her down with the force of a current in the ocean. Her legs, hips, and torso all vanished below before she had time even to string together a coherent realization as to what was happening. Her arms were outstretched above her head, and at the last second she lost her grip on her pouch, the strap slipping out of her hand. She was barely aware of it, though, because the thoughts from the—the whatever it was—were still rampaging through her skull, and she felt utterly helpless to drive it away. She tried to open her mouth to call to Janos, to shout for help, but she felt as if something had paralyzed the speech center of her brain. So over-whelming were the thoughts in her head that she wasn't able to punch past it.

What was bizarre was that it wasn't images *per se* or individual thoughts. It was an overwhelming need, an urgency, and Soleta instinctively tried to pull away from it, tried to sever the mindmeld. But she was in too deep, and it had happened so quickly that she was trapped before she even knew that she was being ensnared. She tried to leave, but every-thing around her howled at her, *Stay with me! You can't leave now! You have to stay with me! Stay forever and ever and ever. . . .* But again, it wasn't in words. It was just her interpretation of the abiding need that had found its way into her soul and was determined to pull her down and make her a part of itself.

At the last second, just before her head disap-peared beneath the surface, she suddenly realized that she had no idea where she was going or how much time she would have underground, if that was indeed where she was going. As a last-ditch measure, she took a deep breath, wondered exactly how much good that was going to do, filled her lungs with air, and then vanished completely beneath the rocky surface.

The strata seemed to melt away before her eyes, and she wondered how in the world she was actually seeing anything as she spiraled downward. There was, after all, no light. Perhaps in some way she was seeing it with her mind's eye, or maybe something was augmenting her view. All in all, though, she had no sure way of knowing.

She was corporeal, though, of that much she was

certain, because she was already starting to feel the air burning in her lungs. She kept her lips tightly sealed and tried to analyze scientifically what was happening. The buildup of carbon dioxide within her was forcing her to want to blast the air out of her lungs. It was simply a matter of willpower, of explaining to her brain in as no-nonsense and reasonable a manner as she could that endeavoring to take in more air was simply suicide. It was not an option, and she was just going to have to hold on to it longer. Unfortunately for her, neither her lungs nor her brain seemed quite open to rational discussion and she knew that this was a contest of wills that she was going to lose.

She opened her mouth, expelling the contents of her lungs, quite certain that that was the last breath that she was ever going to draw.

And that was when she suddenly became aware that her legs were clear of the rock. Her feet kicked in midair, and then she was in free fall, her head and then arms coming free of the rocky strata overhead as she fell through. Fortunately enough, she only fell a couple of feet before thudding to a halt. She went limp, hitting the ground and rolling, and slapping it as she landed to absorb the impact.

The mental assault was now overwhelming, and Soleta's body shook as she was pummeled with desire, longing, loneliness . . . a cacophony of needy emotions.

Soleta gathered her mental resources, pulled them into a ball within her that she could almost visualize in her mind's eye, and then she exploded the ball in all directions as she bellowed with every thought, every fiber of her being, *"LEAVE ME ALONE!"*

And just like that—it stopped.

But she was too wary to assume automatically that it was over. Quickly she promptly rolled to her feet, her hands poised, in preparation for a possible attack.

There was another Vulcan facing her, ready to lunge.

Janos was startled awake.

He wasn't entirely certain what had alerted him, but something most definitely had. He was more than willing to chalk it up to basic animal instinct. It was that instinct that caused him to awaken with a deep, throaty roar. He didn't simply clamber down off the rocky precipice from which he was hanging upside down. Instead he flipped off, landing on his feet, his clawed bared and his lips drawn back to reveal his fangs. He looked right, left, and behind him, reacting to something that he couldn't readily detect. But there was nothing, or at least there seemed to be nothing.

"Soleta!" he called. He waited for a response and when none was forthcoming, he said again, "Soleta!" For good measure he tapped his commbadge and said, "Janos to Soleta," just in case she was simply out of earshot. When still no reply was forthcoming, he murmured to himself, "Bloody marvelous."

His nostrils flared as he assessed scents in the area, and he quickly picked up Soleta's trail. As he tracked her, he growled angrily to himself. It was bad enough that Captain Calhoun had vanished while Zak Kebron was supposed to be keeping an eye on him. That loss had stuck deep in Kebron's stony craw, for Kebron did not take particularly well to failure. How much angrier, then, was Janos for having surrendered to exhaustion but, at the same time, unwisely heeding Soleta's expectations and confidence that she could attend to matters should something go awry. Obviously something had gone out of whack, and he had absolutely no idea what it was. But he was going to find out fast.

He saw the trail was leading him straight to Ontear's cave, and he wasn't the least bit surprised. Although they had been exploring the entire region, Soleta had kept finding herself drawn back to that one place, as if she somehow sensed that all the answers she sought were wrapped up there. And he should have known that if she was going to run into problems, that would be where they would occur. The past, and the truth, were not always prone to yielding up their secrets without demanding a high price in return.

Janos was not a big believer in weapons. He was always more comfortable using his claws and his sheer bulk. But in this case, he decided that this was the time to err on the side of caution.

He pulled out his specially designed phaser. It was an alternate model with larger key pad, controls, and trigger to accommodate the size of his hand. He thumbed the power on and carefully entered the cave, pausing at the cave's mouth to allow his eyes to adjust. He had superb night vision, so it only took a couple of seconds for the interior of the cave to be completely and easily visible to him.

He entered slowly, his claws clicking on the rocky floor, his head moving from left to right and almost turning all the way around, since his flexible neck gave him 300-degree vision. He held his phaser in a relaxed grip, and he no longer was calling Soleta's name. Instead he was trusting his own instincts to guide him to her; if nothing else, he was concerned that calling out to her at this point might alert some enemy.

His eyes narrowed as he saw the small metal device that was her commbadge. He knelt down and picked it up in one clawed hand, turned it over idly like a magician performing tricks with a coin. Then he saw something else . . . a pouch of some sort. He remembered it immediately as the satchel that Soleta had been carrying slung across her chest and over her shoulders.

He knelt down next to it to pick it up, and found, to his surprise, that he couldn't. The strap was inside the ground somehow. He was able to lift the pouch, but it jerked to a halt as if something was holding tight the strap, and he discovered that it was as if the ground had sealed over the strap.

"Bloody hell," he said thoughtfully. He tugged once more to make sure and he remained unable to pull it out. Then he crouched next to the point in the rock where the strap entered and probed experimentally. He expected some sort of sponginess, but instead the ground was, appropriately, rock solid. "Might be some sort of inverse phase transducer," he muttered. "Something that dematerialized the rock around her." He didn't feel in any particular hurry, because if Soleta had been pulled down and then the rock had reformed around her, she was already dead. Expeditiousness is rarely required in the rescue of the deceased. But if she was alive, then rushing unduly might well put an end to the one individual who was in a position to rescue her. Obviously caution was called for.

Something glittered two feet beyond. He did not approach it, though, out of concern that it might be some sort of triggering device for whatever trap had swallowed up Soleta. He decided to ignore it altogether, since obviously the main point of consideration was the place wherein she had vanished.

He rapped on the cave floor. "Knock knock," he said optimistically, and when he received no response, he added, "open sesame?" When nothing happened, he sighed and thumbed the phaser to active status. "Right, then. We do it the noisy way," he said.

IV.

SOLETA WAS POISED, bracing herself in preparation for the charge of the clearly belligerent Vulcan.

It was hard to make out much, because the area around her seemed thick with mist, but as near as she could tell, it was a female, like herself; ready for a fight, like herself; moving left, right, backing up, like . . . herself.

She stopped and simply stood there and waved. Her reflection waved back.

"That was not one of my finer moments," she muttered.

Slowly she approached the highly reflective surface, tilting her head slightly as she got closer. At first she had thought it was some sort of metal, similar to the metal disk that she had touched to first get her into this fix. But now she realized that it was some sort of incredibly polished stone, similar to marble.

She pulled her tricorder from her belt and held it up to get readings. She stared at the device, frowned, adjusted it, and tried it again. In annoyance, or as close to annoyance as she ever got, she thumped the tricorder with the base of her hand. Then she turned it on herself and the tricorder obediently began giving out readings on her. She cleared it, turned it back to the wall, and once again tried to get readings off it.

And once again she got nothing. According to the tricorder, the wall simply wasn't there.

She had been reluctant to touch the wall because the last time she had touched something, it had gotten her into a world of trouble, unleashing a torrent of communication that she had been unable to shut off. When she had hit the floor in this subterranean area, the link had mysteriously disappeared as suddenly as it had first contacted her. Coming into contact with another surface might set it off again, or unleash something even more forceful. But she felt as if she had no choice.

Tentatively she put out her hand to touch the wall. She saw the reflection of herself reaching out as well, naturally mirroring what she was doing . . . and her hand passed right through it.

Impossible went through her head, and she said out loud, "Impossible. If this wall is not here, if it is merely an illusion, there cannot be a reflection of me upon it. Light would not bounce off it, but merely pass through. Light needs something solid for a reflection to occur."

She reached forward again, and once again her

image on the other side did so. Once again she came into contact with nothing, her hand passing through as if she were trying to touch fog. She withdrew her hand. . . .

Her reflection did likewise, but a few seconds later than she did.

"This is insane," she murmured. She paused a moment, considered the situation, and then stepped forward right through the wall. She moved through it without a ripple, of course, but then as she turned, she suddenly heard her own voice. . . . No, not just heard. Felt. Her voice shouting, "Leave me alone!" with tremendous volume and force.

She spun and saw—herself. She was some feet away, crouched on the ground, looking as if she were desperately trying to pull herself together. Soleta watched in amazement as herself from moments ago scrambled to her feet, saw "herself," and froze in a defensive posture.

And Soleta automatically, purely instinctively, assumed the same stance. She couldn't help it, it was completely reflex. Even as she did so, she made a mental note that she truly needed to brush up on her assorted *kata* and other exercises, because the movements of her other self seemed less than sharp to her.

Her "previous self," having ascertained that she was not, in fact, under attack, appeared to relax. Soleta did likewise. And at that point, Soleta realized what was happening: She had never seen a reflection of herself. She had seen some sort of time "phantom," an echo not of what had been, but what was about to happen. Something fatalistic within her prompted her to now make the same movements that she had seen her erstwhile reflection make only moments ago, since she reasoned that she might as well since she had already done it. She might as well keep her own personal history consistent. So she stepped forward toward herself, moved her hand when her past incarnation did, and watched the surprise flicker through her previous self upon realizing that she was not facing a hardened surface that would permit reflections. All the while her mind was racing, trying to understand exactly what it was that she was in and what she was facing.

With great scientific curiosity she watched and waited as her previous self, after some moments more, made the decision that Soleta had really already made and stepped through the wall. For a moment she wondered if a double of herself was going to step through, and wouldn't *that* be cause for conversation once she returned to the *Excalibur* with a mirror image of herself. She could already hear the snide comments. Mark McHenry, for instance, would likely say something "clever" such as, "We like your mirror version better, Soleta, but understand, that's no reflection on you."

But no copy of herself came through, and she quickly understood why. She wasn't dealing with some sort of time machine, physically casting her from one place to another. Instead it was just a sort of viewer, showing her the future on one side and the past on another. It was, in fact, rather confusing, but she didn't have the time to dwell on it further. She needed to try and sort matters out before she inadvertently found herself once more under psychic assault.

She wasn't sure if she was imagining it, but it seemed to her as if the mist around her was thinning somewhat. Slowly she made her way forward and found herself walking down a length of corridor. She started to take tricorder readings once more, and this time something began to register. It was a slow pulsation of energy a short distance ahead of her. The readings were oddly in flux, and she couldn't begin to guess what any of it might mean, but she was game enough to explore it since—after all—that was her job.

Two people were killing each other directly in front of her.

She paused a moment, but only a moment as she realized she was seeing more images. And these seemed to be from a time much farther back than the mere minutes that she'd seen in her own recent passing. It was two Zondarians, and they were garbed in a style of dress that seemed rather unlike anything that modern day Zondarians appeared to be wearing. Granted it was possible that certain sections of Zondarian society were undergoing a "retro" wave of style, but she strongly suspected that she was in fact witnessing something from many years back: two Zondarians battling it out, probably members of the two castes that had been in engaged in a civil war that had stretched back centuries.

One image after another began to flutter past her, some on the floor, others on the wall and ceiling, and still others simply wafting through the air like flights of fancy: women giving birth, people arguing, eating, fighting, dying. They seemed to occur with no particular order, no consistency. It was . . . it was almost as if she was witnessing some sort of stream of consciousness, or perhaps the reverie of a dreamer.

Oh please, she thought, *don't let this world turn out*

to be a sleeping giant who winds up waking up and destroying the entire place. We've been through something like that once already, and that was entirely sufficient for one lifetime.

She turned a corner and it was everything she could do not to gasp out loud. It wouldn't have made much difference if she had, really, since she was alone, but nonetheless it was the principle of the thing. She just didn't like loud exclamations of astonishment. It wasn't proper for a Vulcan woman, even one with Romulan blood in her. That didn't always mean that she was able to prevent herself from displaying inappropriate behavior, but she restrained herself whenever she was able to.

The room she was now entering seemed to go on forever, and there was more of that marble-like material as far as the eye could see. Once again she saw herself, but this time she was quite positive that she was indeed seeing a reflection since her tricorder was giving her readings off the walls.

But there was something in the center of the room—or at least what she fancied to be the center, since she couldn't accurately determine the parameters and so make a mathematical determination—that had completely engaged her attention.

It was a column that seemed to stretch up forever. It bore a general resemblance to the marble-like walls, but it appeared softer, even porous. Perhaps even—and her heart began to race with excitement at the thought—*organic?* Some sort of techno-organism?

The columnar structure was a dark, dusky brown, and as she looked up and up, she saw that it appeared to branch off in its higher reaches. There were cross-connectors that ran off in a variety of directions.

And at its base, there were . . . devices.

They appeared attached to the structure, part of the structure but also capable of separating from it. They were a variety of shapes, made from apparently a variety of materials, and Soleta couldn't even begin to guess what any of them did. The tricorder was yielding no useful information. The alloys were all new to her, the shapes not analogous to anything was in any records.

The energy was definitely coming from within the column, but it was like nothing that she was readily familiar with.

"No," she said to no one in particular. "No, that's . . . not quite right. I've seen something like it," and she tried to remember what it was. The fact that she didn't remember immediately was extremely disconcerting to her; Soleta was not one prone to forgetting things, and there *had* been something, something that was . . .

Suddenly she was struck with a thought, and it was one that made the hair on the back of her neck stand on end. As if she had been physically hit, she spun on her heel, her head whipping around, and she called out, "What did you do to me?"

There was no response.

"What did you do to me?" she asked again, and this time she was actually driven by sufficient irritation that she tossed aside caution and strode with quick steps toward the towering column in the room. She stood before it, her arms folded, and said, "There is information missing from my mind. Information that was pertinent to what I am discovering here today. Were you responsible for its loss? Was that the reason for the connection? To see what I knew and didn't know, and then 'delete' inappropriate information from me? Well?"

Still there was no reply, which was fairly acceptable since she was not truly expecting one. She clapped her hands once and then briskly rubbed them together. "All right," she said. "Despite my earlier experience with you, I am not the least bit intimidated by the notion of a second encounter. If this is what you desire, then it will be on your head . . . or . . . whatever," she finished. And with that announcement, she placed her hands against the column.

She had no intention of forcing her mindmeld upon whatever she might encounter. The mindmeld was a delicate technique at best, and certainly not designed to be utilized as some sort of mind rape or weapon. She was, however, determined to let whatever this entity was know that it had assaulted her, and that she was none too happy about it.

The surface of the column was warm to the touch, but she was not surprised. She felt something within . . . recoil . . . as if it were surprised that she had dared to seek it out.

"Our minds are merging," she intoned slowly. "Our minds . . . are merging."

Go away.

She felt it rather forcefully, and it surprised her. Whatever the sensation in her head, it was speaking with petulance bordering on fear. Certainly not what she had expected.

You brought me here. Why do that and then tell me . . . to go away?

I made . . . a mistake . . . should not have brought you here.

Waves of concern seemed to be rolling off it. Slowly,

gently, she eased her mind probe farther and deeper. She felt as if she were surrounded by blackness, falling ever farther, and all around her there were objects in the darkness skittering away, running in fear, like an army of infants seeking to avoid the advent of a stranger.

You wanted company . . . you wanted to talk . . .

Go away.

I am . . . here . . . we are here. . . . Our minds . . . are merging and we will be one . . . and you will not be afraid.

I AM NOT AFRAID!

It came at her with such force that it nearly knocked her off her feet. This time, though, she was ready for it, and she maintained her footing as she clutched the column.

Tell me . . . who you are . . . what you are.

You do not ask . . . questions of me.

We are one. . . . We are merging. . . . You cannot hold back from me. . . . You took from me . . . give back to me . . . what you took . . . and give to me . . . what you hide . . .

I do not . . . want you.

Yes you do. . . . You would not have brought me here . . . if you did not. . . . That is truly why I am here. . . . You want . . . you want . . .

"What are you *doing* here?"

The voice was loud and sounding quite upset, and it completely jolted Soleta from the concentration necessary to maintain the meld. She looked around in surprise, feeling disjointed and disoriented, which was not uncommon whenever she first withdrew from a mindmeld, and certainly understandable considering the present circumstances.

She saw a Zondarian standing some feet away, but immediately she saw that he was floating several inches off the ground. He "walked" toward her slowly, his feet moving but not touching the ground.

He looked rather old for a Zondarian, although it was difficult for her to be sure in even the best of circumstances, and these were hardly those. He was bald, as were all Zondarians, and his skin was leathery and shiny, with the customary sheen that made it look as if the Zondarians were perpetually wet. Since she was positive that she was seeing a projection of some sort, she couldn't be one hundred percent sure of such subtleties as skin texture.

The newcomer's eyes were set wide apart, and when he blinked, it was with eyelids that were clear. In real life, when Zondarians blinked, their eyelids made very soft clicking noises. They did not in this case, however; perhaps a further indication of the fact that he wasn't really there.

"Who are you?" demanded Soleta.

"I inquired of you first," replied the image. In his 'walking" manner he circled her, never taking his eyes from her. "Will you answer?"

"I am Lieutenant Soleta of the *Starship Excalibur,*" she told him.

The image stopped and appeared to be studying her closely. "Starship?" he asked.

"A spacegoing vessel."

"Remarkable," he said softly. "And your ears—are they a product of this starship? They appear rather unusual."

"I am a Vulcan," she said, "from the planet of the same name. I was exploring the upper regions of this territory, in an area called 'Ontear's cave'—"

"I know what it's called," he told her, sounding a bit arrogant about it.

"And was psychically assaulted and then dragged down here against my will."

The image seemed to look rather surprised. "Is this true?" he demanded.

"You have no reason to doubt my—"

But he waved dismissively. "I was not addressing you," he said rather archly. He paused, waiting for a reply from whomever it was that he *was* talking to.

Soleta took a step toward him, cocking her head with curiosity. "Who are you?" she demanded.

"My name is Ontear," he said in a very distracted fashion. He seemed to be listening to something as if it were originating from very far away.

"Ontear. The Ontear who died five hundred years ago, carried away at the hands of mysterious gods?"

He stopped, his attention suddenly fully back on her. "Say again?"

"Ontear. The noted prophet and seer, lifted away into the skies by a swirling mass of air, commonly called a tornado but believed, in this instance, to be some sort of divine object."

And with an expression of gentle sadness he asked, "Is that what happens to me?"

Soleta had been continuing to approach him, but at that point she suddenly stopped dead in her tracks. *You may have just destroyed a time line,* her mind informed her. *You might well have informed someone from the past of their future . . . and in doing so, have virtually guaranteed he will avoid it.* "I . . . do not know," she said slowly, desperately trying to figure out some way in which to salvage this awful mess that she had inadvertently stepped into. "Not for certain. Reports are varied and conflicting, and there is no sure way to tell what truly happened. There are . . . any number of possibilities and—"

But he was shaking his head, his arms folded, and he merely looked amused at her discomfort. "You need not worry, my dear," he said. "I am too old already to worry about such matters, and my fate—even a violent one—holds no fear for me. Do not be concerned that I shall run from whatever destiny has in store for me, thereby upsetting the delicate balance of the space-time continuum. I shall embrace it, just as I have eagerly embraced all knowledge." He sighed. "We do have another problem, however."

"We do?" asked Soleta.

"I am afraid so. You are here, my dear, due to a malfunction. As I'm sure you've surmised, you see before you a technology representing a perfect synthesis of living and mechanical technology. However, no device—even one of ours—is foolproof. The one here, I am afraid, has broken down. It brought you to itself when it should not have. It mistook you for a . . ."

"For a what?" Soleta wanted to know.

"A lover," sighed Ontear. "It then realized its mistake, but you were already down here and so . . . there it is."

"There what is?" She felt, not for the first time, that she was one half of a conversation and not following the other half.

"The materials you have seen, the valuable hints and glimpses of other technology, the data you have collected with that . . . device. What is that called?"

"A tri—" She paused. She was, after all, talking to an individual from the past. She'd already made a horrible error by mentioning his fate. The last thing she was going to do was compound it by making mention of any other accurate information.

"A tri . . . ?" he prompted curiously.

"A try-trying-to-avoid-explaining-it machine," she said, wincing slightly at how tortured that sounded.

"I see," said Ontear, and she wasn't sure but there appeared to be the slightest touch of amusement on his face. "Very well, then. The point is, none of this was meant for you. And so something must be done about the situation."

"Something." Soleta pondered the significance of this a moment and then asked, very quietly, "Are you saying you plan to kill me?"

"That will hardly solve the problem," replied Ontear. "I have no idea what information you may have already passed along to whomever you arrived with. Even if you never return to your point of origin, there may simply be more people following your lead. No, I daresay that your demise will really attend to none of the difficulties that have presented themselves."

"That is most fortunate to hear." She did not, however, relax her guard for even a moment.

"No, I am afraid this entire installation will have to be destroyed. Your death will simply be an unfortunate byproduct."

And the energy readings on her tricorder suddenly spiked off the scales. The cause was immediately, and painfully, evident, as the energy-filled column began to glow. She could feel the ground vibrating beneath her feet, and the building energy waves were so powerful that she could practically feel them pulsating against her.

"My apologies for this situation," Ontear told her. "It's not fair, but then, life rarely is."

"Stop!" shouted Soleta, but it was too late; Ontear had vanished back into whatever ether he had sprung from.

Seeing that she had absolutely no choice, even though she hadn't a clue as to where she was going to go, Soleta ran. Her arms pumped furiously as she dashed back down the corridor, heading toward the curious wall that she has passed through. She saw something through it, something she couldn't quite make out because she was running too quickly.

All around her the place was shaking furiously. As the marble-like walls whizzed past her, she saw cracks starting to develop in them, and from overhead debris was starting to fall. It wasn't enough that she had to try and stay ahead of some sort of buildup toward detonation—she also had to run an obstacle course, dodging frantically from one side to the other as chunks of rubble fell all around her. One piece grazed her shoulder. She staggered but kept going, keeping her arms over her head to shield her from falling objects.

She made it to the wall and passed through it once more as if it wasn't there . . . which, in point of fact, it wasn't. She emerged on the other side and found herself facing a dead end. She looked up desperately, trying to find some way out, but her entrance had been through the shifting ground above her, and it now appeared to be solid rock once more. The vibrations around her became more and more fierce, and she started to hear explosions.

And, ever so faintly in her head, she thought she heard something else. Something that sounded like a faint sobbing, as if she were detecting a ghostly echo of her previous connection with the telepathic entity that had sought her out. Then, with all the substance that the wall had presented, the sound faded in her mind, leaving no more a trace than evaporated morning dew.

Then another sound replaced it. She looked up, recognizing it immediately; it was faint but growing louder. It sounded like . . .

"Phaser fire?" she murmured to herself, and then her eyes went wide as she realized its significance. And she shouted in a very loud, semi-desperate and extremely un-Vulcan manner, "Janos, here! Down here!"

But she was certain that he couldn't hear her, for the sounds of the explosions from behind her were drowning out everything. She put her hands to her ears, wincing against the overwhelming noise, trying to stay on her feet but failing and tumbling to her knees. She rolled over onto her back, and looked up . . .

She saw the ceiling, about five feet directly above her, heating up.

Realizing she had less than a second to react, Soleta desperately rolled to one side, and then there was an explosion of phaser fire directly above her as the ceiling blasted downward, leaving a pile of rubble about three feet high in the precise spot she had just vacated.

Ensign Janos dropped to the floor, landing in a crouch atop the rubble, and with great alarm he looked down at the rocky pile of fragments beneath his feet. "Soleta!" he shouted.

She ran up behind him, tapping him on the shoulder. He whirled, his teeth bared, his talons extended, and for Soleta it was another reminder of just how unwise it was to startle Janos. But then he realized who it was and said with clear relief, "This is most fortunate!" He held up his phaser. "Not precisely designed to be an excavating tool, but it'll do in a pinch, eh?"

"How do we get out of here?" shouted Soleta over the rumbling.

From a distance down the corridor there was another explosion. This one was louder, more definitive than the others, as if they'd built up to this one. There was a massive flash of light, and it felt like the air was burning around them.

"Quickly, that's how!" responded Janos. And without taking time to explain, he grabbed her arm and slung her over his shoulder. "Right! Hold on!"

She was about to register a protest over being treated as if she were a sack of wheat, but she saw something heading their way. It almost seemed like a tidal wave of energy, and suddenly the notion of getting out of there as quickly as possible, with a minimum of discussion, seemed a damn good one. The only problem was, she hadn't the faintest idea how they were evacuating the area.

Janos very quickly answered that question as he crouched and then leaped upward, his arms extended, his face set in grim determination. Soleta ducked her head, for the hole that Janos had carved wasn't especially wide, and she almost got her head knocked off as he hurtled upward into the only possible escape route.

The tunnel was perfectly vertical. For a moment Soleta found herself second-guessing Janos, figuring that the tunnel might be more accessible for her if he'd carved it at an angle. She wouldn't have to be carted around in this less than dignified manner. But then she realized that he had simply chosen to take the most direct route, not wanting to waste time. He trusted in his own strength and agility to get them back to the surface. Considering what he had gone through thus far and the manner in which things were proceeding, she reasoned that now was not the time to be critical about his strategies.

Janos climbed straight up. There was none of his conversational chatter now, none of his typical pleasantries or occasionally mordant humor. Instead he was entirely focused on the business of surviving. With impressive strength, his talons dug into the rocky tunnel around them and he pulled himself up, hand over hand. There was no sign of any strain on his part, nor focusing of his strength; he simply moved one hand up over the next, without hesitation or slowing. As soon as his body was entirely within the confines of the tunnel he put the claws on his feet to work as well, and it drove him faster, higher.

There was no guarantee that it was going to be fast or high enough as the air continued to broil around them, getting hotter by the second and presaging some massive release of energy that was already in progress below them and in the process of catching up to them. *We're not going to make it,* thought Soleta bleakly. *It is impossible, we simply cannot make it. . . .*

Suddenly they were up and clear. Janos hauled himself out of the hole into the interior of the cave, but he did not slow down even as Soleta tumbled off him. "Come on!" he shouted as he bolted for the opening of the cave. She was surprised to see that, when Janos was really hurrying, he propelled himself with added speed from his knuckles.

"Right behind you!" she replied, slowing only to grab her satchel and commbadge, which were sitting neatly placed on the floor several feet away from the hole.

And then there was an immense explosion behind them, and Soleta was lifted into the air by the force of it, hurled through the air and waving her arms in an impotent fashion. Janos, miraculously, had kept his footing and he spun to face her as she hurtled toward him at the mouth of the cave. Janos put his arms out and caught her and then, before she could say anything, he hurled himself, and her with him, off the rocky precipice that formed the entry to Ontear's cave.

They dropped through the air at dizzying speed, and then Janos's powerful legs absorbed the brunt of the ricochet off a lower outcropping of rock and angled them farther away. Soleta was pressed against Janos, looking over his shoulder, providing her a clear view of Ontear's cave in the upper portion of the cliffside.

The cave trembled for a brief moment, then erupted. An energy force blasted out in all directions, ripping off the top of the cave and then, a moment later, smashing apart the rest of it. Rock rained everywhere, a massive avalanche of rubble cascading all around. Soleta ducked her head down as several shards flew over her, close enough to have parted not only her hair but her entire skull. To the average human looking straight at the explosion, it would have been blinding. For Soleta it was extremely painful, but her Vulcan biology enabled her to withstand looking at the overwhelming whiteness for a few seconds without any significant harm. The energy seemed to whirl upward, to converge and coalesce upon itself as if forming a funnel, and then the intensity became so great that even she had to look away.

Janos thudded to the ground, seeming less light on his feet than he had been a moment before. "Get off," he murmured and she tumbled off him. There was a blast of superheated air from behind them and Janos pulled her to his chest, shielding her with his body, and he let out a roar of pain that was even more deafening to Soleta than anything she had experienced thus far. But she pursed her lips and said nothing, for the bottom line was that Janos had saved her life and she wasn't about to be such an ingrate as to complain about it, even though her head was ringing.

The roar of the unleashed energy high above them continued for what seemed an eternity, and then— just like that—it suddenly stopped. Even so, they remained in the huddled position for a time longer, as if unwilling to believe that they had really survived. Slowly, they began to rise. Soleta stepped away from him and looked up at the area of the cave. The unleashed energy had not only blasted the cave to bits, it had leveled the area.

Immediately she took out her tricorder and began surveying the area. "What are you hoping to find, Lieutenant?" inquired Janos as he dusted himself off.

"Some sign, some trace of—" She stopped as she noticed large areas of red covering Janos's back. "Ensign, you're injured. There appear to be . . . shards of rock embedded in your back."

"It's nothing to worry about. Do your job."

"Ensign—"

"Lieutenant," he said firmly, "finish what you set out to do. I'll be fine, I assure you. This is just a scratch. My pain tolerance threshold is far higher than the human or Vulcan norm. What you perceive as serious injury, I don't even feel. Really, truly, seriously, I'm completely tip-top. Right as rain."

"If you are sure . . ."

"Couldn't be more so."

Soleta nodded briskly and started to make her way up the embankment. The moment she was far enough away, Janos let out a low moan and gritted his fangs against the pain that was so overwhelming, it was all he could do not to black out. "Why do I have to be so bloody brave all the time?" he muttered.

Meantime, Soleta surveyed the area as quickly as she could, for she suspected that Janos was likely in more pain than he was letting on. Since the subterranean chamber had been destroyed, whatever it had been generating that had been blocking her earlier attempts at surveying was no longer in force. Unfortunately, there no longer seemed to be anything worth finding, since it had all been demolished.

Then she picked up something. Ten kliks to her right, there was some sort of metal being detected by her tricorder. She made her way over there and saw it glinting in the rapidly fading sunlight even before her tricorder led her to it. She knelt down and picked it up.

It was the disk. The one that had been embedded in the floor of the cave, with the unusual flame shaped symbol on it.

"After all that . . ." she muttered, but then she shrugged. At least she was coming away with something to show for her efforts. As she made her way back down the slope to Janos, she tapped the commbadge that she had replaced on her uniform jacket and said, "Soleta to *Excalibur.*"

"Excalibur, Shelby here. Go ahead, Lieutenant."

Soleta raised an eyebrow. "Commander. I am gratified that you have been released from sickbay."

"I certainly have. Report?"

"I have finished my survey of the area. The conclusion was somewhat . . . explosive . . . but other than that, it went relatively smoothly."

"Any answers to our little mystery?"

"I am afraid"—and she turned the disk over in her hand thoughtfully—"that we are left with more questions than answers."

"I look forward to the briefing. We'll bring you up."

"Most appreciated, Commander. Soleta out."

She quickly made her way back down to Janos and put a hand up to the joint where his wide head met his shoulder. "What are you doing?" he asked, sounding more irritated than he would have liked.

"Pressure point manipulation."

She located the area she was searching for and

pressed with two fingers. Immediately Janos' eyes cleared of distraction and he looked at her in surprise. "What did you do?"

"Cut off pain impulses you might be feeling. I am, of course, aware of your very high pain threshold, but you seemed in distress and it occurred to me that you might be endeavoring to bravely endure your pain rather than allowing your discomfort to show through. So I felt it appropriate to provide assistance, even though it had not been requested. I hope I have not overstepped myself."

Janos stared at her and never had he so much wished that he was capable of smiling. "You know something, Lieutenant?"

"What, Ensign?"

"If you had claws and a thick coat of white fur, you would be perfect."

She sighed and, as the transporter beams shimmered around them to return them to their ship, informed him, "You have no idea, Ensign, how many times I have been told that."

V.

MOMIDIUMS DIDN'T WALK so much as they oozed.

As a race they were relatively short. Humanoid in general appearance, but bearing more than a passing resemblance to slugs in the general shape and contour of their bodies. They had fairly pale complexions, with skin so light that once could see the thin lattice-work of their veins without too much difficulty. Their arms were deceptively strong since they looked so thin that one would have thought them almost useless. Their legs, however, were virtually nonexistent: vestigial stubs at most, left far behind by evolution. Instead they propelled themselves along by the thick lower halves of their bodies, which undulated along the ground. Their faces were generally round, their eyes uniformly orange. Their noses were horizontal slits, and their mouths were so narrow that they hardly seemed to move when the Momidiums spoke.

It had taken Morgan Primus quite some time to get used to them.

She had not counted, however, on having quite so *much* time.

They had not put her in a prison, at least not in the standard sense. They had not stuck her away in a cell; instead they had given her a rather nice suite of rooms, modestly furnished, although unfortunately scaled to Momidium size. She'd spent her first week there mostly banging her knees or bumping her head.

Unfortunately for her, she'd had five earth years since then to learn how to negotiate the space. She knew every foot, every inch of the place, and could pace it out with her eyes closed. Indeed, she had done so many a time, just to amuse herself, even though it was long past the point when it provided her any amusement at all.

The Momidiums had been polite enough, never referring to themselves as her captors, but rather her hosts. She was never a prisoner, but instead a guest. Nonetheless her imprisonment was quite real . . . thanks to her collar.

She fingered the thin, unbreakable band around her throat without even realizing that she was doing it. By this point she'd almost come to regard it as a permanent piece of jewelry rather than the means of her incarceration. If Morgan made any effort to stray outside the parameters of her accepted environment, the collar simply shut down all synaptic impulses. She would crumple to the floor, her brain trying desperately to fire commands to the rest of her body, and her body simply not getting any of the messages. She had tried it several times, each time certain that she could, through sheer effort of will, force herself to move, to escape.

She'd been wrong. And eventually she'd come to accept her imprisonment, although she had never resigned herself to it.

She heard a familiar noise coming toward her. There were four different primary jailers, and she'd come to recognize each of them by the individual *shlupping* sound their lower halves made when they moved across the floor. "Hail, Kurdwurble," she called before he even came around the corner.

Kurdwurble came around the corner and did that odd facial tic that passed for a Momidium smile. "Hail, Morgan," he replied. "This day finds you well?"

"This day finds me here. Therefore I'm as well as can be expected."

Kurdwurble laughed at that. Momidiums weren't in the habit of laughing outwardly—it was considered to be rather bad manners. Instead his chest simply shook in silent amusement. "Every day we say the same thing to each other, Morgan. You would think we would find something new."

"Well, Kurdwurble," she said, shifting in the recliner that she had presently sprawled upon, "if I am boring you, you always have the option of letting me go. But since it seems to be your intention to keep me here for the rest of my natural life, then I'm afraid that I'm going to have to just keep right on boring you. It's your decision, really."

He shook his head. "Not mine, I'm afraid. I am merely one of your hosts, Morgan. A humble civil servant. I'm not permitted such lofty pursuits as deciding the fate of others. Tell me, does the prospect of spending the rest of your natural life here disturb you? You have not been ill-treated, after all. Your stay has been quite comfortable, in fact."

"It's an enforced stay, nonetheless, Kurdwurble. Whether a gilded cage or no, it's still a cage. I miss my freedom."

"Freedom is an intangible. You have all the tangible considerations and needs you could possibly desire right here," and he made a wide gesture encompassing the whole of the room. "I find myself wondering what more a reasonable person could want."

"If you want to consider me an unreasonable person, you go right ahead." Her lips thinned slightly as she tilted her head to one side. "I've certainly been called worse things in my life than that. You are a very—excuse the expression—down-to-earth people, you Momidiums. You're not among the more spiritual races I've ever encountered, and you don't have much use for ephemera. My people are built a bit differently. I'm not entirely certain why; we just are. We need something else to occupy our minds besides physical objects and creature comforts. We need spiritual matters to comfort us or guide us, we need freedom with which to move, to grow, and thrive. We need the ability to think about that which does not matter at all."

"But why? That makes no sense, Morgan," he said, and he now angled his head in imitation of hers so he could continue to look at her in the same manner. "Why would you care about that which does not matter at all?"

"Because it's only in caring about what does not

matter that we are able to discover what *does* matter, Kurdwurble. Does that clarify for you?"

"Yes, I suppose, somewhat. I . . . well, no," he admitted.

"And in answer to your question: Yes, I'm daunted by the prospect of spending the rest of my life here, for reasons I can't even begin to go into."

"I see." He sighed, which, for him, was an odd, warbling sort of noise. "Morgan, I have never been very much of a thinker. But I have always been able to appreciate people who are, and I'm going to miss our discussions very much."

Morgan was instantly alert. "I'm sorry, what did you say?"

"You're going to be free of this place, Morgan."

Slowly she rose from her chair. "You wouldn't lie to your old friend Morgan, would you, Kurdwurble?"

"Lie to you?" He sounded truly stricken, and he put a hand to his chest looking somewhat aghast. "Morgan, after all this time, do you think I would lie to you? I have been many things, but dishonest has never been one of them. I have never been anything other than truthful with you, and now—as our relationship draws to a close—I certainly have no intention of changing that. Do you remember some time ago when I told you that the Thallonian Empire had fallen into disarray?"

"Yes," she said. "You made it sound somewhat routine, though. A temporary situation at best."

He shook his head. "Anything but routine, as it turned out. The very planet, Thallon, is gone. The Thallonian Empire has crumbled completely, Morgan, and it's a new galaxy that we face. And we Momidiums are seeking our place in it. We have always been willing allies of the Thallonians. Now there are new powers, new forces astride our little section of space. We would ally ourselves with them, and you, my dear Morgan, represent one of the ways that we can do so."

Her eyes narrowed into suspicious slits. "Wait a minute. You . . . you said I was going to be free."

He shook his head. "Free of this place, Morgan. Not free simply to walk away, however. But be of good cheer; for we are turning you over to your own kind."

"My own kind? What do you mean?"

"There is a starship in the sector now, representing the United Federation of Planets. We have contacted the vessel, informed them of your presence here, and have stated that we are willing to turn you over to them in exchange for several fairly reasonable considerations. They have agreed to our terms and, so I am given to understand, are on their way here even as we speak."

"A starship. After all this time." She shook her head in amazement. "Well, that is the equivalent of being free, I suppose. If it's a Federation vessel . . ." She stopped. "Which one. What's her name?"

"I believe it is called the *Excalibur,* which, I am told, is named for an Earth weapon. Rather odd name for a vessel if you ask me, but then, no one did."

"The *Excalibur.* All right, that's a relief."

"A relief?" He looked at her askance. "Should it make a difference which vessel it is?"

"No, no, not really. I just . . . didn't want it to be the *Enterprise,* that's all. I have some difficult memories attached to that one. It doesn't matter, though. If it's a starship from the UFP, then I'm as good as free," she said, clapping her hands together briskly in undisguised glee. "I'm going free, Kurdwurble. I'm going free!"

"It would appear so. I have a message for you, actually." He held up a small recording chip. "It came in through our comm center not twenty minutes ago. Two messages, actually. One was to our government, accepting our terms. The other was a personal message directed to you." He gestured to a playback unit along her wall and she turned to face it as he undulated over to it and slid the chip in. "It is from the assistant to the official ambassador."

"How very bureaucratic. I'm honored."

A picture appeared on the screen. It was a young woman, with a serious expression and her hair pulled back. Morgan sat forward, her interest piqued. The young woman looked familiar. That was very unlikely, of course. This girl appeared to be in her midtwenties, and Morgan hadn't run into any Starfleet personnel in nearly a decade.

"Hello, Morgan," said the young woman. "It's me. Cheshire."

Morgan was across the room as if she'd been springloaded. She punched the machine, popping out the chip and catching it in her hand. She turned to face a remarkably startled Kurdwurble, who stared at her in open surprise. "Morgan—?"

"I want another ship."

Kurdwurble couldn't quite believe he'd heard her properly. "You want—?"

"Another ship, yes."

He shook his head. "Impossible."

"Why?"

"That is the only Starfleet vessel in the area, Morgan!"

"Fine, then if you're of a mind to turn me loose, let me go and I'll find my own transportation off this rock."

"It's not that simple, Morgan," he said, unable to comprehend what her problem could possibly be.

"Then make it that simple, Kurdwurble. You can do it. I know you can. You have friends, you have influence, you have—"

"Morgan, perhaps I haven't made myself sufficiently clear, although I thought I had. I have no say in the matter. Your release is part of a much larger picture. The *Excalibur* has offered us help and aid in exchange for your release."

"They'll help you anyway!" she told him flatly, pacing the room. "That's what they do! Starships go around helping people! Just tell them that I escaped, but ask for their humanitarian assistance. They'll aid you; you have my word."

He put his hands on his hips and looked at her in a slightly scolding fashion. "First of all, Morgan, you're asking us to take the word of someone who, if she has her way, won't be around to make good on that word should it prove to be unsupported. And second, we are people of our word. We have told the star vessel that you will be here to be turned over to them. You wouldn't wish to make liars of us, would you?"

"What I wish is . . ." But then she reined herself in, putting her fingers to the bridge of her nose and endeavoring to compose herself. "I just . . . do not wish to board that particular vessel."

"That young woman . . . she seemed to know you. What was her name? Cheshire? You seemed to react quite strongly to it."

Morgan said nothing, and Kurdwurble studied her

closely. "Is Cheshire a particularly emotional name?
A very rare one, perhaps, among humans?"

"It's . . . not common, no. Not as common as John
or Bill or . . ." She repressed a smile, which was
something she did by habit since she was not particularly inclined to display amusement. "Or Kurdwurble."

He looked at her skeptically. "Kurdwurble is a
common human name?"

"Absolutely, yes," she said in such a no-nonsense
tone that for a moment he almost believed it.

But then he shook his head and said, "I think you
are attempting to confuse me. Yes, most certainly. I
shall miss that, Morgan, as I've said. You have made
my time with you . . . most interesting."

She bowed slightly in a rather gracious pose, and he
returned it. He then made it clear that he was not
easily distracted as he asked again, "So, 'Cheshire.'
Again, your reaction was excessive. You are a very
reserved individual, Morgan. You do not display
emotions easily; indeed, you seem to consider them
rather distasteful on the whole. I would be most
curious to know what provoked your response. You
know that I have found your race to be intriguing,
based on your descriptions of humanity. Is there
something about Cheshire that is—?"

"It simply brought back memories," she said stiffly,
turning away from him. "There was a creature called
the Cheshire Cat . . . in a work of fiction entitled
Alice in Wonderland. The Cheshire Cat would speak
in tantalizing ways and then would slowly vanish, one
part of his body at a time, until only his smile
remained."

"His smile? I do not think such a thing is possible."

"Well, it *is* supposed to be a work of fiction."

Kurdwurble looked at the blank screen where, only minutes before, the young woman's face had been. "I am not an especially knowledgeable judge of human expressions, Morgan, since I have only had yours to study. But it is my purely amateur opinion that the young woman in the message would have a rather attractive smile if she was so disposed. 'Attractive' by human standards, of course."

"Of course," agreed Morgan neutrally.

"In fact, if I were to use my imagination—which would be a problem since, as you know, I am most unimaginative—I would almost think that it would bear a passing resemblance to your own . . . were you ever to smile."

She didn't turn back to look at him for a long moment. She was trying to figure out what to say, or even if she should simply say nothing at all. Finally, though, she turned to face him . . .

But he was gone.

She looked down and saw the slight trail of slime on the floor that always seemed to be left in the wake of Momidiums. It tended to evaporate very quickly, however, and so presented minimal risk of slipping. Still, it was unusual for Kurdwurble to simply disappear that way. Perhaps he wanted to make a dramatic exit; or perhaps, she realized, he felt she simply wanted to be alone with her message.

She stared at the chip in her hand and considered grinding it into dust. But finally she realized that it would only prolong the inevitable. So she placed the chip back into the player and stepped back.

How could she not have known the face immediately? Granted it had been ten years, and granted she'd been barely a slip of a girl at the time, but even so, the face was almost entirely unchanged. A bit rounder, a bit more mature, but that was all.

What was she going to do now? What the hell was she going to do?

Steeling herself, she activated the message chip and the face of Roblin Lefler appeared on the screen once more.

"Hello, Morgan," it said just as it had before. "It's me, Cheshire. I imagine you're surprised to see me. Imagine how surprised I am to see you. Imagine my amazement upon seeing that my dear mother, who died ten years ago, is hale and hardy and in one piece on the planet Momidium, deep in the heart of Thallonian space."

Morgan wanted to look away, but she wasn't able to. She was fixated by the stare of her daughter: a bizarre combination of cold fury stoked with flames of anger.

"Well," continued Robin, "I'm sure you're curious as to everything that has happened since your . . . departure. Dad died, a little piece at a time, and finally all of him died. And I joined Starfleet, as you can see, living under the assumption that I was an orphan." She paused a moment, appearing to give the matter a good deal more thought, and then she shrugged. "That is more or less it, I guess. The *Excalibur* is on her way to pick you up, and then we'll take the opportunity to get reacquainted. I'm sure you're looking forward to that almost as much as I am. I don't know about you, but I . . . right now . . ." For a moment it seemed as if she were gong to lose her composure, but she kept her chin rock steady and maintained it. "I . . . right now . . . knowing that you disappeared . . . knowing that you abandoned Daddy and me, and that I mourned you when it was just a joke, and that the last ten years of my life have been a complete lie . . . Right now, mother, I wish I were dead. And I hope you're feeling the same way." And the screen blinked out.

Morgan slowly sank into a nearby chair, staring at the screen even though it was blank. Her fingers strayed over her chest as if she were trying to massage a stopped heart back to life, and as she did so she felt the coolness of the medallion she wore pressed against her. For the umpteenth time she wondered if it had all been worth it.

And then she leaned forward, still in the chair, and replayed the message, over and over again. And it was, of course, the last words that struck most closely to her heart.

I wish I were dead. And I hope you're feeling the same way.

"Darling," she said to the screen, "for what it's worth, I do. And I just wish to God that it were that simple."

VI.

Dr. Selar stretched on her bed in a manner similar to a cat, starting at her toes and slowly elongating her spine, her hands over her head and her fingers outstretched to the utmost. Then she let out a low sigh and shook herself slightly.

She simply lay there, the hissing of the shower in the next room only faintly making an impression on her as she gazed out the window of her quarters at the stars as they passed by. Not for the first time, she wished for some other view. The peaceful deserts of Vulcan would have gone down fairly well about then, or that glorious red sky. For that matter, although she had long ago become accustomed to the carefully maintained atmosphere aboard starships, there was part of her that missed the arid air of home.

She wondered if this was all part of *Pon farr*.

Whether there would be some sort of internal drive that would try to get her to go home, now that she was . . .

Pregnant.

She felt a strange sensation on her face, muscles stretching that didn't ordinarily move, and there was a faint pressing together of her teeth. It took her a moment to fully understand what was happening to her, and she had to reach up to touch her face to verify the fact for herself.

Yes, there it was, big as life: a smile. A broad, beaming, totally unhidden smile wide across her face.

There was no logical reason for it, but there it was all the same. She was smiling so widely she felt as if it would split her face in half. She was relieved that no one was watching her, because it was extremely embarrassing. She fought the smile, commanding the muscles in her face to relax and smooth out, but it was there all the same. This was ridiculous. This wasn't her.

She heard the shower stop, and that immediately wiped the grin off her face. Furthermore, she suddenly felt a degree of modesty sweep over her. She had not felt that way for several days, particularly not whenever Burgoyne was around. Selar had been rather demonstrative with her lusts; in fact, to some extent she couldn't even remember everything that had happened. She could recall skin against skin, and Burgoyne looking down at her with a look of determined exhaustion on hir face, her fingernails digging into Burgoyne's back, and a lot of sweat—which was most unusual since Selar didn't customarily sweat—and heat like exploding suns that seemed to blast out of every pore of their bodies . . . and laughter. Her laughter, which was something she never heard. She realized how odd it was not to know what one's own laughter sounded like. She had no basis for comparison, really, and had no idea at all whether she had a good laugh, or a stupid laugh, or what.

But she had made love for days, having taken time off from her duties as CMO for medical reasons. That had certainly been a legitimate enough claim; the demands of *Pon farr* had been overwhelming and a medical necessity: she would have died had she not satisfied them. She had felt almost hedonistic during that time. She had wanted Burgoyne constantly, and not just on a physical level. She had bonded with hir on an emotional level as well as physical, had felt a closeness to hir that she never would have thought possible. She felt complete trust in hir, that there was nothing she couldn't tell hir, that s/he . . .

But . . . but if Selar truly did feel that way, she wondered, then why had she pulled the blanket up under her chin? Why did she now feel a certain degree of dread that any moment Burgoyne would emerge from the bathroom? Why did she suddenly not have the faintest idea of what to say?

Something about readouts of the phase generators as they interfaced with the coils. Selar didn't care, or want to listen to it. In her state of urgency, it was simply unimportant. Burgoyne had been trying to tell her about it, but Selar had been too busy pulling off Burgoyne's clothes to pay all that much attention.

In any event, Burgoyne had been essentially doing double duty over the preceding days. S/he'd been with Selar, doing hir level best to satisfy the Vulcan's seemingly insatiable needs, and when Selar had fallen into exhausted sleep, Burgoyne had somehow managed to haul hirself out and attend to engineering responsibilities. In a way, Selar couldn't help but admire hir stamina. Indeed, there was much that was admirable about Burgoyne. She'd heard about how Burgoyne, seized with righteous indignation, had gone after the individual who had been responsible for badly injuring Selar down on the surface of Zondar. It had been an amazing display of stamina, daring, bravery, and utter moral outrage. In the subsequent word-of-mouth retelling, Burgoyne's feat had only become more and more impressive. It had been the last element that had broken down Selar's resistance to Burgoyne's "charms." Selar had originally thought to have the captain serve as her sexual partner, and he had been willing if not overly enthused. But Burgoyne had been making overtures to Selar since they had first met, and between Burgoyne's incredible display of devotion and her own hormones driving her to make a choice, well . . . Burgoyne had won out.

Yes, there were a lot of positive things to say about Burgoyne 172, the Hermat engineer of the *Excalibur.* The only thing was . . .

Selar wasn't sure if she was the one to say them. She wasn't sure how to phrase it, she wasn't sure how to put across the emotions that she was feeling because her old training, her old personality were starting to take hold and the concept of emotions were, once again, anathema to her.

If her mate had been a Vulcan, this would have been understood between the two of them. Indeed, he'd probably be feeling exactly the same way. But Burgoyne . . . Burgoyne was a Hermat. Burgoyne was someone who rejoiced in emotion and displays of affection, tendencies that had been so overwhelming to Selar at first that she had tried to do everything she could to distance herself from hir. Now she had gone in the other direction, becoming so intimate with hir that there was nowhere she could hide any part of herself. She felt . . . she didn't know what she felt. She only knew that she wanted that emotional distance that would be automatically conferred upon her by a Vulcan partner. With Burgoyne, she had no idea where she stood.

At that moment, Burgoyne emerged from the bathroom. S/he was adjusting the top of hir uniform, and s/he was shaking hir head in puzzlement. S/he caught Selar looking at hir and smiled, displaying just a hint of hir fangs. "Feeling rested?"

Selar nodded, not taking her gaze from Burgoyne, her mind still racing as she tried to sort out the unwanted feelings tumbling through her mind.

"By the way, Selar . . . damnedest thing, I think I forgot to mention it . . . at least, I was going to mention it when I came by earlier, but we got a bit distracted . . ." S/he smiled at the memory, but then noticed that Selar didn't seem to be reacting one way or the other, so s/he continued. "That problem in Engineering? The one I was telling you about, with the energy wave that we couldn't figure out? It stopped. Just like that, no warning. We still hadn't quite figured out what it was, although I had some pretty far-fetched theories. And then for no reason at all, we couldn't detect it anymore. I've had my people working on it, but I—"

"I am pregnant," she interrupted.

That left Burgoyne speechless for a moment before

s/he had a chance to compose hirself. "Are you . . . are you certain?" s/he finally managed to get out.

She nodded slowly. "It is curious. My mother told me that she was aware of my existence from the moment I was fully conceived and gestation was under way. She claimed many Vulcan females were capable of that. I was . . . skeptical. It seemed most illogical to me, and I did not see how it was possible to have awareness of a being so . . . so small. But she was correct. I sense it. I am aware of it as an extension of my being: separate, yet as one. It is a most *compelling* sensation."

Burgoyne couldn't take hir eyes off her. S/he strode to Selar's side, knelt down and said, "Can I . . . feel?"

"There is nothing to feel," Selar said matter-of-factly. "The infant will not be detectable to the touch for seven point five weeks. There is no logical reason for you to place your hand on my stomach."

"Maybe. I just wanted to anyway," Burgoyne said tonelessly.

Selar looked at hir with curiosity. "Burgoyne, we need to speak. There is much that we—"

"No, we don't need to," Burgoyne said. S/he rose, finishing fastening the top of hir uniform jacket. "Because I know exactly what you're going to say, because it's what I was going to say."

"I do not quite comprehend," Selar told hir.

"Well, then, I'll make it clear to you. We've had our fun, Selar. Both done what we wanted and needed to do. And now it's time to move on. So we just end it clean. Go back to being crewmates, and that's all."

"Are you . . ." Selar couldn't quite believe she was hearing what she was hearing. "Are you saying that you are not interested in pursuing any further relationship?"

"Of course not," Burgoyne replied. "I'd have thought that would be obvious. You don't know much about Hermat psychology, Selar."

"Yes, so you have told me on previous occasions," she said carefully. "What aspect of that psychology is pertinent to this moment, may I ask?"

"We're not built for long-term relationships. It's just not in our makeup. We're a free-spirited group, we Hermats. We're not especially monogamous. We prefer a variety of partners, and to savor whatever it is that life has to offer us. It would be natural for you to fall in love with me—"

"I?" She cocked an eyebrow. "I . . . fall in love . . . with you?"

"Well, you had this whole *Pon farr* thing going. You weren't thinking especially straight. You left yourself vulnerable to me. It would be natural for you to form an attachment to me, but I'm telling you right now, there's no point to it. We wouldn't have a prayer together. Not even a prayer of a prayer."

"I find it . . ." She sought the right word, since "stunned" and "shocked" expressed more emotion than she desired. "I am intrigued that you would feel this way. It is not how I perceived you."

"Perceived me?" S/he laughed curtly. "I'm not entirely sure what you mean by that."

"It means that I . . . thought I had a sense of the person that you were. And now it would appear that I was mistaken. I emphasize that it appears that way. However—"

S/he raised a long tapering finger, momentarily

silencing her, and s/he said, "Was I, or was I not, there for you when you were ready to get physical."

"It is not quite that simple—"

"Was I," s/he repeated patiently, "or was I not?"

"You were," she admitted.

"And you were about to tell me that you weren't really comfortable in continuing our relationship as it was. That, in effect, you wanted to end it. Correct?"

"There is more than—" But when Burgoyne once again interrupted her with a slightly scolding gesture, she sighed and said, "Once more you are, in essence, correct."

"Don't you see, Selar?" asked Burgoyne as s/he backed up toward the door. Impressively, s/he managed to do so with something of a swagger. "That's why we were perfect together. We always know exactly what's going on in the other's mind. I was—and remain—everything you ever needed in a man. And in a woman, for that matter." And with that, Burgoyne touched hir forehead with hir finger in a signal of departure, turned, and walked out of the room.

Selar sat there for some time longer, amazed that it had been that simple. Burgoyne had taken it perfectly well, had not made a fuss over the situation, had even beaten her to the punch by ending the relationship before it began to get uncomfortable. She should be happy that it worked out as smoothly as it had.

Still, for some reason that she couldn't quite articulate, she suddenly felt a bit cold. She placed her hand on her stomach and felt warmth radiating upward from it.

And she looked around right and left, as if afraid that someone might somehow see her (illogical as that concern was) and when she had satisfied herself that she was, in fact, alone in her quarters, she allowed herself to smile once more.

Burgoyne's first impulse was to go straight to hir quarters, but s/he was not, by nature, a solitary individual. Besides, s/he would have felt as if s/he was hiding, which would not have been far wrong. And so, deciding firmly to take matters in the other direction, s/he headed straight for the single most populated area of the ship that s/he could find, namely the Team Room lounge.

It was busy, as it often was this time of day when the day shift had just come off duty. The noise and chatter from within hit hir like a solid wave. S/he looked around carefully, spotted Robin Lefler and Si Cwan off in a corner by themselves, and Lefler seemed somewhat intense in whatever she was saying to Cwan. Then s/he noticed the captain and commander seated at one table, involved in what seemed like a rather animated discussion. For a moment s/he considered endeavoring to join it, but then s/he spotted the person s/he was looking for. He was seated at a table by himself, calmly nursing a drink and staring off into space as he so often was. There was no one on board ship whose mind was always a million miles away quite like this individual.

S/he made hir way across the room to the bar, and then procured a shot of scotch. Then s/he headed for the table, stepping between people who were heading to or from the bar, and dropped into a seat opposite him. "Hello, stranger," s/he said.

Mark McHenry looked up at hir with momentary

surprise, and then he smiled in amusement. "Come up for air, did you?"

"A very large lungful," s/he replied. "So how are you? Haven't seen you around in a while."

"Possibly because you haven't been around," McHenry told hir.

S/he leaned forward, dropping hir chin into hir upraised hand. "Do I detect a tone of annoyance, Mark?"

"Not at all," he said easily.

"I think," said Burgoyne leaned forward, looking playfully at McHenry with that decided cat-and-mouse manner that McHenry frequently found annoyingly attractive, "I think that you are jealous of the good doctor and myself."

"That is ridiculous."

"I think that you picture me in her arms and it drives you completely crazy nuts with envy. Yes, I do." Burgoyne was now grinning widely.

"Burgy," McHenry sighed, "if you're wrong about that, as I assure you you are, then you're just wasting your time. And if you're right about it, then what you're saying now is kind of . . . what's the best word?"

"Sadistic? Torturous?"

"I was gonna say 'silly,' but those are fine, too."

Burgoyne studied McHenry for a long moment, and then leaned back in hir chair, way back. "Doesn't matter," s/he said. "The doctor and I are *pffft* anyway."

"What?" He looked at hir in surprise. "That one didn't come down the rumor mill yet. When did that happen?"

"Just now. It was a long time coming though."

"A long time? You were together less than a week."

"Really? Seemed so much longer."

"Well, that's . . . that's really surprising, Burgy. And a . . . shame, I guess."

Burgoyne hadn't been entirely sure what s/he expected McHenry to say, but that wasn't it. "A shame? Why a shame?"

"I don't know. I just felt like you had wanted her, fought for her. You really seemed to like her, that's all."

And Burgoyne ran hir tongue over hir upper ridge of teeth. "I like you, Mark."

He stared at hir as if he couldn't quite believe what he'd just heard. Then, with a slight laugh, he said "Ooooohhh no. Oooohhh, I get it."

"Get it?"

"Yeah. Yeah, I do. You and Selar had some kind of fight, that's it." He pointed an accusing finger at hir. "You had a fight, and because you can't stand being alone, you're coming back to me. Good old reliable McHenry. You must figure, 'Mark, he's such a flake, he probably didn't even notice I was gone.' Well you know what, Burgy? I did notice. And I'm not completely the flake you assume I am."

"Oh, Mark—" s/he sighed.

"Don't 'Oh, Mark' me. What am I, your life preserver? Your way of avoiding solitude? I don't think I'm comfortable with that, Burgoyne. Go off to other people, have your flings or your affairs, and then come back to me, the safe harbor, the port in the storm. I feel used," McHenry said indignantly.

"Aw, come *on*, Mark. What the hell are you talking

about? Are you completely flutzed in the head or what?"

He was about to reply, but then stopped. "I don't know," he said honestly. "No one's ever asked me if I'm flutzed. For all I know I might be."

"Take my word for it, you are. We had fun together, Mark! You and I, we had some great times."

"Great times." He chuckled softly.

"What's so funny? We didn't have great times?"

"We had fun, Burgy. That's all we had."

"Yes! Exactly!" S/he thumped the table for emphasis. "Wasn't that great?"

McHenry leaned back and shook his head. "Burgy, you just don't understand, and I don't think you're culturally capable of understanding. So let's just leave it, okay?"

S/he shrugged. "Fine. So you wouldn't be interested in seeing me tonight?"

"No way. You just don't get it, Burgy. Maybe I need someone who cares about more than just using me as an object to satisfy hir. Maybe I want someone who won't make me feel like a Ping-Pong ball, or a toy to be picked up when s/he feels like it or put aside when s/he finds someone else, only to be grabbed later when s/he wants another guiltless 'good time.' Maybe I want someone who cares about Mark McHenry the man. Who cares about my hopes and dreams and aspirations more than my body. Maybe I need someone who'll treat me better than you do.

"Then again," he said, the memory of their last interlude coming back to him, "maybe I don't."

"Your place or mine?" s/he inquired, looking completely innocent.

"Whichever," he managed to choke out, "is closer."

"Mine, then." S/he put down the drink. "Shall we go?"

Robin Lefler and Si Cwan sat undisturbed in a corner of the Team Room, and Lefler hadn't been saying a word for some time. Si Cwan stared at her in silence and finally he asked, "Was there something in particular you would like to discuss?"

"What gives you that idea?" she asked sullenly.

"Well, to start off with there was that rather scathing communiqué you sent to your mother."

She looked up at him, her dark eyes snapping. "How do you know about that? Were you reading my personal communications? Who do you think you are?"

"Well, when the Momidium government first got it, I was the one whom they came back to and asked whether we really wanted it delivered. I told them to transmit it back to me so that I could 'review' it. In point of fact, I hadn't seen it at all."

"It was sent as a private transmission. They had no business viewing it."

"It was sent to a prisoner. They had every business viewing it, and you should have known that, Robin. Considering the fact that I authorized its delivery to the intended recipient, and considering that I am choosing not to make a further issue out of an extremely inflammatory message, I would mind my tone a bit if I were you. Do we understand each other?"

"Yes," growled Lefler, "I understand."

"If I may make an observation, it seems to me that you have a great deal of anger toward her."

"She abandoned me! She—" She stopped and shook her head in frustration. "You wouldn't understand."

"I might."

She considered that possibility a moment, drumming her fingers on the table as she thought about it. "This stays between us?" she asked after a time. "Doesn't leave this table?"

"Yes, presuming you feel that you can trust me."

"Yeah. Yeah, I think I do. Okay," and she shifted in her seat, "you have to understand, I never really felt like I knew my mother. I never felt as if she was really there for me. There were always other things on her mind, and when she spoke to me it was like she was a million miles away. She was sad much of the time, and I never knew why. Every night—every single night of my life—she would always be outside come nighttime, sitting there and staring up at the stars. I don't ever remember her going to bed. I'm sure she did, but not so I ever saw. I always figured that something terrible had happened to her. Some sort of trauma in her childhood that made her that way. And I wanted to work past it. I mean, she was my mother. You're supposed to love your mother, right? You're supposed to do whatever it takes.

"So I made it my job to try and be her personal jester. No matter how down she was, how depressed or melancholy, I made that much more effort to be upbeat and cheerful. I'd joke with her, clown with her. Broke my back just to get a smile out of her. And she knew I was doing it, of course. She was a brilliant woman, my mother, I mean absolutely brilliant. Dad said that when she did sleep, she relaxed herself by doing complex equations in her head. He could hear her muttering them to herself. So there I'd be, her little Robin, dancing and smiling and saying, 'Let's have a party, Mom!' She called me her 'Party Girl.' 'The Walking Grin.' There was a character called the Cheshire Cat in that book I mentioned to you, *Alice in Wonderland,* and he always had this big smile. After mom read me that book for the first time, she started calling me Cheshire because I always had this big, stupid smile plastered on my face all the time. I felt I didn't dare ever let her see me sad, because I didn't want to take any risk that I might ever depress her. I'd always be looking for the upside. Laughing hyenas would have looked morbid next to me. I started doing that whole 'Lefler's Laws' thing because she seemed to think it was funny when I would just come up with these crazy rules of mine.

"But with all that, my mother never seemed to try and make any time for me. Not ever. She seemed amused enough by my antics, but she seemed to regard me as a curiosity, like she was studying me through a microscope. Like she was afraid to get too near me. I think, bottom line, she never really liked me much. I was just this pathetic little thing practically killing herself just to get a laugh out of her mother. How pathetic is that?"

"I don't think it's pathetic at all," Si Cwan said softly. "Clearly you cared a great deal for her. Certainly she must have known this. I'm sure it made a difference to her."

"Not enough of a difference to get her to change," replied Lefler bitterly. "And then, when I was still a teenager, just like that, *poof.* She's out of my life. I spent years mourning the loss, Si Cwan. Not just mourning the fact that she was taken from me, but mourning the fact that I never really got to know her. That I had been deprived of a normal mother-daughter relationship when she was with me, and that I'd never have the opportunity to try and fix things. I've carried that with me, that base sense of failure, for a decade now. And you know what the worst thing was?" He shook his head and she continued. "Deep down . . . waaaaay, way deep down where smart people don't go, I almost felt as if she had gotten killed because she wanted to get away from me. How is that for a completely screwed up way of viewing the world? That this was a woman who was so tired of having me around for a daughter, that she was actually ready, willing, and able to shrug off this mortal coil rather than have to deal with me anymore. The thing is, you can chalk this up to the overstimulated and angst-ridden imaginings of a teenager, but now here I am, I'm all grown up, and look what we've got. We've got my worst nightmare come true. She's alive, Si Cwan. She's alive, and it looks for all the world like I was dead right. That she went and faked her death just to find a way out. Part of me is screaming, 'Good move, Lefler. Not only did you drive away your mother, but you cost your father his wife. You cost him his life, because he died of a broken heart!' It's beyond belief! It—"

He took her face in his hands. She was amazed by the warmth of his skin, and when he looked into her eyes she felt as if she were being pulled into them.

"Now you listen to me," he said forcefully. It was the voice of someone who was not only accustomed to giving orders, but to having them obeyed instantly. "Whatever happened with your mother was not your fault. Whatever happened with your father was likewise not your fault. You are carrying whatever burdens they may have had upon your shoulders. There is no point to that, no reason for it. Whatever reason your mother had for disappearing had absolutely nothing to do with you."

"You don't know that."

"I do not have to. I know you. I know the wonderful kind of person you are, Robin. I can see it in your eyes, in your heart. You're kind and compassionate, and if you wish to ascribe to your mother all the reasons for your most positive qualities, then that is entirely your privilege. The important matter is not how you got this way, but that you are this way. She missed you growing up, and that is your loss, but it is also hers. And she was the one who set that into motion.

"Listen carefully to me, Robin. You are being given a rare opportunity here. My entire family was slaughtered in the fall of Thallon except for my younger sister, who is lost somewhere in this gods-forsaken space sector. My relations with my family members were extremely acrimonious, and there were many points of disagreement between myself and them. There is so much that I wish I had said to them, so many pointless hours wasted in argument and vituperation that could just as easily, and preferably, been utilized for some positive pursuits. But all those hours are lost to me, as is my family. You have been blessed, Robin. You thought resolution, closure, maybe even personal growth were all lost to you. Instead, you have been given a second chance. Most of us would kill for that second opportunity. I certainly know I would. You've been given that chance, and the optimistic and bright-eyed Robin Lefler would probably have a rule to cover that. Does she?"

"Lefler Law One hundred and eight," she said without hesitation. "It's not over until it's over, and sometimes not even then."

"I'm not sure I understand it," Si Cwan told her, "but you say it with conviction. The most incomprehensible pronouncements of our time have been said with that sort of conviction, and subsequently accepted. In fact, there are any number of laws that have been made that probably originated in just that way."

"You think I'm being ridiculous," she sighed.

"I think you're being Robin Lefler," he replied. "And that is more than enough for me. It would be nice if it could be enough for you as well."

"You flatterer," she said with a shake of her head.

Suddenly he drew her face toward his, and she knew that he was going to kiss her. For a wild moment, she wondered what it would be like. Would it be soft and loving or hard and rough? Which way did she want it? Part of her wanted to be swept off her feet by this rather dashing and romantic fallen monarch. But another part wanted to take it slow, to have the relationship meet its full potential. To . . .

He kissed her chastely on the forehead.

She stared at him.

"You know," he said, sliding back into his seat and patting her hand warmly, "in so many ways, you remind me of her."

"Her who?"

"My sister. Same enthusiasm, same joy of living, same social consciousness and feeling that the problems of the galaxy are all caused by her. Being with you reminds me of her, makes me feel like we're together, just for a little bit."

His sister. Great. I'm his surrogate sister.

"Robin, are you quite all right?"

"Oh, fine," she said quickly. "I'm perfectly fine. Your sister, huh? Well, that's certainly what I was aspiring to. And you're certainly like the brother I never had. Well, the brother I never had if he'd turned out to be red-skinned and have tattoos on his forehead. That kind of brother."

"I see."

"I want to tell you, Si Cwan," she said as she started to rise from her chair, "this has been a really wonderful, revealing chat."

ELSEWHERE . . .

HER LOVER IS SPEAKING TO HER.

It tells her of a loss. Another of its kind is suddenly gone, just like that. It causes her, just for a moment, to cease her singing. She feels her lover's sadness, and she mourns the loss of others like it.

And then a fear begins to pervade her. She does not realize its origins at first, because she thinks it may be coming from within her. But then she realizes that such is not the case. It is, in fact, coming from her lover.

The realization is startling to her. In all this time, her lover has been her strength, her salvation. All of her own confidence and certainty comes from the protection that her lover provides her. For her lover now to feel fear, it must be a most terrible state of affairs indeed.

She reaches into her lover, probes gently, to learn what disturbs it.

She finds fear of being kidnapped. Fear of forced abandonment. Her lover senses something, senses that some change has occurred. That something new has been introduced into its personal environment. A variable, an x factor that threatens to disrupt the status quo. And once something like that has been introduced, it is impossible to determine what the outcome will be or where it will all end up.

It is possible, of course, that there will never be any disruption to her lover. That their little world of Ahmista will remain undisturbed and unaffected by whatever is happening elsewhere in the galaxy. It is more than possible, in fact. It is extremely likely.

But there is still a chance, of course. An outside chance that something could happen. Someone might come to try and take her lover away.

She will not let that happen. She knows that for a certainty. If someone should come along and try to deprive her of her lover, she will fight back with every bit of ability at her disposal. Mercy will be an alien concept to her. She will destroy anything and everything that attempts to separate her from that which she adores, that which she could not live without.

She strokes her lover gently and speaks to it with the power of her mind. She reassures it, lets it know that she will never abandon it or turn away from it. *You are mine. You will always be mine, and I yours. Nothing can ever change that. If others try to . . . I will destroy them. I will obliterate them. It will be as if they had never existed. You can trust me on that, I swear to you. I swear it.*

And her lover believes her. It knows that she is sincere, and accepts her without hesitation.

She will be one with her lover. She will stay with her lover.

She draws it tighter to her, and in her mind she calls out defiantly to any and all who might try to separate them. *Come to me,* she challenges any and all potential threats. *Come to me and I will show you what happens to anyone who would hurt me, or who would try to come between my lover and me. We are together, forever. Come to me, if you will. Come to me . . . and know my love . . . and know your death.*

And she waited eagerly for the chance to prove her love by destroying whomever might approach.

VII.

"IT'S BACK, SIR."

Leaning over the console in Burgoyne's office, Ensign Beth tapped the readouts dancing across the screen, the energy spikes being generated by the engines. Burgoyne shook hir head in disbelief as, all around hir, the day shift in Engineering came on duty.

"You see? During a routine diagnostic, it suddenly spiked as if it . . . it . . ."

"Woke up," Burgoyne murmured. "That'll teach me to start a day with anything approaching a good mood."

"A good mood?" Beth smiled wanly. "Another wild evening with Dr. Selar?"

Burgoyne immediately fired her a look that fairly shouted to her that she'd overstepped herself. "I'm disinclined to be grist for the rumor mill, Ensign, if it's all the same to you," s/he said sharply.

"I'm—" She quickly looked around as if hoping that she could suddenly spot someplace else she should be. "I'm sorry, sir."

But Burgoyne simply regarded her as if from very far away for a moment, and then said wistfully, "No, no, it's all right, Ensign. You're just being human, with all the attendant problems that brings with it. If we could design a starship that was fueled by rumors, we could probably crack Warp Ten with it." S/he scratched hir chin thoughtfully. "I should have known it wouldn't be that easy, that the problem wouldn't just disappear."

"You were speculating earlier, Chief, about the possibility of there being something . . ." She looked uncomfortably in the direction of the warp core. "Well, something alive in there? And now you're talking about maybe something woke up. Do you really think that—"

"I'm not sure," admitted Burgoyne. "But I'll tell you one thing, Beth. If there really is some sort of energy being or creature rumbling around in the engines, this has suddenly gone beyond being an engineering problem. I'm going to have to bring in science on this." S/he tapped her commbadge. "Engineering to Soleta."

"Soleta here. Go ahead."

"We have a situation down here that I'm having trouble resolving—and you did not hear me say that, since everyone knows I have the answers for everything."

"Understood, Chief. I am about to brief the captain

and commander on the details of my excavation on Zondar, but I will be down directly."

"I'll be waiting. Burgoyne out." Burgoyne turned to Beth just in time to notice that Ensign Christiano was walking past Burgoyne's office and he seemed to be trying to sneak a very nonchalant look in. Beth was pointedly looking in the other direction. This exchange, or lack thereof, was hardly lost on Burgoyne, who said, "Trouble in paradise with Mr. Christiano, Ensign?"

"Lieutenant Commander," Beth said stiffly, squaring her shoulders, "if you are permitted to keep the details of your private life private, then I would think that you would allow me the same courtesy."

"By all means," Burgoyne assured her.

"Whatever is going on between Ensign Christiano and myself, or whatever is not going on, is not something that I really wish to discuss at this time."

"I understand completely."

"I don't want to talk about him or my ring, all right?"

"I'd be happy to honor your . . ." Burgoyne blinked a moment in confusion. "Your ring? What ring?"

"Well . . ." She cleared her throat. "Since you asked . . ."

In the conference lounge, Calhoun was holding up the disk, carefully examining it front and back. Standing directly behind him, looking over his shoulder, was Shelby. "I take it, Lieutenant, that despite your time already spent in this sector of space, that you've never seen anything like this?"

"No, sir, I have not," said Soleta. "The symbol on it has no particular meaning. The material itself is not especially abnormal. An alloy with a mix of at least twelve different elements to it. No internal circuitry that I can detect; it appears to be solid throughout."

"Looks like a metal hockey puck," Shelby observed.

"Since I'm unfamiliar with that device, I will take your word for it," Soleta said.

"And you said that it talked to you somehow? That it channeled some sort of a . . . a mind?"

"So it seemed, Captain. But to be honest, everything happened so quickly that it is difficult to know precisely what happened. It's as I described in my report: I touched it, I felt some sort of warmth, and suddenly there was this . . . this voice in my head. Events unfolded rather quickly after that."

"Yes, so you said. Nice that you made it back in one piece." He sat back and said sadly, "I just wish that there had been something left there for us to study."

"As do I, Captain. Unfortunately, there's definitely nothing left. The force blast that blew off the top of the mountain was rather comprehensive. It was designed to obliterate everything that was there. From my firsthand observation, I would have to say that it more than did the job."

"And you're convinced," Shelby said, slowly walking along the interior of the room, "that the image you saw was Ontear. *The* Ontear of Zondarian history."

"That is my conclusion, yes."

"And mine as well," Calhoun reminded her. "I saw him, too, when I was a captive down there."

"You're not going to tell me this was a ghost, are you?" Shelby warned, clearly not sanguine over that prospect.

"Far from it. I think he was all too real," said Calhoun.

Soleta was nodding as well. "From your accounts, Captain, and from my own experience, I believe that what we saw was a crude form of observational time travel. Ontear utilized technology that enabled him to project himself forward in time, to observe and, if he desired, interact with whatever he encountered while never truly leaving his own period of time. Since he amassed himself a considerable reputation as a seer, I would surmise that he pursued these endeavors within his local arena of time as well. There is not all that much difficulty in being a soothsayer—"

"If you have firsthand access to the sooth," Calhoun said. "Charming little deal he has worked out. He goes to the future, watches it unfold, then in his own time he predicts its coming."

"But he had to be judicious about it," Shelby pointed out. "He had to do things in such a way that it wouldn't result in the future actually being changed. That could have jeopardized the entire time line that he was trying to observe."

"From my preliminary research," Soleta told them, "at least half of his predictions involved natural disasters. Warning people of floods, quakes, and such. Nothing that foreknowledge could possibly have made any difference in."

"I disagree," said Calhoun. "Let's say that Citizen X was destined to die in a volcano. If Ontear targets the volcano, and Citizen X knows to get the hell out of there or he winds up roasted in lava, then history could indeed wind up being changed."

"We will never know for certain," Soleta admitted. "Although I would like to think that, at the very least, he was selective in whom he dealt with and what particular moments, if any, he chose to interfere with. He might have been bright enough to target the potential focal points in time that could seriously have disrupted the path of Zondarian history."

"We can only hope," sighed Calhoun. He slid the disk back across the table to Soleta. "Check this with Si Cwan. See if he knows anything about it or has ever seen anything like it. This is supposed to be his home turf, after all."

"As you wish, sir."

With a glance at the both of them that seemed to indicate they were finished with their business, Calhoun rose and headed back to the bridge. Soleta was about to follow when she heard her name spoken very quietly, just under someone's breath. She turned, mildly surprised, to see that Shelby was whispering her name, barely mouthing it. Shelby knew that Soleta's rather sharp hearing would detect it. She hung back since Shelby's desires were clear: She wanted to speak to her privately for a moment. As soon as Calhoun had departed, Soleta turned squarely to face Shelby with a questioning eyebrow raised.

"Soleta, may I ask your opinion about a personal matter?"

"Of course you can, Commander."

"I just . . ." Shelby's hands seemed to move in vague patterns. "I . . . wanted to talk to another woman for a moment."

"Do you wish me to find one for you?" Soleta inquired.

"No, I—" Shelby laughed softly. "I meant I wanted to talk to you. You're the highest ranking woman on the bridge aside from me. Maybe that's a silly criterion, but nonetheless I feel a sort of . . . of connection with you in that respect."

"It is flattering that you think of me with such regard. Very well, Commander, how may I be of service?"

Shelby walked slowly around the table with a bit of a swagger to her step, as if endeavoring to bolster her confidence, as if she were discussing something that was mere silliness at best. "You seem to be a fairly sharp judge of character, and you've had a chance to observe the interactions of all concerned fairly closely since the launch of the *Excalibur,* and I suppose that one of your strengths is analysis, which would make you an ideal person to ask about this. I fully admit, I'm not entirely comfortable discussing it, but I'm a strong believer in talking things out, getting opinions and feedback. You understand, don't you?"

"Understand what? I confess, Commander, I am still uncertain as to precisely what it is that we are discussing."

"Love. Desire. Attraction. That kind of thing."

She looked at her askance for a moment. "Commander, are you propositioning me?"

"What?"

"I admit that science is synonymous with experimentation, but I—"

"No!" Shelby put up her hands as if shoving the notion away. "No, Soleta, that's not what I'm talking about at all."

"I see. Then clarification might be in order if we are to proceed."

"Look, I just want to check how something might be perceived, that's all. In your opinion, would you or any members of the crew . . ." She shifted uncomfortably in place. "Does anyone think that I have romantic intentions toward Captain Calhoun?"

"I do not know," Soleta said, sounding no less puzzled than she had before. "Are you asking me to conduct a survey? If so, as soon as I have completed my current studies, I shall embark on a survey of—"

"No! No, I don't want you conducting a survey, Soleta! I just want to know if I come across to you as being enamored of Captain Calhoun! That's all."

"Commander," Soleta said slowly, "to be perfectly blunt, it has never even entered my mind. Your performance as second in command of this vessel has been above reproach. Your interactions with the captain on the bridge have been nothing less than professional at all times. If you are indeed possessed of some sort of intense romantic feelings for him, it is not evident to me. Granted, I am not the ideal individual to form commentary in regard to human mating or sexual habits, but I would have to say in my assessment as a Starfleet officer that, at the very least, whatever emotional feelings you may possess for the captain have not in any way compromised or interfered with your ability to do your job." She paused and cocked an eyebrow. "Is that sufficient response for you, Commander?"

"Yes," smiled Shelby. She raised a hand for the purpose of placing it in a friendly manner on Soleta's shoulder, but then thought better of it and simply turned it into an apparently casual scratching of her own neck. "I appreciate the time, Soleta, and I also know I can count on you to keep this discussion between ourselves."

"Of that, Commander, I can most uncategorically assure you."

Shelby walked out of the conference room as Soleta gathered up the disk. The science officer watched her go, then shook her head and murmured, "Commander, you are so in love it borders on the ludicrous."

Soleta walked up to the turbolift and the door hissed open. She was mildly surprised to see Dr. Selar in there, and she nodded her head slightly to her fellow Vulcan in greeting as she entered the lift.

"Soleta," Selar said after a moment as the doors hissed closed, "I do not believe I have properly thanked you for your help with my difficulties during the time of *Pon farr*. Any discussion I had with off-worlders about the matter was most . . . difficult. Your aid, to say nothing of your efforts in mindmelding to provide diagnosis of the situation—"

"No thanks are required, Selar," replied Soleta. "You were in distress and I provided assistance. To do any less than what I did would have been illogical."

"Nonetheless, your aid is appreciated. And you will be pleased to know that the matter has been successfully concluded. I believe I am indeed pregnant, and the mating urge has passed."

"My congratulations, Selar." She turned to face her formally and raised her fingers in the customary gesture of blessing. "May your child live long and prosper."

"Thank you."

"I am about to see Lieutenant Commander Burgoyne on another matter. Would it be good form for me to extend congratulations to hir as well?"

Selar seemed to study her a moment, and abruptly she said out loud, "Computer, halt lift." The turbolift promptly came to a halt and Soleta regarded her with open curiosity. "Soleta, may I ask your opinion about a personal matter?"

"I'm beginning to feel a bit like ship's counselor."

"Pardon?"

"Nothing. Of course you may, Doctor."

"I simply feel that, due to our mindmeld and your involvement earlier, I feel a sort of connection to you. And I am . . ." She appeared to be searching for the right word. "I am conflicted in my attitude toward Burgoyne."

"Conflicted in what way?"

"In every way," she admitted. "The bond of *Pon farr*—" Selar paused, then continued. "The point is, I am accustomed to having distance from others. Not simply physical distance, but the emotional distance not only granted me by my nature, but demanded of me by my profession. I abandoned that distance when I gave myself over to Burgoyne. I am not certain now if it is possible for me to recapture it, nor am I certain that I am even desirous of doing so."

"The gate has already been opened, Doctor. I am not altogether certain it is possible to close it."

"Perhaps it is," replied Selar.

"Selar, you believe that you are bearing Burgoyne's child. That would seem to give hir some sort of permanent place in your life. Or did you not consider that?"

"To be honest, I had not. I had many considerations driving me, Soleta, but long-term planning was oddly enough not one of them. I do not know if I subscribe to your belief that Burgoyne's presence in my life is mandated. It is not at all impossible for me to raise this child on my own. And tell me, as a Vulcan, Soleta, can you envision Burgoyne as a lifemate for me? S/he is so different, so very much the antithesis of all that we are. Let us say that I were to return to Vulcan, on a temporary or even permanent basis. There would be no place for Burgoyne within our society. Nor would I easily fit in with Hermat society. We are too different, Soleta."

"Is that your real concern, Selar? How each of you 'fits in' to your respective worlds of origin?"

Selar considered it a moment and then slowly admitted, "No."

"I did not think so. In my opinion, Selar—since you asked—I believe that you feel rather vulnerable in the presence of Burgoyne. That it is that vulnerability you consider to be the most daunting aspect of your present situation, and that might be a problem whether you were with Burgoyne or any member of our own race. The problem that presents itself is that, while another Vulcan might be equally and comfortably withdrawn, Burgoyne would require continued displays of intimacy, both physical and emotional. You are not at all certain whether you are capable of providing those. Am I correct?"

"I would have to say that your assessment is more or less accurate."

"More? Or less?"

"More," sighed Selar.

"Selar, if I may be so bold, do you love hir?"

"I do not know if that is a particularly relevant question."

"I disagree, Selar. I think it may well be the only relevant question."

Selar seemed to be staring intently at the door of the lift, as if she were capable of seeing straight through it and down to Engineering. "I do not know," she admitted.

"Then it seems to me," Soleta said slowly, "that once you have worked out the answer to that question, the rest of the answers should be forthcoming on their own."

Selar said nothing for what appeared to be a very long time, although Soleta knew internally that it was only eleven seconds. "Computer, resume lift function." Obediently the turbolift smoothly reengaged on its path as Selar said, "I believe you are correct, Soleta. I shall give the matter careful consideration and endeavor to come to a logical conclusion."

"If I may be so bold, Selar, might I suggest that, when pondering questions of this nature, logic is the very last discipline you would want to apply." And she stepped out of the turbolift and headed to Engineering.

"Soleta, may I ask your opinion about a personal matter?"

Soleta stared at Burgoyne across hir desk. They had been going over the energy readouts and mysterious percolations of the engines for nearly half an hour, and Soleta had agreed to give the matter a good deal more study, particularly searching for potential analogs to other such occurrences in assorted vessels. It had almost been something of a blessing for her, spending an entire thirty minutes dealing exclusively with matters that pertained to her job description. But now Burgoyne was seated behind hir desk, hir long, tapered fingers interlaced, and s/he was staring at Soleta with those remarkable dark eyes.

Apparently under the impression that Soleta hadn't quite heard hir, Burgoyne repeated, "Soleta, may I ask your opinion about a personal matter? I mean, perhaps this is being a bit forward, but after our having worked so closely together when the captain was gone and the commander was out of commission, I feel that we established a kind of connection."

"If you say so," Soleta said.

"Sure," Soleta said more loudly. "Go right ahead, Chief. I assume that this is a question regarding matters of a delicate romantic nature?"

"How did you know?"

"I'm science officer and chief data analyst of this ship, Lieutenant Commander. Would this pertain to Doctor Selar?"

"Partly. Mostly, it's about Mark McHenry. That's why I was asking you. You went to the Academy together, worked closely, so I figured you would have some further insight."

"Oh." That surprised her slightly, but she took it in stride. "Very well. What is the nature of your situation with McHenry?"

"It's just that he may very well have pegged me on something, and I don't completely want to admit it. I'm very fond of him, and I just wanted to know if you thought that, in the long term, I might be doing him damage."

"Damage? Of a physical nature?"

"No, of an emotional nature."

"Ah, well, yes, as a Vulcan, naturally I would be the ideal person to voice opinions on human emotional durability."

"I'm sorry, Lieutenant," Burgoyne said, looking genuinely apologetic, and s/he started to rise from behind hir desk. "I shouldn't be dragging you into this."

"Perhaps not, but here I am in any event," said Soleta as she gestured for Burgoyne to sit down again. Burgoyne did so. "And McHenry is indeed a longtime associate, although 'friend' may be too strong a word, for in many ways he is almost as incomprehensible to me now as when we were cadets together. Still, of all humans that I have ever encountered, he has always shown a remarkable degree of resilience. Oftentimes it seems to me that almost nothing phases him. Do you wish to tell me precisely what is the nature of your situation?" and she added silently to herself.

"Soleta, you have to understand I'm a very physical person."

She stared at him. "As opposed to a being of pure consciousness, like an Organian?"

"No, I mean . . ." S/he let out a long, unsteady breath. "What's the best way to put this? I had . . . have . . . very strong feelings for Selar. From the moment I met her, I felt as if we could be something special together. But you understand, I'm hardly a virgin in these matters. There have been other women and men that I've had similar feelings for. I'm very driven by my physical and emotional makeup. I feel an attraction for someone and it's practically over-whelming. And I will do everything I can to make that attraction clear . . . until the physical aspect has been attended to, at which point I feel—what's the best word? Sated. I'm a very curious individual, Soleta."

"I would have to agree with that, Burgoyne."

Burgoyne was about to continue, but then hesitated and clarified. "I meant 'curious' as in 'inquisitive,' not 'curious' as in 'strange.'"

"Oh. Well, that, too, I suppose."

"And along those lines, I have . . . I had . . . extreme curiosity about Selar. That curiosity drove all other aspects of my personality, as it always does."

"I see. And under ordinary circumstances, having had your curiosity satisfied, you would now be moving on elsewhere."

"That doesn't seem unreasonable to you, does it, Soleta?" Burgoyne leaned forward, and it seemed to Soleta as if s/he was urgently looking for some degree of understanding. "I mean, let's be blunt: It's not as if my lovers aren't curious about me in turn. Don't try to deny it. I'm the only Hermat in Starfleet. I'm used to the looks, the speculation, the whispered discussions that suddenly stop whenever I enter a room. And I'm fine with that. It's understandable. It's even human. I always assume when I take a lover that he or she is motivated primarily out of curiosity as to what sex with a Hermat is like. My peers are Starfleet personnel. Investigation and exploration is our business. So it only makes sense that exploring each other would be a natural extension of the package. But with Selar there was . . ."

"Something more?" When Burgoyne didn't readily reply, Soleta continued, "The depth of connection that *Pon farr* can foster can be quite intense. To a non-Vulcan, it can even be overwhelming if you are not prepared for it."

"Could *anything* have prepared me for it?"

"Probably not," admitted Soleta.

"So, as I was saying, my curiosity should have been satisfied, and I . . ."

Burgoyne seemed to be having problems phrasing

it, and Soleta stepped in. "You had problems moving on. Loving her and leaving her, as it was."

"Yes."

"You found you wanted to stay with her. To stay close to her."

"Yes."

"And the problem with that was—?"

"Don't you understand? I didn't know if it was real!" Burgoyne said urgently. "It might have been something forced on me because of *Pon farr*. I didn't know. I don't know even now . . . if the feelings that I'm having are genuine or fake. If I had to go based on my previous involvements, I'd have to say they're not remotely genuine because I've never felt like this before. But if they are . . . but I don't know . . ." S/he leaned forward, hir head in hir hands. "It's totally disrupting my peace of mind."

"And so you went running back to McHenry?"

"Mark is familiar. Mark is safe. I understand Mark, understand how he makes me feel. It doesn't have to mean anything with Mark."

"I see. What you wish," Soleta said, "is a succession of partners, one after the other. A variety of assignations that have no more meaning than a passing gust of solar wind. An endless parade of intrigued sexual playmates to satisfy your endless fascination with physical pleasure."

"Exactly," Burgoyne said. "Is that so wrong?"

"I'm not judging good or bad, Burgoyne. I'm not judging at all. To be honest, I'd rather be anywhere else discussing anything else."

"And besides, who are you to talk about emotional attachments? It's not as if that's something at Vulcans are particularly renowned for."

"Perhaps not in the standard human way, no. But we know love."

"That's an emotion. Vulcans don't believe in emotion."

"Oh, honestly, Burgoyne. You make it sound as if Vulcans accord emotion the same level of credibility as we would The Katha Legend. Of course we believe in emotion. Of course we possess emotion. If we didn't have emotions, our lives would be that much easier. What we do is control our emotions, to the best of our abilities. Love, like any other emotion, is something that we regulate. We do not fall in love based upon romantic and fairy tale notions as other species do. Love is a state of mind that is carefully developed. We make a decision with whom we will fall in love and then proceed in a logical, carefully reasoned fashion. Mates are selected through a conscientious process of compatibility in thirty-seven different areas, ranging from social equatability to opinions on matters of deep philosophical meaning. A relationship is built upon intellectual discourse, rational conversation, and lengthy interaction that elevates the spirit and leads toward a clearer and greater comprehension of the disciplines of logic and the many responsibilities inherent in being a Vulcan."

"At which point your biological drives kick in."

"It is not a perfect system. Nothing ever is." When Burgoyne laughed at that, she added, "I'm pleased to see that you are amused by all this."

"No. No, I'm not amused," Burgoyne said sadly. "Soleta, what am I going to do? I went running back to McHenry because I was scared off about how I felt about Selar. Mark knows that's why I did it, I think.

But he took me back anyway, and it all seemed a great game to me, but now I'm suddenly worried about hurting him. And I'm worried about hurting Selar, except I don't know that I have any basis or that I could hurt her, but it worries me. And I'm not used to worrying about hurting anyone. What do you think I should do?"

"Be prepared to hurt someone," she replied without hesitation.

"Thanks," said Burgoyne a bit sourly.

"I apologize, Burgoyne. This area is really not my specialty. Although, if this day keeps up as it is, I may wind up changing my discipline from science to interspecies romance. There's been a good deal written about that over the years. Quite a few in-depth studies done."

"Really?" This seemed to intrigue Burgoyne, and with hir pale blond eyebrows knit together in a puckish manner, s/he commented, "I'd love to read them."

"Somehow," Soleta told hir, "I just knew you would."

Si Cwan's quarters were becoming rather impressive. Soleta wasn't quite sure where he had managed to acquire the assorted thick cloths, trappings, and brocades that seemed evocative of his homeworld of Thallon, but she had to admit that it was looking more and more impressive.

At that moment, Si Cwan was studying the flame image on the disk while Robin Lefler watched him. "Well?" Soleta asked after a moment, her arms folded.

"I . . . do not know anything . . . for certain," Si Cwan said after a time. "And all that I do know is a child's story."

"Pardon?" asked Soleta. She exchanged glances with Lefler, who shrugged.

"There was a book in Kallinda's library," he said. "A book of tales of ancient Thallon. Originally handed down via oral tradition, spun by various storytellers throughout the centuries. There was one story I remember in particular: It was about a trickster god named Imtempho. He liked to do things to enrage and annoy the other gods, pulled all manner of tricks on them. The story went that the gods had created the Thallonians to be their playthings, their objects of amusement. But Imtempho, although he was merely a trickster, truly hated the gods and wanted to see them all done away with. But he was unable to lift a hand against them himself. So he stole something from the gods that was the property of them and them alone, and that was fire. He brought fire down to the Thallonians, and the Thallonians began using it to accomplish all manner of wonderful things. This angered the gods, who demanded that the Thallonians return the fire to them. The Thallonians retaliated by setting fire to the Great Hall that the gods lived within, and all the gods were burned up. In that way, the Thallonian people left behind their ancient beliefs and moved forward toward a time of reasoning and self-reliance."

"That's a very charming story," Soleta commented. "Is it remotely relevant?"

"It might be in one respect." He held the disk up. "The book carried with it illustrations that were reproductions of the tale done in ancient times. And I could swear that Imtempho was always pictured wearing an emblem quite similar to this around his neck, like a medallion."

"I see," Soleta said slowly. She considered it a moment, and then said, "Very well, Ambassador. Thank you for your time."

"My pleasure. I wish I could be of more help to you than simply recounting an old children's story."

She nodded thoughtfully and headed out the door. It took her a moment to realize that Robin Lefler had fallen into step beside her and was accompanying her down the corridor. She looked questioningly at Lefler, who said, almost defensively, "I'm heading back to Ops."

"Of course you are," said Soleta reasonably.

They stepped into the turbolift, the door hissing shut behind them. "Bridge," Soleta said.

"Soleta . . ." Robin said after a moment.

"Yes?"

"May I ask your opinion about a personal matter?"

Soleta stared at her.

"Computer, stop lift," Soleta said immediately. The car promptly halted and she turned to face a puzzled Lefler. "Love?"

"What?"

"Is this about love?"

"Well, yes."

"Mm-hmm. Let me guess: Si Cwan."

Lefler blinked in surprise. "How did you know?"

"Process of elimination. Marry him."

"Soleta!" Robin laughed in a very uncomfortable manner. "It's a little more complicated than that."

"No, it's not."

"But I don't think he even knows I'm alive!"

"Lieutenant, if you marry him and he still doesn't know you're alive, then you have bigger problems than I could possibly solve."

"Soleta, for God's sake! I thought you'd understand! I mean, you *were* responsible for getting Si Cwan on the ship in the first place, and you met him years ago when he spared your life, and you saved my life on Thallon, so I just felt as if you'd be a good person to talk to about this because I feel you have a, you know . . ."

"Connection, yes. That is becoming painfully apparent to me. If I had any more connections, I'd have my own subspace radio frequency. Lieutenant, look, it is not as if I am unsympathetic. Well, actually, I *am* unsympathetic by this point, but you should not take that personally."

"I'll try not to," Robin said uncertainly.

"Marry him, don't marry him. Tell him how you feel, don't tell him how you feel. Sort out your problems, throw yourself into his arms, tease him, taunt him, decide he is not right for you or that he is perfect for you. I do not care. It is not my problem. It is not my specialty. It is not my area."

"Soleta, I thought we were friends." Robin said, sounding a bit hurt.

"I am aware of that, Robin, and understand that I am not averse to the notion. However, if we are indeed friends, you will then be willing to be sympathetic when I say that I really, truly, do not wish to discuss these matters. Will you honor my request?"

"Well, sure. I guess."

"Thank you. Computer, resume lift operation."

The turbolift promptly continued on its way to the bridge, and they rode most of the rest of the way in silence. But just before they got to the bridge, Lefler turned to Soleta and said, "Are you going into that Vulcan heat thing?"

Soleta turned and stared at her with undisguised incredulity. *"What?"*

"It's just that you seem awfully testy."

Soleta tried to find words but, uncharacteristically, they eluded her. She settled for holding her tongue as she stepped off the turbolift. She drifted toward the science station, slowing only as she passed Zak Kebron. He looked at her with vague curiosity. "Problem, Soleta?" he asked in a low voice.

"Is it my imagination, Kebron," Soleta asked slowly, "or is everyone on this vessel preoccupied with romance?"

"Not me."

"No?" she asked.

"I don't need romance," Zak Kebron told her confidently. "I have goldfish."

Soleta wisely didn't pursue it.

VIII.

THE DIPLOMATIC RECEPTION CHAMBER of the Momidiums was scaled to accommodate Momidium needs, as was indeed most of the other furniture and architectural design of the place. Nonetheless, it was still a rather impressive structure, and Shelby found the Momidiums themselves a rather pleasant people, easy to get along with . . . even if they did remind her a bit of slugs.

Once the *Excalibur* had settled into orbit around the planet, Shelby, Si Cwan, Selar, Lefler, and Zak Kebron had beamed down to the planet's surface at the coordinates provided. Kebron, as was his habit, spent most of the time looking around suspiciously and trying to determine if there was anyone hiding who might be prepared to spring out and launch a trap. Si Cwan, for his part, immediately fell into easy conversation with Cudsuttle, the head of extraterrestrial relations.

"I'll be blunt, Ambassador," said Cudsuttle. "I never had much patience with, or use for, the rest of your clan. But you were of a very different stripe, and I was pleased to learn that you had survived the insurrection. Rumor has it that you seek the whereabouts of your sister as well."

"The rumors are quite correct," allowed Si Cwan.

"I hope for the best, then, for her and for you," said Cudsuttle. "Commander Shelby, you have a good man here," he said, nodding approvingly toward Si Cwan. "You should take care not to lose him."

"We're very aware of that, sir, and have no intention of losing track of him," Shelby assured him. "So, I understand we can be of help to each other. Dr. Selar here is more than willing to get together with your medical personnel immediately to run tests on this vaccine of yours. With any luck, we'll be able to verify its fitness for use in . . . three hours, was it, Doctor?"

Selar nodded. "I believe that is what Dr. Maxwell said. In fact, he tends to be conservative in his estimates, so we may very well be able to handle it more quickly."

"Excellent. And you wished help from an agricultural specialist regarding an irrigation system."

"Correct, Commander. Will that person be forthcoming?"

"You're looking at her," Shelby said. "Believe it or not, Cudsuttle, I grew up on a farm. I doubt there's anyone on the ship more experienced in these matters than I am. I'll be more than happy to give you whatever guidance I can."

"That is most kind of you. And we will be happy to

escort Ambassador Cwan and Lieutenant Lefler to the Primus prisoner."

"Why did you hold her?"

The question came from Robin and, unlike the quite cordial tone of voice that was the norm up until that point, she sounded tense, almost angry.

"I beg your pardon?" asked Cudsuttle politely.

Seeing potential for problems, Shelby stepped in quickly. "The lieutenant was simply asking, in a rather intense fashion," she noted in a warning tone that was not lost on Lefler, "why precisely the woman, Morgan Primus, was held here, particularly for so long. Did you believe her to be a spy and, if so, what exactly was she spying on?"

"You mean are we hiding something of interest?" Cudsuttle said, sounding rather amused at the concept.

"Something like that," Shelby replied guardedly.

"Would that we were that devious a people, Commander. We might have gotten farther than we have in galactic politics. No, I am afraid it's nothing quite as intriguing as that. It was simple caution. We were not concerned that she was spying on us so much as that she might be some sort of provocateur or emissary for an alien race, out to stir up trouble. We Momidiums are a peaceful people, Commander. We do not seek out problems, either within our own sphere or with powerful potential opponents such as the Thallonians. Perhaps she was an enemy of the Thallonians. Perhaps she wished us harm. We did not know for certain, and we did not desire to take the chance. All we knew is that she showed up on our world, asked a goodly number of questions regarding ancient artifacts, and violated one of the basic laws of Thallonian rule, which was: No out-worlders. Based upon all of that, we didn't so much make her a prisoner as take her into protective custody."

"Her protection," asked Si Cwan, "or yours?"

"A bit of both, I daresay," admitted Cudsuttle. "In any event, that time is now gone. She is yours to do with as you will. I officially release her to Captain Calhoun, with you serving as his representative. Kurdwurble!" he called, and from the sound of that Si Cwan momentarily thought that he had something caught in his throat. But a moment later another Momidium emerged from nearby. "This is Kurdwurble," Cudsuttle said by way of introduction. "He will bring you to her."

"Right this way," Kurdwurble said, gesturing for them to follow.

"Ambassador," Lefler said suddenly, "perhaps it'd be best if you accompanied the commander. I'm certain I can handle this on my own."

"Lieutenant—" Si Cwan began.

"I'm certain that I can," Lefler repeated, and her glance took in everyone in the away team, but most particularly Shelby, in a manner that could almost be considered challenging. It was as if she was saying, *I have to do this myself. Please don't mix in.*

As if in silent acknowledgment, Shelby nodded. "Very well, Lieutenant. And good luck."

"Thank you," she said, adding silently, *I'll need it.*

Morgan Primus was sitting squarely in the middle of her quarters, her hands resting in her lap. Except for a slight rise and fall of her chest, she might have been mistaken for a statue. At her feet were her packed bags, which didn't contain all that much since she had not arrived on Momidium with an excess of luggage. She had, after all, been trying to travel light.

She heard a soft footfall approaching the suite of rooms that had been her prison for all these years, and even though they were the footsteps of someone she'd never known as an adult, she was still able to recognize them. She braced herself, knowing that she was going to have to manage with all her strength to hold herself together. She was bound and determined not to let the slightest weakness show through.

Robin stepped into view in the entranceway.

They stared at each other. Simply stared. Morgan wanted to say something, wanted to explain. She was ready for the outpouring of anger and vituperation, prepared to handle questions although she had every intention of being as vague as possible about many of the replies. She was ready for the cold stare, the icy assessment, a bellow of rage fueled by pain, a shout of disbelief, a continuation of the earlier transmission. Hell, for all she knew, Robin would be so infuriated that she would simply pull out a phaser and start shooting. Stranger things had happened, certainly. A crime of passion, that's what they'd call it. Any board of inquiry in the world would look the situation over and simply pronounce it temporary insanity. They wouldn't immediately put her back in place on a starship, but neither would they stick her in a camp for the rest of her life.

What she was not prepared for, in all of that, was the simple flat stare that greeted her. There was no emotion in her eyes. She might just as easily have been a Vulcan meeting a total stranger for the first time.

Morgan realized that Robin was going to wait for her to say something. Stubborn little thing, that Robin. Probably got it from her mother. Well, there was no use for it. She was going to have to say *something,* or they might just stand there regarding each other for the rest of the day.

The silence was fortunately broken by Kurdwurble, who finally felt compelled to ask, "Are you a telepathic race?"

"What?" asked Morgan.

"I was just wondering if perhaps you were communicating by thought alone. We Momidiums are limited by our ability to articulate. I thought perhaps between members of your own species . . ."

She shook her head.

"I see," said Kurdwurble, who didn't quite, but he wasn't about to admit it. He shrugged, which for a Momidium was more a sense of one's head sagging down between the shoulders. "Well, none of my affair. Not anymore." He held up a small round electronic device. "Turn around please."

Morgan did as she was instructed, presenting her back to Kurdwurble, and Kurdwurble placed the device against a small panel on the collar. Morgan felt a slight electronic jolt and then the collar fell away from her, clattering onto the floor deactivated and harmless.

"You are free to go. It was good speaking with you, Morgan. In another life," he said with that odd shrug again, "who knows what we might have been to each other?"

"Who knows indeed. Thank you for making it bearable, Kurdwurble."

He looked to Robin and said, "Be good to her. She is a very special woman." And then, with no further words, he turned and undulated away, leaving the two women once more to their silence.

"You must have a lot of questions," Morgan finally said, unable to take it anymore.

"Yes," replied Robin in a voice that bordered on total disinterest. "Are you coming or not?"

Morgan stared at her incredulously. "That's it?"

No reply.

"Robin, let's not kid each other. You must have a million questions. You must have a great deal of anger in you; you certainly made that clear enough in your little love note. So go ahead." She got to her feet and stood there, braced. "Let me have it, right between the eyes. Tell me what's going through your mind."

Nothing.

"I see. The silent treatment. That's what it's going to be. All those questions, all that anger and hurt and whatever else tumbling around inside your head, and you're going for the silent treatment. Very mature, Robin," she said sarcastically.

"I like to think I'm very mature," Robin said in a voice that could have been originating back on Mars. "I had to grow up at a rather early age, what with my parents being dead and all."

"I'm . . ." She drew a deep breath. "I'm sorry about your father. I had no way of knowing—"

"Don't." Robin pointed a finger at her and Morgan could see that it was everything she could do not to let it tremble. The effort she was expending to control herself was having a massive effect on her. "Don't apologize. I can handle anything except that. Because there is no apology in the galaxy that can even begin to cover it, and if you try, Mother, so help me God, if you try, I will snap. Do you understand me? I will snap like a rotting twig. After everything else you've done to me, I would like to think that you'd at least have sufficient compassion not to do that to me as well."

Slowly Morgan nodded. "All right, Lieutenant." As she was about to leave, she accidentally stepped on the collar that was on the floor where it had fallen. She stooped, picked it up, and turned it over in her hands. "Hard to believe that this is what kept me here all these years."

"Perhaps they considered saddling you with a child, but they knew that wouldn't be enough to keep you in one place."

"Cheshire," she turned to face her, "you don't—"

"Shut up! Don't you dare call me that! You've lost the privilege, do you understand me? DO YOU?!?"

The volume, the intensity, the fury of it was so great that Morgan took a step back as if she'd been shoved. Robin had to visibly fight to pull in her fury and then, very quietly, she said, "Come. It's time to go."

Without a word, Morgan picked up her bags and followed her daughter to freedom.

Calhoun sat on the bridge, watching the planet turning beneath him, and wondered for what was hardly the first time if he hadn't made a mistake. He was so much happier leading away teams than staying on the bridge and allowing others to seize the day. It wasn't that he didn't trust Shelby to do the job; he did. But damn, he missed doing it.

Then again, he couldn't help but notice that whenever he did get involved with setting foot on planets, disaster seemed to strike. Thus far his two major accomplishments planetside had been having one disintegrate under his feet and being kidnapped while in residence on the other. Neither incident, he felt, was destined to win him any away team performance medals.

Shelby emerged from the turbolift and Calhoun turned in his chair and looked up at her expectantly. "Well, Commander?" he asked.

"All done, sir," she replied briskly. "I gave them a few pointers on their irrigation system that initial estimates show will improve their harvest yield by nineteen percent. And Dr. Selar reports that their serum checks out. I took the liberty of authorizing our synthesizing of a quantity of it, since the doctor reports that their facilities are, at best, barely adequate and we can accomplish the reproduction of the serum approximately five times faster than they can. Within twenty hours, maximum, this epidemic they're fighting will be completely under control."

"No sign of civil unrest?" he asked. "No outbreak of war? No one kidnapped? No giant flaming bird appearing on the horizon?"

"You mean none of the usual stuff, Captain? Nope. This was a horrifyingly simple assignment." She descended the ramp and walked around to her chair . . . and then hesitated a moment before sitting.

He caught the movement, or lack thereof, and saw her look at him with just a hint of suspicion. He smiled and shook his head, and said in a very low voice, "We're even, okay? Let's let it go."

She nodded and sat confidently in her chair. "Now, as to the matter of Morgan Primus—"

"Yes, I notice that Lefler isn't with you."

"I've assigned quarters to Primus—or Lefler, or whatever her name is—and Robin is getting her installed there. Kebron is running a security check on her now, but nothing seems to be turning up beyond what Robin already told us. I assume you want to meet with her."

"As soon as possible," Calhoun said firmly. "Her presence on this ship provides a mystery, and I generally like to have mysteries attended to as quickly as possible."

"Understood, sir. Conference lounge?"

"No," he said after a moment's thought. "Captain's ready room. The conference lounge seems more appropriate for an interrogation and, for the moment, let's remain friends."

"Considering what Lefler's going through," Shelby observed, "that's going to be a trick and a half."

"Captain," McHenry now turned in his chair. "We've just received word from the *Seidman*. She's on her way to the designated rendezvous point and wants to know if we're still going to make that as scheduled."

"If we're done here, then we certainly are. Set course, Mr. McHenry, warp factor three."

"Aye, sir."

Calhoun looked regretfully at Shelby, and she knew what he was thinking. The *Seidman* was a transport vessel sent by Starfleet to carry away the first two men that had been lost under Calhoun's command. Two security men, a highly dangerous job to be sure, but that didn't make the loss any more palatable. Hecht and Scannell: Hecht was simply dead, and as for Scannell, his mind had been totally destroyed. He writhed in the throes of madness, and although there was some hope for rehabilitation, to achieve that required facilities that were more than the *Excalibur* had to offer.

"So soon," he said with clear regret on his face, and she knew precisely what he meant. It seemed far too soon into the mission to lose any crewmen. And she also knew that, no matter what she might say, Calhoun would still hold himself responsible.

As much as she herself wanted command, there were times when Shelby didn't regret in the least that she had not yet landed in that chair.

Morgan looked around her quarters, unpacking her bags as she did so. She glanced out her view window at the starscape and said, "Stars. Now that's something I didn't think I was ever going to see again." She tore her gaze away from it and looked around the quarters. "Nice to see that guest quarters are still respectable."

Si Cwan stood nearby, leaning easily against a wall. "Have you been on a starship before?" he asked.

She paused a moment, and it looked to Si Cwan as if she regretted having said anything. But then she appeared to shrug mentally. "From time to time," she said vaguely. She turned and looked him over from top to bottom. They openly studied each other, and he couldn't help but notice what a handsome woman she was. "So, what do they call you again?"

"Si Cwan. Ship's ambassador."

She was momentarily impressed. "*The* Si Cwan? Of the imperial family?"

"Formerly."

"Now serving as a Federation ambassador. My, how times change, don't they?" She sat down on the edge of the bed and looked up at him. "Why are you here, Ambassador?"

"A variety of reasons. I felt it necessary to return to—"

"No, I mean why are you *here?* In my quarters? Are you here to pump me for information?"

"You are a blunt woman, Morgan. That is a pleasant change. Very well. It was felt by Commander Shelby that you should not be unattended until such time as Lieutenant Kebron has run a full security check on you. Locking you into your quarters seemed rather hostile, and consigning you to the brig was likewise inhospitable. In point of fact, I believe that she was expecting Lieutenant Lefler to stay with you, but she declined the honor. So I offered my services."

"How very gallant of you. Do you work closely with Robin?"

"She is my part-time aide-de-camp. She graciously volunteered her time."

Morgan sized him up once more and then laughed. It was not an open laugh, but merely a short, even slightly disdainful chuckle, in the base of her throat. "How gracious indeed."

"Meaning . . . ?"

"Meaning you're rather attractive for a man with red skin and tattoos on his head."

"Lieutenant Lefler is a thorough professional, madam," Si Cwan admonished her. "And I will thank you not to ascribe any other motives aside from her interest in serving the best interests of the *Excalibur*."

She put up her hands in an overly apologetic manner. "I offer my humble pardon, Ambassador. I did not mean to insult my daughter or you. If it's all the same to you, we'll keep my little gaffe to ourselves."

"I would far prefer that we did."

Si Cwan's commbadge beeped on his tunic and he tapped it. "Si Cwan here."

"Ambassador," came Shelby's voice, "would you be so kind as to escort Ms. Primus to the captain's ready room?"

"At your service, Commander." He bowed slightly and indicated the door with a wave of his arm. "After you, madam."

"At your service, Ambassador," she said in a deep, throaty tone. And as she headed toward the door, she stopped and momentarily ran her fingers along the curve of his beard. He blinked in surprise. "Between you and me, Si Cwan, I don't blame my daughter one bit."

Lefler was at her station when Shelby stepped in behind her and said softly, "The captain would like to see us in his ready room."

Automatically, Robin glanced in the direction of the captain's ready room and saw Si Cwan escorting Morgan through the door. Immediately Robin looked back at Shelby and said, "Commander, if it's all the same to you, I'd rather not."

"It's not all the same to me, Lieutenant," Shelby said, firmly but not unkindly. "What is all the same to me are orders from the captain, even the ones we'd rather not follow. He wants to see you. You get seen. So do I."

"But—" Then she saw the look in Shelby's eyes and sighed, "Aye, sir." She rose from her station as Ensign Scott Fogelson automatically took her place. When she stood face to face with Shelby, she said very softly, "I hate this."

"Understood," said Shelby neutrally. "Let's go."

Calhoun couldn't help but notice that Morgan Primus moved about the captain's ready room as if she felt she belonged there. He had chosen the ready room for a reason: He'd wanted to feel as if he had a psychological advantage. A conference lounge had the feel of neutral territory, but the ready room was the captain's home court. Unfortunately it didn't seem to have much relation to the present situation, and Calhoun—who was generally an impeccable judge of character—had the distinct feeling that Morgan was not someone who was readily, or easily, intimidated.

Si Cwan remained with them and, moments later, Shelby and Lefler joined them. There wasn't quite enough seating space for everyone, but Si Cwan made a point of simply standing over in a corner of the room, arms folded. Calhoun had noticed that Cwan preferred standing to sitting whenever possible. As if he wasn't tall enough, it appeared that he liked to loom. Shelby and Lefler sat in chairs opposite each other, and Morgan settled comfortably into the small couch. "So," Calhoun said amiably, "here we all are. So . . . Ms. Primus. Or do you prefer Ms. Lefler?"

"'Morgan' will do, if that's all the same to you." He

noticed she was running a finger along the back of the couch. Checking for dust. Who the hell *was* this woman? "I see little need to stand on ceremony."

"Very well, Morgan. Mr. Kebron has finished running his security check on 'Morgan Primus,' and it is very much as Lieutenant Lefler had told us. According to records, you died ten years ago. Your body was never recovered despite best efforts by the authorities."

"Well, Captain, it appears you succeeded where the authorities failed. You found it."

"And may I ask, Morgan, where you've been all this time? We can account for the last five years, obviously, but the five years intervening are something of a mystery."

"Captain," Morgan said slowly, "I believe that these questions are somewhat outside the parameters of your job."

"It's a funny thing about me, Morgan," Calhoun said with a thin smile. "I'm one for stretching parameters. The longer you're with me, the faster you'll realize that."

"That is good to know, Captain, but I do not anticipate being here all that long."

For the first time, Lefler spoke up. "That eager to get away from me again, Mother?"

Slowly Morgan's gaze swivelled toward her daughter. Her expression was very severe, her face beginning to darken as if a storm cloud was setting in. "Robin," she said, "do you wish to continue with sniping comments that accomplish nothing or do you want to just get it out in the open where we can discuss it?"

Si Cwan put a restraining hand on Robin's shoulder

as Lefler looked as if she were about to leap out of her chair. He held her steady for a moment, but then she pushed his hand away and was on her feet. "All right," she said sharply. "You want to get to it? Let's get to it."

Shelby glanced over at Calhoun, but he made a small gesture indicating that they should do nothing to interfere. She sat back and watched with concern.

"Bottom line, Mother, you ran out on me. On Dad and me."

"Yes."

"You faked your own death."

"Yes again."

She took a deep breath. "Why?"

"It was necessary."

And that was all she said. Robin waited for her to expand upon it, but as the silence lengthened she realized that Morgan was apparently under the impression that that was all the explanation required. "It was necessary?" echoed Robin. "Ten years I think you're dead. Dad dies of a broken heart. And the only thing I'm entitled to is 'it was necessary'?"

"You're entitled to far more than that, Robin, but that's all I'm prepared to tell you at the moment."

"At the moment?" Lefler couldn't believe it. She started pacing around the chair, Si Cwan stepping back to give her room. "What the hell are you waiting for? Until you're a grandmother? Until I'm on my deathbed? That's when you're going to come around and say, 'Oh, honey, by the way, I'm now prepared to explain to you why I *screwed up your life!*'"

At that, Morgan was on her feet, her fists curled tightly at her sides, and said, "I gave you life, child! I gave you life, and you seem to have survived my departure just fine. And I'm sorry that your father 'died of a broken heart,' but people die, Robin, that's just a statistical fact. And I miss him, but the strong survive, and that's just a fact of nature. That's natural selection. And if he wasn't strong enough to withstand my loss, then nature selected him not to survive, and that is not my fault."

"How dare you!" Lefler shouted, and leapt to her feet.

"Okay, that's enough!" said Calhoun. "Lefler, back off!"

Lefler didn't move, even though her whole body was trembling. Si Cwan seemed about to try and draw her back away from Morgan, but Robin caught his movement with a sideways glance and froze him in his tracks. Si Cwan wisely decided to stay exactly where he was.

For her part, Morgan's face was flaming red, as if she'd been slapped hard. "Did that make you feel better, Robin?" she asked quietly. "Did that make up for anything?"

"No," admitted Lefler, looking no less angry. "I want to know what's going on, Mother. You owe me so much. At the very least, you owe me that."

"Perhaps you're right, Robin. But we don't always get everything we want, and sometimes there are some things that remain mysteries. Believe me when I say that it's far better for all concerned if we leave it that way."

"I can't."

"Well, I can. And unfortunately, if I'm not willing to say more than I have, then you are just going to have to be prepared to live with that. You've lived with my death for all these years, Robin. Live with my life for all your remaining years and let it go at that. Captain," she continued before Robin could even say anything, "it is my understanding that we will be meeting up with the transport *Seidman*. Is that correct?"

"Yes."

"Very well. I am officially asking you to put me aboard her. I'll make my own way from there."

"You're intending to leave Thallonian space?" Si Cwan asked.

"Perhaps," replied Morgan. "I haven't made up my mind yet."

"You know," Shelby said, "for some reason that I can't quite put my finger on, I don't entirely believe you. I have the sneaking suspicion that you have indeed made up your mind, Morgan. Do you agree, Captain?"

"I do indeed, Number One."

Morgan did a momentary double take. Then she cleared her throat and said, "To be honest, Commander—"

"There's a change of pace," murmured Lefler.

"I do not especially care what your opinion of me is," she continued as if Lefler hadn't spoken. "What I care about is continuing about my business. I have been delayed for five years. I have certain goals, certain things I desire to accomplish, and there is no way that I can get that time back. I would ask you to cooperate with me now by not delaying me any further. Now I am asking you for, and frankly I expect to receive, a means off this ship."

"Permission to show her the back door, sir," said Robin.

"Lefler, that's not going to accomplish anything," Calhoun said sharply. "Morgan—"

"Captain, if you give the matter some thought, I'm sure you'll see that you have no choice," Morgan said reasonably.

"I already have given the matter some thought, and until this situation is resolved to my satisfaction—in short, until I know why you faked your death and showed up in Thallonian space ten years later— you're going to stay put right here on the *Excalibur*."

"What?" Morgan fairly exploded. "What did you say?"

"After all," Calhoun said, "we haven't received formal confirmation of your identity from the Terran data net. Until then, you could be anyone."

"At this distance," Morgan said grimly, "that will take . . . ?"

"At least two weeks by subspace. Not counting any bureaucratic problems on the other end."

"Robin," Morgan said, turning to her daughter, "tell them I'm your mother."

Lieutenant Leffler replied to her mother's request with an angry glare that said "so now you want to be my mother!"

Calhoun noted that Shelby's face had gone slightly ashen, although Si Cwan, from long years of practice, kept his face properly inscrutable. "You will be treated as an honored guest, of course," he assured her. "You will not be kept under lock and key, but given free access to the ship, within the limits imposed on all guests. But I have absolutely no intention of simply turning you loose. For all I know, you had some sort of mischief planned toward the Momidiums that you would implement the moment we released you."

"Captain, I assure you, if I never see Momidium again, it will be too soon."

He came around the desk and leaned against it in an almost avuncular fashion. "Morgan, I'm sure you understand why your assurances do not mean a hell of a lot to me. Not only have you been less than forthcoming, but you're almost proud over your ability to hide the truth. That does not sit well with me. Until such time that you are forthcoming, you can stay aboard this ship until you rot. Do I make myself clear?"

"This is extortion!"

He clapped his hands together briskly. "Yes, I'm clear, all right."

"You're blackmailing me, Captain! Blackmailing my right to privacy!"

"One person's blackmail is another person's negotiation," he said calmly. And then he took a step toward her and it was Calhoun whose face was darkening. The scar on his cheek stood out in sharp relief against it. "Now listen to me, lady," and his voice was low and intimidating. "I don't know you. You're just an object to me, a body to be transported. But Lieutenant Lefler here is a valued crewmember. I do not like the way you have treated her in her life. I do not like the aspects of her—the anger, the boiling fury—that you're bringing out in her now."

"Then let me go so I don't continue to be a bad influence," said Morgan.

He shook his head. "Ohhh no. No, Morgan. Whatever demons drove you away from her ten years ago don't matter to me all that much, but you don't get off that easily here. What you did to her was unjust, and there will be justice now. I will see it done."

"Captain Calhoun, trying to right wrongs and save the galaxy," Morgan asked, her voice dripping with sarcasm.

"Not the entire galaxy," he said tightly. "Just my little piece of it."

For a long moment the air between them seemed to crackle with energy and then, slowly, Morgan found she couldn't help but look away from the piercing fierceness of those stormy purple eyes of Calhoun's.

"Are we done here?" she asked, still looking away.

"It would appear that we are, yes. Ambassador . . . Lieutenant . . . if you wouldn't mind escorting Morgan to her quarters, she can begin her stay with us."

"So I've gone from being a prisoner of the Momidiums to a prisoner of Captain Calhoun, is that how it's to be?" asked Morgan.

"You're a prisoner of your own heart and deeds, Morgan, and of your own coldness. I'm just the facilitator."

She seemed about to respond, but apparently thought better of it as she turned and walked out. Si Cwan and Lefler followed her out, and Lefler paused for a brief moment to look back at Calhoun. The captain couldn't tell whether she was looking at him in gratitude, in anger, in confusion, or perhaps a combination of all three.

Shelby was about to speak when Calhoun quickly raised a finger to silence her as he tapped his commbadge and said, "Mr. Kebron, a moment of your time, please."

"Mac, you can't be serious about this."

"You seem to say that a lot, Commander. And you keep finding out that I'm perfectly serious. Sooner or later I think you should really stop saying that. It's making you predictable."

"Mac, for the love of—"

Kebron entered the ready room and stood there, arms casually draped behind his back. "Yes, Captain?"

"I want a level two security watch kept on Morgan," Calhoun said.

"All security personnel to keep an eye out for her at all times," Kebron said easily. "No single team or teams to watch her, but instead to trade off in pass-the-baton fashion. Check in with security head every fifteen minutes to keep me apprised of her whereabouts."

"That's it. Inform all guards. I want it done yesterday."

"Aye, sir." He tapped his commbadge. "All security units, this is Kebron. Security watch, level two, subject Morgan Primus, immediate institution. Go. All units confirm at security board," and he walked out of the captain's ready room with more speed than Calhoun would have given him credit for.

Calhoun then waited for Shelby to lay into him. His back was to her, but he was quite sure that it was gong to be coming any moment. When there was nothing but silence, he turned to face her on the assumption that she was waiting to be able to look straight at him. Sure enough, there she was, her arms folded and with a neutral look on her face that could only be covering what he was certain was a sense of complete and utter exasperation.

"Go ahead," he sighed. "Say it."

"Mac," she told him, "I think what you're doing is very sweet."

He looked at her as if she'd grown a second head. "Pardon?"

"I said I think it's very sweet."

Slowly he walked toward her with a bit of a side-to-side motion. "You know, Eppy, somehow of all the things I expected you to say, that wasn't among them."

"Look, I know you've got your heart in the right place. You see that Lefler is suffering, you feel a degree of moral outrage at the woman who's causing it, and you feel you are obliged to do something about it."

"That's mostly it," he admitted. "Oh, sure, part of it comes from the fact that she annoyed the hell out of me. That I can deal with, though. But you saw what she did to Lefler. Lieutenant Lefler is one of my people, and I won't see any one of them being abused if I can help it."

"Within the context of the ship and her mission, Robin Lefler is one of your people, no question, Mac." She took a step closer toward him, looking sympathetic. "But when it comes to dirt done to her ten years ago, and how she chooses to deal with it now, Robin is her own person. You can't make it better for her simply because you're refusing to let her mother run away again."

"The ability of each and every crewmember to function at full capacity most certainly is my business," Calhoun pointed out. "If this business with her mother diminishes Robin Lefler's ability to function, then that makes it my concern. And I will attend to the mental welfare of my officers as I see fit."

"That's a reach, Mac, and you know it. If a couple

of former lovers were aboard the same ship and were sick of each other, and one of them wanted a transfer off, would you refuse to do so because you wanted them to—"

He stared at his ex-fiancée incredulously.

"Okay, bad example," she admitted.

"I should say so."

"The point is, Mac, you can't force people to get along. You have this King Arthur complex. You want to come riding on your brave white horse and right all wrongs, save damsels in distress, and make the world safe for chivalry."

"You used to compare me to a cowboy. Now you say I'm a knight."

"Whatever fits the moment. Mac, Morgan is right. You can't keep her here against her will on a tecnicality just because it seems like a good idea to you. She hasn't done anything. Hasn't broken any laws."

"She broke Thallonian law by coming to Sector Two twenty-one-G. Lord Si Cwan is furious over the transgression, and has demanded that justice be done. He has requested that she be held until trial."

"Oh, he has," Shelby said skeptically. "Considering that he is a deposed lord and his empire fallen, his jurisdiction in this matter seems questionable. And when was this burst of indignation, may I ask?"

"Five minutes from now, after I tell him about it."

"This isn't a joke, Mac. Your motives are pure . . ."

"As befits the ruler of Camelot."

She nodded in acknowledgment and then continued, "But you don't have the right to do this. You're trying to twist the legitimate concerns a captain may possess about a crew's well being into a shape that will allow you to do anything you want. You can't just run roughshod over regulations whenever you feel like it. The rules exist for a reason."

"I know that, Commander. And I know that you're right. I should be making more of an effort to live within them. Often I consider rules and regulations to be unworkable and, to be perfectly blunt, if I can find a way around them in order to do what's right and proper, then I'll do so."

"Right and proper by your definition."

"Yes. Because I'm the one who's out here, Eppy. Not the paper pushers and nameless bureaucrats who made the rules that I'm supposed to follow. Something is going on with Morgan Primus, Commander. Something that, in my opinion, goes beyond her abandonment of her daughter and husband ten years ago. I don't know if it presents a threat to Federation security, to this ship, or to the whole of Thallonian space, but until I do know to my satisfaction, then here is where she is going to stay. I'm sorry if that upsets you, Eppy."

"No, it doesn't upset me particularly. Saddens me a bit, but doesn't upset me. You could be a great officer, Mac. One of the best there ever was, if you could only learn to live within the rules that other officers do. Mac, do you think I enjoy constantly having to be your conscience? To be the voice of reason? I knew signing on that I'd be serving that function to some degree, but I didn't quite expect it would be this much. Sometimes I think you never listen to me."

"I always listen to you, Eppy. Not necessarily doing what you say is not the same as not listening to you. Look, when it comes down to it, and if I have to choose, I'll settle for being the best man I can be rather than the best officer, and let everything else sort itself out."

"You can have that attitude now, Mac. But sooner or later, there's going to be fallout over it. You're flaunting regulations and someday you're going to flaunt the wrong one. And when that happens—"

"When that happnens, then what? Tell me, Eppy, if they call you to testify, whose side are you going to be on? Would you sit there and tell a board of inquiry that you support me or that you're against me?"

She shrugged. "I don't know. Maybe I'll have Captain Binky come and testify in my stead."

"I'm serious, Commander."

"So am I, Captain."

She turned to go, and he smiled wanly as he called after her, "Besides, Eppy, you shouldn't be upset. It's appropriate, really."

"Appropriate? You lost me, Mac. How so?"

"You said I had a King Arthur complex. Well, what better ship to have me than the *Excalibur?*"

She shook her head as she walked out, and as she went she said, "Mac, I just hope to hell you know what you're doing."

He waited until she was gone, and then he said to himself, "So do I, Eppy. So do I."

IX.

SOLETA AND BURGOYNE STUDIED the readouts from the matter-antimatter reactor assembly as the *Excalibur* moved through space at warp three. "You see?" Burgoyne said, noting the energy spikes. "There it is again. Some sort of rhythmic pulse."

"And you seriously believe it could be a biologic?" Soleta asked. "That seems rather far-fetched, Chief."

"More far-fetched than a gigantic flaming bird smashing apart a planet?"

"No. I will grant you that. And the theory," she said, looking over the case history of the problem, "is that somehow it's becoming energized whenever we use the warp engines."

"That is essentially correct."

Soleta stepped away from the consoles and looked at the massive matter-antimatter reactor assembly.

The M-ARA stood ten decks tall, with the matter reactant injector at the top and the antimatter reactant injector at the bottom. The core of the reactor was a series of doughnut-shaped pressure vessel toroids, surrounded by phase adjustment coils and coming together in the dilithium housing and reaction chamber in the middle. The crackling energy of ionized gas, hotter than the sun, pulsed within.

"Something existing in that?" Soleta said in wonderment. "Something feeding off it?" She weighed the situation for a moment, and then said, "Well, there is one way I can think of to test it."

"That being . . . ?"

"Well, when an infant is feeding at its mother's bosom, if you remove the food source, you get a reaction. The child demands to know where its food source is."

"You're not suggesting shutting down the engines cold."

"It shouldn't be necessary. We can scale the engines down and very likely generate the same reaction."

"Yessss," Burgoyne said slowly, stroking hir chin and studying the reactor core thoughtfully. "Yes, we could. And I'll have my people running scans all over the M-ARA to see if they can localize some sort of anomaly. It might very well stand out against the lessening energy and, at the very least, make its presence known. While we're at it, we can run a PPT—a pressure port test—at either end of the assembly. I'm worried that damage might have been done to the port seals during all these energy spikes. Besides, with the ports open, we'll have an easier time running scans to see what, if anything is in there, and we can only run PPTs when we're operating the engines at a fraction of normal capacity."

"Won't you have to remove the magnetic fields in order to do that?" Soleta said, sounding a bit concerned. "We could flood the entire engine room with radiation."

"No danger of that. We'll put a temporary containment patch on it. That'll be more than enough to hold everything in place. Only problem is," s/he said thoughtfully, "we won't be able to run at warp speed. Impulse will have to do."

"Do you think it wise to delay?"

Burgoyne shook hir head. "Something is going on in my engines. The sooner we know what, the better off we'll be."

"All right," Soleta said in a no-nonsense tone. "I'll get the necessary clearances from the captain. We'll be a bit late for our rendezvous with the *Seidman,* but that's hardly a matter of extreme concern. You get your team assembled and we'll start the procedure at . . . thirteen hundred hours?"

"Done," said Burgoyne.

Morgan Primus sat in the Team Room at twelve-fifty-five hours, trying to figure out just what in the world she was going to do next. She had a large pitcher of synthehol on the table in front of her, and she was lifting it carefully as if judging its heft.

"May I join you?" came a voice from nearby. She glanced up and saw Si Cwan standing next to her, looking politely interested in her.

"Be my guest," she replied, gesturing to the empty seat opposite her. Si Cwan took it and she couldn't help but notice how upright he sat. Ramrod straight. "I feel so loved."

"Indeed. And why is that?"

"See him?" she said, angling her head toward one side of the Team Room. A security guard was there, with a hand on a drink and an eye on her. "Followed me in here. And before he followed me, another guard was following me. I counted about eight switch-offs."

"Why would they be doing that?"

"Because that's what I would do. Security watch, level two, in all likelihood. Nicely effective way of keeping an eye on somebody if you don't want to look like you're keeping an eye on somebody."

Si Cwan fixed his gaze on the security guard. He looked up after a moment, noticed that Si Cwan was watching him, and quickly endeavored to look anywhere else.

"He's not particularly good at it, this one in particular. But he probably hasn't had a lot of practice." She swirled the drink she had in the glass and said regretfully, "Synthehol. Never developed much of a taste for it myself. Romulan ale is my drink of choice."

"I believe that is illegal, is it not?"

She put a finger to her lips and said "Shhhh" in a conspiratorial manner. Then she put her glass down and asked with grim amusement, "Are you here to plead my daughter's case?"

"I am here because you have a difficulty, and I wish to simplify it for you."

She leaned forward, her interest piqued. "Can you get me off the ship?"

"No. But you can get you off the ship."

"Oh. This again." She looked out the main window,

and then frowned. "We're slowing down. I wonder why."

"Are you certain?"

"Believe me, I know. We've come out of warp and now we're reducing speed even further. I wonder why they cut the warp engines. It's not as if we're near anything."

"I don't know. I'm sure they have their reasons."

"Really." She turned to look at him. "Tell me, then: If you are so certain that the people in Engineering have their reasons for what they do, why can't you make the leap that I have reasons for what I do?"

"Because I know them and have confidence in them," Si Cwan said reasonably. "You are asking for that same degree of trust and have done nothing to earn it."

"You're saying I should go spill my guts to my daughter."

"I am saying you have a problem that is not going to be solved simply by sitting in the Team Room and complaining about the quality of the beverages served here. Talk to your daughter. Talk to the captain. Explain yourself."

Her dark eyebrows knit. "And how often did you have to explain yourself in your lifetime, Si Cwan, hmm? How often did you have to explain the orders you gave, to cite chapter and verse as to why your instructions should be obeyed. Not very often, I should think. In fact, all during your reign I would venture to guess that you never had to. You simply voiced a wish and it was obeyed."

"For one thing, you are not royalty."

She waggled a scolding finger. "Never assume."

"And for another," he continued, ignoring the

reprimand, "I indeed had to explain myself any number of times to my peers. To those who were capable of judging what I had to say; people whose support I depended upon in order to get things done."

"Ahhh," said Morgan, "then that's where the problem is stemming from. You see, I have no peers on this ship."

"Oh, is that a fact?"

"Yes. More of a fact than you could possibly believe. Even if I explained it to you, it is most unlikely that you would believe me."

"I don't know about that," retorted Si Cwan. "I have seen and done quite a few things of amazing variety. You would be surprised as to what I would believe."

"Not this. You'll never believe this."

"And what precisely is the nature of this thing I won't believe?"

She seemed to be sizing him up once more, as if she were considering being completely honest with him. "I wish I could trust you. I wish I could trust someone. I can't even trust my own daughter," she said, looking rather depressed over the entire matter. "You'd think I could, wouldn't you?"

"I can be trusted, and so can Robin."

She shook her head. "She hates me. She hates me, and I can't blame her. She feels I ran out on her, and she doesn't understand. She just doesn't. How could she?"

"How could she understand what?"

And it was at that moment that the lights suddenly went out.

Immediately everyone was on their feet, looking around in confusion. The lights came back on again, but then dimmed, and there were noises of bewilderment, everyone asking everyone else questions.

Suddenly the ship shook violently, staggering everyone in the Team Room. Alarms began to klaxon all over the station.

And Morgan was already on the move.

The pitcher in her hand, she was charging for the door of the Team Room the moment the lights had gone out the first time. Si Cwan, looking elsewhere and distracted, didn't see her go. But the security guard had her firmly in his sights and, already certain that she had spotted him, tossed aside caution and moved to intercept her.

She got within two feet of him and suddenly she was swinging her arm around full speed. The guard didn't have any time to react as the pitcher of synthehol smashed against the side of his head. The pitcher was relatively unbreakable, but the guard's head was not. He went down, the world swirling around him and spinning away into blackness as blood poured from a large wound on his head. Morgan, for her part, didn't care. She tossed aside the pitcher and was out the door within seconds.

The plan was already running through her head even as she heard the alarms began to wail. She looked left and right and saw dozens of crewmen running to the positions assigned to them at times of shipboard emergency, which this most certainly was, whatever was causing it. There was not going to be any time for anyone to pay attention to one little passenger.

She noticed a medtech heading quickly down a corridor. The medtech had equipment attached to a belt looped around her waist, and Morgan saw possibilities. The techie was doubtlessly heading for sickbay. That was the same general direction that Morgan was going, and so she wouldn't need to go far out of her way at all to obtain potentially useful items.

Smoothly and unhurriedly, as if she had all the time in the world, Morgan Primus blended in with the running crewmen of the *Excalibur,* moving quickly after the medtech and hopefully, after that, toward her destination . . . and freedom.

On the walkways above the matter reactant injector, Ensign Ronni Beth was heading in one direction, energy survey instruments in hand, and looked up in annoyance to see that Ensign Christiano was coming toward her in the other direction. For a moment, just a moment, her heart fluttered at the sight of him—the tall, lanky body, the flowing brown hair, and the ready grin—and the memory of what she'd once had with him, but then she remembered the hurt that he had given her and her heart hardened against him.

Christiano didn't appear to notice her at first, because he was looking over his own instrumentation readings. But then he looked up, saw her and said cheerfully, "Beth, hi!"

She stopped a few feet away from him. About six feet below them, the top of the matter reactant injector pulsed slower and slower as the engine capacity was reduced. The core itself seemed, from the angle they were at, to stretch downward into infinity, the ionized gas within swirling around like a captured nova. " 'Beth, hi'? That's what I get? After the hell you put me through?"

"Look," said Christiano, "it's not what you think . . ."

"No, it's never what I think," she shot back at him. "You and I, we were never what I thought."

"Ron, don't be like that."

"I can't help the way I am!" she said, thumping the railing in annoyance. "And what the hell are you doing up here, anyway? I'm supposed to be running the scans on the MRI."

"No, that's what Burgy told me to do."

In annoyance, Beth tapped her commbadge. "Beth to Burgoyne."

"Burgoyne here. We've got the engine down to five percent of capacity, and the temporary containment patch is in place. You should be able to start running the pressure port tests."

"Will do, Chief. But I've got Christiano up here as well."

"What's he doing up there?" Burgoyne sounded confused and annoyed.

"That's what I was wondering. Did you intend to have us both up here?"

"No! Christiano, can you hear me?"

Making out Burgoyne's voice wasn't easy over the *thrumming* of the engine below, but Christiano was just able to manage it. "I hear you, Chief."

"You're supposed to be running the port test at the *antimatter* reactant injector. Not the MRI, the AMRI. You're at the wrong end of the M-ARA."

Christiano looked rather chagrined. It was bad enough being in the wrong place, but having made the screw up with Beth present and knowing about it . . . well, that was more than he would have liked. "Sorry, Chief. I'll get right on it."

"See that you do! Burgoyne out."

* * *

Burgoyne shook hir head in annoyance as s/he monitored the readouts. Soleta was next to hir and asked, "Problem?"

"Crewman's in the wrong place. At least," s/he said, frowning, "I think he is. Frustrating thing is, I hope it wasn't my screwup. I might have accidentally assigned him to the wrong place. Just had a lot on my mind lately, I guess."

"Do you wish to discuss it?" asked Soleta.

"No. No, I don't think so."

"Good," Soleta said firmly. "Because I do not believe I wish to hear—"

Then her eyes widened. "Burgoyne!" she said as the readings began to spike.

"I see it!" replied Burgoyne. Hir heart was pounding against hir rib cage as hir mind fought to understand what s/he was seeing. "Look at that! Something's driving the energy readings back up again! But that's impossible! Nothing can override the flow from the power transfer conduits! It's got twenty seven fail-safes!"

"Apparently that's one less than it needed," Soleta told hir sharply. "The engines are powering up, the matter-antimatter feed is coming back on line."

"Blast and damn!" shouted Burgoyne even as s/he hit hir commbadge. S/he looked up at the ten stories of the M-ARA as s/he called, "Burgoyne to Beth! Burgoyne to Christiano! Get the hell out of there! We're removing the containment patch and replacing the pressure ports! Get clear in case something else goes wrong!"

That was when Burgoyne heard the screams. Alarmed shouts coming from throughout the engine room, reacting to something that did not seem as if it could possibly exist.

And then s/he saw it.

In the heart of the matter-antimatter core, it began to take form. The ionized gas within moved about it, and whether it was feeding off it or whether the gas was actually constituting its body, s/he couldn't even begin to guess.

It didn't have eyes or any discernible feature. It seemed almost embryonic, as if it were trying to decide what shape it was going to take. Burgoyne could almost imagine that s/he heard some sort of distant roaring, although that was flat-out impossible. But then again, so was this.

"Soleta to bridge!" Soleta was shouting over her commbadge. "There is some sort of being in the M-ARA! Repeat, some sort of creature, possibly sentient, definitely hungry!"

"On my way!" came Calhoun's voice.

And then the alarms began to go off, systems shutting down and starting up again all over the ship. Burgoyne wasn't sure where to look first, and then s/he looked up and s/he saw something truly horrifying. Something that made the situation seem like the death throes of Thallon all over again, except this time it was the helpless *Excalibur* that found herself squarely in the middle of the situation.

Something was punching its way up through the top of the matter reactant injector. Although the magnetic patch was still in place, some*thing*—a talon, a claw, a tentacle, a roiling combination of all that and more— stretched through it and upward, toward the terrified forms of Ensigns Beth and Christiano.

* * *

Lieutenant j.g. Michael Houle never knew what hit him.

Houle, a tall, handsome, and freshly promoted flight deck officer at shuttlebay two, at that moment was trying to figure out why all the systems were going insane in front of him. One indicator said that the bay doors were open, another said they were closed, a third said that the annular force field that prevented depressurization of the bay had come on, another said no. It was as if the entire array had gone nuts, as if something was blowing out energy all over the ship and creating havoc with the systems.

He heard a footfall behind him and turned to see if it was someone who was going to explain to him what was going on. He didn't even have time to fully register that a fist was coming his way before it struck him cleanly on the chin. Houle's head snapped around and he sagged to the floor without having managed to say a single word.

Morgan stepped past him, shaking out her hand to remove the tingling from her fist. "Never hit bone on bone," she scolded herself. "I simply must remember that."

From the Ops booth, she looked down over the shuttlecraft available to her. There was not quite the assortment available as there was in the main shuttlebay; on the other hand, she knew it was considerably less guarded and more open to attack. Besides, she didn't need much. Then she spotted the ideal vehicle for her needs.

"A type six," she said briskly. "Will give me warp two for thirty-six hours, warp one-point-two for two days if I'm moving at full bore. Excellent."

Her intention had been to reroute the bay door

commands so that she could activate them from the interior of the shuttle, but she quickly found herself falling victim to the systems blackouts that were devastating the rest of the ship. Clearly the unexpected distraction of the systems problems was a double-edged sword. It had caused enough confusion to allow her to slip by the security guards, but it was now impeding her intended means of egress.

"All right," she said to no one. "Not a problem. I have a backup plan."

Quickly she exited the Ops deck and headed down to the shuttlecraft that she had selected. She emerged from the stairway to the Ops level, ran several feet— and stopped.

Si Cwan was blocking her way, standing between her and the shuttlecraft.

"You left right in the middle of our drinks, Morgan," he chided her. "You struck me as a woman of better breeding than that.

"One side, Ambassador, or I'll strike you in a worse way than that," she said. Slowly she walked toward him, her arms swinging in leisurely fashion. "This is none of your concern."

"Yes, so you believe. Unfortunately for you, I do not." He did not appear the least bit concerned about her advance. There seemed little reason for him to be. He was a head taller than she, with broad shoulders and muscular build. And he was someone who had proven himself any number of times in battle; indeed, he had even managed to fight the formidable Zak Kebron himself to a standstill. "Do not try it, Morgan. The outcome will not be pleasant for you."

"Yes, so *you* believe," she tossed back at him.

"Trust me, Si Cwan, you do not want to get between me and the shuttle."

"I already am, and trusting you seems to be the root of our problem, doesn't it?"

"It would seem so."

And then, with no further preamble, Morgan launched herself at Si Cwan.

He admired her form. She moved quickly, confidently, and although she didn't have nearly the reach that Si Cwan did, she more than made up for it with speed and aggressiveness. But Si Cwan's confidence never wavered. He sidestepped as she came at him with that graceful economy of movement he always displayed, and he swung his leg in a roundhouse kick that was designed to catch her squarely in the back and knock her to the ground.

But then Morgan made a sudden movement with her hand, something so subtle that he almost didn't spot it. When he did, it was too late. His leg was already in motion, and then Morgan had out the spray hypo that she had grabbed off the medtech and secreted up her sleeve. She jammed it squarely into his inner thigh and it hissed its contents into him.

"You . . . !" Si Cwan managed to get out, and then the world twisted around him. He sank to his knees, desperately trying to fight off whatever it was that she had pumped into his system. There appeared to be three of her in front of him and he made a desperate lunge toward the one in the middle. One would have thought it was the logical choice, but his hand went right through her and then the one on the right slammed a fierce kick into the side of his head.

And still Si Cwan would not go down. Instead he

crawled on his hands and knees, trying to go after her even as she opened the door of the shuttle. "Oh, for God's sake," she said in irritation. Displaying amazing strength considering her size, she grabbed Si Cwan by the back of his tunic and yanked him toward a freight container that was anchored to the floor. It was exactly what she needed as she yanked it open and saw that it was empty. She hauled him up and shoved him into the container, snapping the lock shut on top. "You won't suffocate," she said. "I'll let them know you're in here after I'm safely gone. Trust me, this is for your own good, although you probably can't hear me or else don't believe. But as you said, trust has always been part of our problem, hasn't it?"

Si Cwan couldn't manage any sort of articulate response, which wasn't all that much of a problem since she wasn't listening to him. With the ambassador safely stowed, she headed back for the shuttle and climbed in.

Quickly she fired it up, bringing the engines on line with practiced ease. She had to hurry the systems check, but she was confident in Starfleet compulsion to keep everything in top working order.

For the briefest of moments she regretted taking off on Robin yet again. But she would just have to understand. "You're a big girl now, Robin," Morgan said, "and you can certainly live without your mommy. Heaven knows you've done it for long enough."

The bay doors remained sealed, but Morgan did not see that as being a problem for much longer. As the engines roared to life, Morgan brought the phaser array on line. Standard equipment for the shuttle did not include any weaponry, but Morgan had quickly spotted this one rigged with a type IV phaser array.

Clearly this was a shuttle reserved for special operations. Well, she had just such an operation in mind.

She targeted the bay doors and opened fire. The phasers blasted outward, pounding into the doors and easily smashing through them, sending large pieces of the triple-layered duranium doors tumbling into space.

She prepared to lift off, but something ricocheted off the front of the shuttle, tumbling away. It caught her attention and she realized that it was the top of a freight container. Then she heard something else, something much fainter, bump against the lower section of the ship. She might not have heard it at all, for the vacuum of space and the roar of the engines was almost deafening, but the moment she saw the piece from the container spiraling away into space, she had known with hideous certainty what was going to be next. A quick exterior scan confirmed it for her.

"I don't believe it," she said.

Si Cwan was clutching the right warp nacelle of the shuttle, and he had mere seconds to live before the howling vacuum of space dragged him to his death.

X.

THE TENTACLE (for that was the shape that it had
assumed at that moment) stretched up out of the
matter-antimatter core. The magnetic seal reconfig-
ured around the tentacle, preventing any of the intense radiation and heat—hot enough to blast a
gaping hole straight through the side of the
Excalibur—from escaping.

"You go this way, I'll go that way!" screamed
Christiano as it snaked upward. But Beth was paralyzed, staring down at the tentacle in undiluted horror. No textbook had ever prepared her for this, no
tall tale or fable of an expedition had ever mentioned
something akin to a Lovecraftian monster taking
refuge inside of the warp core. It was like nothing
anyone had ever seen, a horrific thing composed of
energy plasma, glowing and shifting, undulating hide-

ously, and she could swear that it was letting loose with some sort of ungodly howling that was ripped from the primordial origins of humanity.

"Go!" Christiano shouted again, and he shoved her, and this time she started to move. Christiano bolted in the other direction and then the tentacle snaked out and wrapped around Christiano's leg. Christiano barely had time to let out a cry of terror and then he was yanked clear off the catwalk. The tentacle started to retract, hauling Christiano down toward the magnetic seal and, inevitably, toward the warp core itself. Through the clear containment of the core, Beth could see the being within writhing about, upset, confused, furious, trying to come to terms with its very existence in an environment that defied the ability of anything to live within it.

Christiano howled Beth's name, and Beth had no time at all to make a snap decision. She lunged off the catwalk, snagging the lower half of the rail with one hand and stretching her other hand to the utmost just as the tentacle descended past her with a frantic Christiano writhing in its grasp. The containment patch yawned wide beneath them, not letting the radiation out, but not stopping anyone from going in. The ionized gas roiled below and then Beth snagged Christiano by the wrist.

"Don't let go!" he screamed. *"Don't let go! Don't let me go!"*

The tentacle yanked downward and Beth's grasp slipped as she was jolted before she was able to get a firm grip on the catwalk railing. She snagged Christiano's hand, holding on with every bit of willpower she had, as she was hauled halfway forward and her ankles wrapped desperately around the lower strut of the railing. Now she had no support at all, forming a human bridge between the catwalk and Christiano. There was no way on Earth she could possibly get the leverage to haul Christiano back up.

Not that it mattered.

For with that abrupt yank downward, Christiano's lower body was yanked down into the warp core. Ironically, Beth's endeavors to help him transformed what would have been a quick death into an agonizing one. Had he simply fallen in, he would have been vaporized instantly. As it was, the lower half of his body was immediately incinerated, but the upper half—including a piercing and terrifying death scream—had time to register what was happening while it was happening.

There is no more horrifying sensation than knowing that one is already dead and there is nothing one can do about it.

Without Christiano to anchor her, Beth simply hung there, held only by the locked position of her ankles. She was stunned, her mind unable to accept what she had just witnessed, and then her entire body simply shut down and her legs went limp. Beth began a headfirst dive toward instant death.

And a taloned hand reached down from above and snagged her ankle.

On the catwalk overhead, Burgoyne 172 held on for all s/he was worth. S/he was only slightly out of breath despite the fact that s/he had scaled the emergency ladder along the reactor core shaft, up ten decks, in just under sixty seconds flat. S/he paused a moment to gather hirself and then pulled Beth up and out of harm's way.

And the tentacle writhed up toward them.

"Pressure port seals!" shouted Burgoyne at the top of hir lungs. "Bring engine up to seventy-five percent capacity and keep it there!" And the emergency systems kicked in, slamming the pressure ports into place, sealing off access to the injectors.

The tentacle immediately dissipated, but not without giving off a massive blast of heat that Burgoyne feared, for just a moment, was capable of incinerating them where they stood. But after a few moments had passed, Burgoyne was happy to realize that they were still there and still in one piece.

S/he held a trembling Beth tight against hirself, displaying considerable agility as s/he made hir way down the ladders toward the main engineering room. Every one of hir people was gathered down there, looking shaken and confused. They were staring at the warp core with undisguised fear, for although the danger seemed momentarily to have passed, it was still all too present and all too real.

Trapped within the confines of a cargo container, Si Cwan fought desperately to shove away the lethargy that was seizing his mind. The drug injected into his system was a powerful one, but whatever it was, it had apparently been set to effect human physiology. Thallonian physiology, on the other hand, was made of sterner stuff.

It was not easy for him by any means. It was everything he could do to fight it off. His overpowering temptation was to sleep, to just give in to the darkness that threatened to envelop him. But he kept muttering, "No," over and over to himself, forcing himself to focus, to ignore the temptation to give up.

He began to pound on the lid of the container. It seemed solid, and the ringing of the noise he generated as he struck it seemed so loud that he thought it was going to split his head wide open. But he did not cease, did not give in, would not give up. "Won't . . . get away," he murmured. "Won't get away, won't get away." It became his mantra as he repeatedly pounded on the lid, over and over, determined not to lose. He felt the lid begin to loosen, bit by bit. Once more he started to tire but he knew that if he surrendered the momentum now, he would never attain it again. With both his fists he smashed upward, sending the lid flying up and off, and he started to clamber out of the container . . .

Just as the shuttlecraft blasted open the bay doors.

The vacuum of space howled around him while he was still hauling his numbed lower body out of the container. Instantly he let out much of the breath from his chest, because he knew that if he inhaled deeply, as was his reflex, the air would explode out of his lungs in a rather forceful fashion. The powerful suction hauled him out of the container and he skidded across the floor. Only seconds lay between him and ejection into the depths of space.

He pushed up with his powerful arms, angling himself in a desperate move, and slammed into the warp nacelle of the shuttlecraft. Urgently he wrapped his arms around the nacelle, braced his slow-to-function legs against the support strut, and hung on with all the strength he could muster.

The shuttlecraft lifted clear of the floor, and it was then that he realized that seeking salvation from death in space by clutching on to a vessel about to head into that very same void was probably not the best strategy he had ever developed. Unfortunately, by the look of things, he wasn't going to be around long enough to formulate any more.

"Damn the man!" snarled Morgan. "*God*damn the man!"

All she had to do was hit the forward thruster, and the shuttlecraft would be out and away. She would be clear of the *Excalibur,* gone to the safety of space and away from her imprisonment, and by the time they realized what had happened she would be long gone. Granted, they'd probably be able to follow her, but she had places she could get to, resources she could tap. Coolly she ranked her odds at about 70/30 in favor of making a clean getaway, and those were odds that she would happily take.

But it was going to be at the cost of a man's life; a man who had wanted nothing more but to try and patch things up between her and her daughter and obey the captain's dictates that she was not to leave the ship. Was her freedom worth killing Si Cwan for?

Hell yes! Morgan's mind screamed at her. *You don't owe him anything! Punch it and let's go!* But even as her mind celebrated her freedom, she powered up the reverse thrust. The shuttle backed up under her careful guidance, slowly and carefully bringing Si Cwan toward the door that led to the Operations control booth. She knew that if she could get him to that point, and if he could just hold on until she did, he could worm his way through the door and to safety.

And the drug in Si Cwan's system picked that moment to release its full potency.

Si Cwan suddenly felt his arms and legs go completely limp. He retained consciousness, but commands from his brain to his limbs simply didn't go through. He slid off the nacelle and didn't even have the opportunity to thud to the floor as the suction of deep space picked him up and hauled him toward the void. And there was absolutely nothing that Morgan could do about it.

So it was with complete astonishment that she saw Si Cwan slam to a halt just as he was about to plunge into space. An invisible barrier had sprung into existence, and Si Cwan slid off it and fell to the ground, looking somewhat stunned.

Up in the Ops control booth, Lieutenant j.g. Michael Houle had come to when he heard the phasers blast open the doors. Forcing himself to full consciousness, he had desperately tried to reroute the malfunctioning systems for the purpose of activating the forcefield, which was the normal backup when the bay doors were open. With seconds to spare, Houle had managed to bring the systems back on line and turn on the forcefield.

Instantly the suction of space's vacuum had been thwarted, although Si Cwan still looked somewhat amazed to discover that he was, in fact, alive.

Morgan, however, was left with a problem. If she tried to open fire on the forcefield, she might or might not be able to punch through it. But if she did, she'd be faced with the same problem she had before: Si Cwan, who in this case was lying in stupefied confusion, still trying to sort out what had happened, was now smack in the way. Her hasty exit meant his untimely death.

She had already faced that decision once, and she knew what it was going to be.

With the frustrated grunt of one who knows she has lost, Morgan settled the shuttlecraft back down into its place. Then she opened up the side hatch and stepped out to see if Si Cwan was all right.

What she discovered instead was half a dozen security men with phasers drawn and leveled at her.

"Hi, boys," she said with a cheerfulness she didn't feel.

A medical team had been dispatched immediately to Engineering. Aside from some minor radiation and heat burns as a result of the strange, energy plasma tentacle that had extended from the heart of the warp core, the single greatest injured party seemed to be Beth. She sat in one corner of Engineering, trembling uncontrollably, her arms drawn close together and her legs drawn up in an almost fetal position. Dr. Karen Kurdziel was administering a sedative to her as Burgoyne stood nearby, looking on and feeling more helpless than s/he had ever felt before.

"There you go," Kurdziel said. "Now come on, relax. Just relax." And slowly she forced open Beth's arms, which were still frozen in a sort of rictus.

Something wet and fleshy plopped to the floor, causing several crewmen who were nearby to jump back, startled and repulsed. It was Christiano's right hand. Even to the end, Beth had not let go of it. She'd been clutching it even beyond the point where she was aware that she was doing it. Then the sedative fully kicked in, and she slumped over. Moments later an antigrav gurney had carried her away.

Burgoyne watched it go, and then Calhoun was at hir side, a hand resting on hir shoulder. "Nice save of Ensign Beth, Chief," Calhoun said.

"Not nice enough to save Christiano as well, though."

"You did the best you could." He raised his voice to address the other members of Engineering. "All right, people. I know this was a rough one. And I know our neighbor there"—and he indicated the warp core within which something completely unknown seemed to be lurking—"is somewhat disconcerting. But Lieutenant Soleta assures me that we can keep it under control for the time being, so we shouldn't have to evacuate the ship. I'm asking you now to be the professionals I know you are, and carry on your duties with the efficiency that I've come to expect from you as the crew of the *Excalibur*."

There were still nervous stares, and fearful glances at the core, but slowly the Engineering staff went back to their assigned posts. Calhoun, meantime, immediately went with Burgoyne to hir office, Soleta accompanying the two of them. The moment they had seclusion, Calhoun said flatly, "You're not going to tell me I misspoke, are you, Lieutenant? You *can* control the thing."

"Yes, I believe so, at least for the time being. We can supercool the matter-antimatter mix, basically slow down the thing's metabolism, whatever that may be. It will still receive energy from the ship's engines, so it won't have another fit. But it'll be sluggish and, with any luck, unable to cause any damage."

"Did you have any idea that it would retaliate in the way that it did when we cut the energy consumption?"

"No, sir," said Soleta flatly. "But I should have allowed for that possibility. The responsibility is mine and I accept full consequences for the outcome."

"Now wait a minute," Burgoyne contradicted her. "This is my engine room, the final decision mine. If not for me—"

"This was a scientific mishap, Chief. Mine was the oversight that might have prevented—"

"Shut up," Calhoun said sharply, silencing both of them. "It doesn't matter whose fault it is. The responsibility is mine . . . and always is. And that's all. Besides, all the placed blame in the world doesn't bring back a single life. Are we clear on that?" When they nodded silently, he said, "All right. What the hell have we got in there, anyway?"

"In simplest terms," said Soleta, "something planted by the energy creature that we encountered during the destruction of Thallon. Possibly an offspring of the creature itself. I've compared the energy resonance of the bird-like energy creature we encountered with the entity that's in the warp core. There are variances, but sufficient similarities to indicate that there is some sort of relation. It is my belief that it is presently in the natal stages. But once it 'hatches,' its birth will very likely destroy the ship. And as it continues to grow, the effect it will continue to have on us is unpredictable."

"When does it hatch?"

"Unknown. It could be days, months, perhaps years. Its progenitor, if such it is, took centuries. There is simply no way to tell at this time."

"All right. And how do we get it out of our engine?"

"We don't know that either."

"Great. What *do* we know?"

"That we're screwed?" suggested Burgoyne.

Calhoun looked tiredly at Burgoyne. "Yes, Chief. I think we figured that one out all on our own."

XI.

Si Cwan stood outside the brig and looked at Morgan inside of it with more than a little sadness. "I did my best, Morgan," he told her. "I pointed out to the captain that you could easily have made your escape at the cost of my life, but you chose not to. I thought that would weigh in your favor. Unfortunately the captain did not choose to view your generosity in the same manner as I did."

From within the brig, Morgan shrugged. "That's all right, Si Cwan. You tried. And to be honest, I can see your captain's point of view on this one. There's just something about having someone blast open a door in one of your shuttlebays that makes you less than likely to think kindly of that person."

"That's a very philosophical way to look at it," Si Cwan noted. Then he stopped speaking, apparently noticing someone coming his way. "Why, Morgan, I believe you have visitor."

Morgan knew perfectly well who it was going to be even before Robin appeared in view, for the tread tipped her off. She realized belatedly why she was able to pinpoint it so easily. It was because it sounded just like her own step.

"Hello, Robin," she said.

Lefler stood on the other side of the forcefield door, her hands behind her back, simply staring at her mother. Judiciously, Si Cwan said, "Perhaps you'd prefer that I left so that you ladies could have some time alone."

"No, that's quite all right," Lefler said. "Mother, I know about the circumstances that resulted in your being here, and although I know that you were in the process of committing a crime . . . a crime for which you deserve to be punished, and frankly, I don't care if you're left here until you rot, and . . ."

"Robin, is there going to be something remotely uplifting in this dissertation anytime soon?" asked her mother. "Because if—"

"Mother, just be quiet, okay? I just . . . I wanted to thank you for not killing Si Cwan. God, I can't believe I said that. Thanking someone for not committing a murder, as if that shows any sort of incredible moral character. No one was ever thankful to me because I didn't kill anyone."

"Our tenth anniversary," Morgan said promptly.

Robin stared at her in confusion. "What?"

"Our tenth wedding anniversary, your father and me," Morgan explained. "You were five years old. And you decided that you wanted to make us breakfast. You were very excited about it. You couldn't decide what to make, so you made everything. While we slept, you destroyed the kitchen. You made eggs, pancakes—peanut butter pancakes, as I recall—French toast, cereal, bacon that was fried so tough you could have chipped a tooth on it, fresh-squeezed orange juice that still had the pits in it, and some other things. I think I've blanked them out. You brought the whole thing up to our bedroom on a tray," and she demonstrated, imitating the proud walk of a five-year-old confident that she has just performed the greatest service of her entire young life. "You woke us up, showed us how you had made breakfast for us, and then sat there and expected us to eat it."

"My God, I vaguely remember this," said Robin, putting her hand to her mouth. She looked completely embarrassed, and Si Cwan was happy to see it. It was the first time he had seen her looking anything other than angry in days. "Your hair was all standing every which way because you'd just woken up."

"That's right. And you were so adorable in this little white nightgown you had then. So you marched over and put the tray down and then plopped onto the floor with that Cheshire Cat grin and waited. And your father and I, we had absolutely no choice. So we plastered smiles on our faces and we ate everything. Every damn thing. And then we spent the next few hours taking turns running to the bathroom. It was the single most hideous meal we'd ever eaten."

"Oh, my God," laughed Robin. "I'm so sorry."

"It's okay," Morgan assured her. "In many ways, it was also the best. You were such an adorable child, the best, you . . ."

And then she saw that Robin's lower lip was trembling. "Oh, Ches'," she said sadly, invoking that childhood nickname of days gone by.

"Why did you leave me, Ma?" Her voice sounded very small and very defenseless.

And Morgan walked toward her, her arms outstretched, and Si Cwan barely had time to shout a warning before she would have hit the forcefield.

She fought to keep tears from her eyes.

"Ma, are you okay?!" asked Lefler.

Morgan fought to bring herself under control. "Oh, fine. Just fine. A little shaken. Nothing I can't handle."

"I'm sorry, Mom. That was . . . unprofessional." She forced the tears to stop flowing from her eyes, drew her arm across her face in a large and rather dramatic smear.

"That's . . . quite all right, dear," Morgan said, feeling as if her teeth had been severely rattled. "I probably had that coming. That and a good deal more, I should suspect. Look, Ches', tell me what happened before. When the whole place was going crazy. No one's speaking to me about anything."

"There's nothing you can do about it, Mom. They're handling it in Engineering."

"Well, honey, I don't quite believe that's all of the story. I'd very much like to know more of what's going on, and I'd appreciate it if you would bring me up to speed. And maybe—just maybe—I can solve some of your problems if you help me solve some of mine. You know me, Ches'. You know I've got some serious brainpower, if you must force me to boast of myself."

"We have top minds working on it right now, Mom."

"Then what's one more? Go ahead, you've nothing to lose. Tell me."

So she told her. She laid it all out for Morgan, the entire story as Lefler had managed to hear it in bits and pieces. As the narrative went on, Morgan's face became more and more serious, and her eyes seemed to come into even clearer focus as if the only way that she could possibly view the world were through the prism of a problem that required solving.

Robin was silent for some time after she finished, and still Morgan said nothing. Finally, though, after having apparently given the matter considerable thought, she said, "I need to see your captain."

"Whatever for?"

"Because," Morgan told her with a hint of impatience, "I think that I can actually get this mess settled. I think I may—just may, mind you—be able to save this ship. But I'm going to have to discuss it with your captain first, and I don't think I'm exactly very high on his list."

Now it was Robin's turn to appear to ponder all that had been said. Finally she said to Morgan, "You have to understand, Mom, you're asking me to crawl out on a limb here. Not only, as you say, are you not high on the captain's list, but you're asking me to risk my own status on that very same list. Because if I crawl out on that branch along with you and then it winds up getting sawed off behind us, there is going to be a very considerable crash when it hits the ground. I have no desire to be on it."

"What are you saying?"

"I'm saying, Mother, that you're going to have to be forthcoming this time." She leaned forward to the very edge of the forcefield, resting with her hands on either side of the door frame. "Before you're given the opportunity to convince the captain, you're going to have to convince me. Do you think you can do it?"

"Do I have a choice?"

"Not that I can see."

This time Morgan didn't have to give it any thought at all. "All right," she said without hesitation. "I'll tell you. Not everything, mind you, but enough to get us started."

And she told her.

The narrative took a few minutes, and as she spoke the eyes of both Lefler and Si Cwan grew wider and wider. By the end of it, they had turned and looked at one another with conviction on both their faces. "The captain," said Si Cwan, "has definitely got to hear this."

"Do you think he'll believe it?" asked Morgan.

"If you were in his position, would you?" Si Cwan asked her reasonably.

Morgan pondered it a moment and then said, "No chance in hell."

"In that case, he probably will. Because if there's one thing I've noticed, it's that whenever one tries to second-guess Mackenzie Calhoun, one inevitably finds oneself squarely in the wrong."

"I don't believe it," said Calhoun.

"Captain, I'm deadly serious," said Morgan as Calhoun paced the conference lounge. As opposed to Morgan's earlier meeting with him, when he had appeared utterly unflappable and relaxed for the vast majority of the meeting, this time around he seemed tense and cool. She couldn't blame him, really. He had a creature living in his warp core. That would be enough to put anyone on edge.

Also present in the conference lounge were Shelby, Soleta, and Burgoyne, as well as Lefler and Si Cwan, who had organized the meeting. They likewise seemed preoccupied, and every so often Burgoyne would, as quietly as s/he could so as not to disturb anyone else at the table, receive reports from Engineering. S/he had demanded that s/he be updated every ten minutes as to any changes that might have occurred with the creature. In a uniquely odd endeavor to lighten the situation, Burgoyne had named the creature, for no discernible reason, Sparky. When Soleta had asked, "Why Sparky?" he had retorted that the creature had to be called something, and Sparky was as good a name as any. Soleta hadn't quite understood exactly why the creature needed to be called anything other than the creature, but she didn't see much point in arguing.

"Your skepticism is understandable, Captain," Morgan said. "But I'm telling you that your only hope of solving this problem lies with a race of beings—the same beings who are the reason I wound up coming here in the first place."

"Yes, so you said," Calhoun replied. "Since you are the one who's making this rather outrageous claim, Morgan, I will thank you either to try and prove it, or else stop wasting the time of everyone concerned here."

"Captain, if you'll just listen . . ." Robin began.

"I believe, Lieutenant, that I've done more than enough listening to this woman."

Morgan sat in the chair nearest the captain and

leaned forward, her fingers interlaced. Speaking with a newfound urgency, she said, "Whatever they call themselves, I couldn't begin to say. I call them the Prometheans, a highly advanced, technologically superior race. I came to Thallonian space in the company of a friend named Tarella. We'd been tracking these mysterious Prometheans, and the research trail led us to Momidium. What we found there led us to believe that the Prometheans could be found on a world called Ahmista. But before we could set off, the Momidiums wound up capturing me. Tarella got away, however, and I half expected that she would come back for me. In fact, I spent my entire first year in captivity waiting for her to return and free me. But she never came back. I don't know whether she was killed, or whether she found something so incredible that she . . ." Morgan shrugged. "It could be anything. Any of a hundred reasons why she didn't come back."

"And we're supposed to go searching for your friend, is that it?"

"I don't come to this party offering a lot of guarantees. The only thing I know is that we were heading for Ahmista. What has happened to her since then, I couldn't even begin to tell you. If I had to guess, I'd say that the odds of her still being on Ahmista are pretty slim. Chances are that I'm going to have to start from level zero to try and pick up the leads to the Prometheans."

"How do we know," Shelby asked, "that this isn't simply another ploy to try and escape?"

"Don't kid a kidder, Commander. We both know that if you don't do something about junior in the warp core, there isn't going to be a ship left to escape from. You can't survive indefinitely. You might not even survive into next week."

"Considering the gestation period of the last energy creature we encountered, we might survive into the next century," Soleta said.

"True enough, Lieutenant. Are you willing to risk your life, and the lives of everyone on this ship, on that possibility?" fired back Morgan.

"None of us are," cut in Calhoun. "But neither are we willing or interested in committing resources to a false lead to a race of beings so mythic you don't even have a definite name for them. We could be chasing fairy tales for all we know."

Si Cwan stepped forward. "And yet these fairy stories have a ring of familiarity to me, Captain. I described earlier the tales of my youth, of the gods and the firebringers. Morgan's own naming of her mystery race is after a similar fire-to-humanity story that exists in our own mythology. Don't you find it curious that both of our civilizations share a mythology having to do with the acquisition of flame?"

"That is not at all unusual," Soleta replied. "There are many core concepts that prompt similar myths. Many cultures have end of the world scenarios, flood scenarios, and different mythologies explaining different aspects of nature. No, it is not uncommon at all, and hardly proof of any connection. Unless you are about to claim that these mysterious Prometheans were responsible in some way for technological advancement on the part of mankind."

"Anything is possible."

"But not probable," said Calhoun. "We could use some sort of proof about this race aside from your suppositions and guesses. Otherwise my assumption will be that this is merely an elaborate ruse that, for some reason, Lieutenant Lefler and Ambassador Si Cwan have bought into."

Si Cwan glance down at Morgan and said simply, "Show him."

"Now is the time, Mom," agreed Lefler.

She nodded and reached under her shirt, sliding something that was round and hard up toward the collar. And then she pulled out, mounted in a black casing, a small amulet with a raised image of a flame on it. "We came upon two of these through a trader on Momidium who didn't realize what he had," she said. "Tarella and I believed that they were markers of some sort. Perhaps even beacons, a means of summoning the Prometheans, although we were not entirely sure how they would function."

There was stunned silence in the room for a moment.

"Look familiar?" Morgan asked drily.

Calhoun turned to Soleta and said quickly, "Go get it." Soleta was out of her chair like a shot.

This prompted a confused look from Morgan, who turned and stared up at Si Cwan and Lefler, who were standing nearby. "What am I missing?" she asked. "You told me they'd be interested in the medallion. You didn't go into any detail beyond that. Is there something I should know?"

"Perhaps," said Robin. "But you've been so busy being mysterious and hard to comprehend, that I thought it only fair to give you a bit of mystery right back. Seems equitable to me, don't you think?"

"Yes," Morgan said slowly, and clearly slightly amused by the situation. "Yes, I suppose it does at that."

Moments later, Soleta had returned, and to Morgan's utter astonishment, she placed down on the table a disk that likewise had a flame emblem on it. Slowly, her hand trembling, Morgan reached toward it.

"Captain . . ." Shelby said warningly, but Calhoun decided to go with his gut and waved Shelby off, indicating that they should let Morgan touch it. She picked it up, turned it over in her hands, and ran her fingers along the flame symbol engraved on it. She noticed immediately that, as opposed to the medallion she herself bore, the flame emblem was indented on this one.

Burgoyne, for hir part, seemed unimpressed. "We're wasting our time with this, Captain," Burgoyne said urgently. "The smart move is to try and get back to a starbase out of Thallonian space. Some sort of facility that can help us in extracting Sparky from the warp core."

"There is no guarantee that any facility short of the shipyards in San Francisco would be capable of accomplishing such a feat, nor do we know if even they could do so," Soleta said reasonably. "Furthermore, we do not know the full abilities of this creature. Can you imagine if the efforts of unknowing Starfleet engineers should cause the creature—"

"Sparky," Burgoyne corrected her.

"The creature," continued Soleta, "to flee the containment of the *Excalibur* only to take up residence within the core of Earth itself, as the energy creature did on Thallon? That scenario would be catastrophic, to say the least."

"You're saying we're stuck out here?"

"I am saying, Chief, that if there are other options it

would be wiser to explore them first, no matter how far-fetched."

"Captain," Morgan said cautiously, holding the faces of the medallion and the disk opposite each other. "Do you have any objections if . . . ?"

Her intention seemed self-evident and Calhoun weighed the possible consequences. "From where I sit," he finally decided, "I don't see as that we have a lot to lose. Go ahead. Let's see if rubbing the lamp will pull the genie out."

With a deep breath, Morgan slowly brought the two metal disks together. She couldn't help but notice that the diameters were a perfect match. And not only that, but with the slightest of turns to adjust, she clicked the flame emblem of her medallion into the recess of the disk handed her by Soleta.

She wasn't sure what she had expected. A flash of light, perhaps, or a sepulchral laugh. A surge of energy or a massive telepathic bolt that would cut straight to the very core of her soul and bond with her at a spiritual level. A Chinese gong. She had no idea, really.

Unfortunately, what she wound up getting was nothing.

She simply sat there, the disks in her hand. Nothing trembled, nothing vibrated. Nothing, in short, happened.

"Are we rescued from Sparky yet?" Calhoun asked drily.

"I don't understand it," Morgan said. But then, with more firmness of tone, she added, "But then again, I didn't necessarily expect to understand it. There has to be more to it than this, Captain, and with any luck at all, the answer is on Ahmista."

"Any luck at all is something we haven't had in abundance." He sat back in his chair, considering the matter a moment. "Ambassador, do you know anything about this Ahmista?"

"Not really," replied Si Cwan. "A fairly small population, the planet had no particular strategic value, and the residents were not especially advanced. It was never considered a worthwhile use of Thallonian resources to have much to do with them. We knew of them, but we never bothered with them."

"Fair enough," said Calhoun. "Do you know where Ahmista is?"

"I'm not McHenry, Captain," Si Cwan said with slight amusement. "I don't carry these matters around in my head. If I could see a starmap and our relative position on it . . ."

"Soleta?" prompted Calhoun.

Soleta punched it up on the computer terminal next to her and, moments later, the desired information appeared on the conference lounge viewscreen. It displayed all the known information about Thallonian space that they had, and a blinking spot that marked the *Excalibur*'s location. He studied it for a moment, and then pointed to a system that was not especially detailed. "Right here," he said. "This is it."

"There's no indicator of any planets there," Soleta noted.

"I think you'll find that the Federation is not in possession of any complete starmaps of Sector Two-twenty-one-G," said Si Cwan, using the Starfleet designation rather than referring to it as Thallonian space. "My people tended to be circumspect about such matters, even after the point that such circumspection was of any use to the greater good. Nonetheless, it is most definitely here. Three planets, with the outermost being the one she refers to as Ahmista."

Shelby leaned forward, studying the location. "At warp nine, it's still three days' journey from here. That's a best guess on my part; McHenry could probably tell you down to the second. But that seems about right."

"Can we afford to go to warp nine, Burgy?" asked Calhoun.

"I think so," said Burgoyne slowly, although s/he didn't appear all that enthusiastic. "As near as we can tell, increased warp activity makes Sparky more active. Doesn't make him more hostile though. The only hitch is . . . well, it could accelerate his development or growth. In trying to track down someone who can help us with this situation, we may be exacerbating it."

"This entire business is a long shot at best, Captain," Shelby observed.

"Are you saying we shouldn't do it, Commander?"

"No. I'm just saying it's a long shot."

Calhoun considered the matter for a moment, drumming his fingers on the table in thought. And finally he said, "I don't want to have to give up this ship, people. Abandonment remains an option, but it's not one that I accept gladly. To say nothing of the fact that, if we do abandon, we have no guarantee that once we shove everyone into the saucer section and cut the Engineering hull loose, Sparky might not come out of the warp core and take up residence in the saucer section impulse engines, and then we'll be worse off than when we started. A long shot is better than no shot. Commander, have McHenry lay in a course for Ahmista. Burgoyne, monitor Sparky even more closely than you are now. Eat, sleep, and breathe in synch with his cycle if you have to, but stay on top of him. Understood?"

"Aye, sir."

"Captain," Lefler asked, "may my mother leave the brig?"

He studied Morgan appraisingly for a moment. And then he said, "Your mother, Lieutenant, blew a hole in the door of shuttlebay two and almost cost Si Cwan his life, her subsequent actions notwithstanding. I don't trust her yet."

"I'm right here, Captain," Morgan commented. "You don't have to speak of me in the third person."

"I don't trust you yet," amended Calhoun. "And until such time that I do, if ever, you can take up residence back in the brig where I don't have to expend any security forces for the purpose of keeping an eye on you."

Lefler started to protest, but Morgan was already on her feet and nodding her head in acquiescence. "I understand fully, Captain. Were I in your position, I would likely be doing the same thing. And I find that I have a fairly good track record at this point in noting what you will and will not do. Robin, Ambassador, I appreciate your efforts on my behalf. And now I believe my escort is waiting for me. Captain, may I keep this?" she asked, holding up the joined medallion.

"I would rather you didn't," he told her. "Keep your half if you wish, but return the other to Lieutenant Soleta, please."

She nodded and, with a slight effort, pulled the two

apart. She handed the indented side back to Soleta and then said to Calhoun, "I appreciate your indulgence in this matter, Captain."

"May I ask, Morgan, why you are suddenly being cooperative?" Calhoun inquired.

The others looked to her, clearly interested in the answer. "I wish I had an easy answer for you, Captain. Perhaps I simply see more advantage in cooperating than not cooperating. Perhaps I think we can actually be of help to each other. Or perhaps . . ." She looked at Si Cwan. "You know, I thought, for all the time that I was incarcerated on Momidium, that I would do anything, absolutely anything, to achieve my freedom. And I discovered that, no, that wasn't the case. There are some things that I wouldn't do to gain freedom. And I found that to be . . . heartening. Does that answer your question, Captain?"

"Not completely, no."

"Well, you may just have to live with that, Captain. We all do to some degree or another."

He nodded in agreement, finding himself liking her in spite of himself, which was more than a little annoying.

XII.

Si Cwan, in his office, studied the picture of Morgan Primus that remained on his computer screen. There was a slight flicker of power, but then the couplings righted themselves as the rerouted systems Burgoyne had cobbled together righted themselves. By this point, Cwan was barely noticing such fluctuations. Like victims of any war-torn environment, difficulties that would once have seemed oppressive now had faded into mere background inconveniences.

He studied the woman's face carefully. Damn, but she was a striking individual. There was something within her, though, something that seemed to cry out of secrecy. Some deep and unending mystery at which he could only guess.

"She has old eyes," he said at last. To a Thallonian, that was a comment that had deep meaning. To have old eyes meant that one had an old soul, and was a rather experienced and spiritually elevated individual. Either that or it made a great pickup line when one wanted to compliment a female that one was interested in bedding.

He hadn't entirely made up his mind which it was for him yet.

There was a chime at the door. "Come," he said, leaning back in his chair.

To his utter surprise, Zak Kebron was standing there. As always, the massive Brikar seemed to fill the doorway.

Si Cwan's first thought was to wonder what sort of trouble he was in. He and Kebron had had a mutual antipathy, underscored by a sort of grudging respect for each other's personality and accomplishments. The closest they had come to a true understanding was the realization that they would both far rather have each other as allies than enemies. Consequently they endeavored to minimize their conversation, limiting it to missions at hand, missions in the past, and missions in the near future. It made for fairly succinct discussions that consisted mainly of the imparting of specific data. This was a relationship that worked fine for both of them.

So it was with great surprise that Si Cwan saw Kebron standing at his door. "Is there a problem, Kebron?" he asked without hesitation.

"There is," Kebron said slowly. Kebron was the mortal enemy of the term "gregarious," likely to try and eliminate it from any dictionary in any language. When he spoke it was with short, spartan sentences, although he was occasionally capable of a fairly morbid wit that even Si Cwan had to admit that he admired. "A problem that has to be addressed."

"A problem with me?" asked Si Cwan.

Kebron nodded. Since Kebron had virtually no neck, one of his nods more or less consisted of a slight bow.

"All right," said Si Cwan, slowly rising from behind his desk. "What is the nature of the problem? If there is anything I can do—"

"There is. When I point, say 'You're welcome.'"

"What?" Si Cwan stared at him. "I don't understand."

"I don't need your understanding. Just your cooperation." Kebron hadn't moved from the doorway. "Can you do it?"

"Well, yes, of course, a child could do it."

"Very well." Kebron paused as if steeling himself and then said, "Thank you." And he pointed.

"You're welcome," said a bemused Si Cwan on cue.

Kebron turned and walked away, the door sliding shut behind him.

"Now hold on a moment!" called Cwan, not about to let it go at that. He followed Kebron out into the hallway. He didn't walk right next to him, because Kebron's size, stride, and general swing of his arms as he walked usually precluded that. So Cwan hung about a foot or so back and to the right. "What was that all about? You can't just come in, say 'Thank you,' and leave."

"I just did." As was not unusual when he was walking with a purpose, the floor under Kebron rumbled slightly under his footfall.

"You didn't say why you were thanking me."

"Unnecessary."

"Not to me it's not," and he grabbed Kebron by the arm.

The massive Brikar stopped and, without looking at Si Cwan, rumbled, "You so very much do not want to do that."

Si Cwan released Kebron's arm like a fiery briquette, but he took the opportunity to step around Kebron and stand squarely in his path. This could, of course, have backfired somewhat since Kebron could had walked right over him without too much difficulty, but he was hoping that wouldn't happen. "Kebron—Zak—what's going on?"

Kebron made a sound in his chest that came across like rocks tumbling around in a clothes drier (although neither of them had ever seen, or even heard of, a clothes drier, so the comparison would have been lost on them). "I feel constrained to thank you . . . for your help."

"My help?" Si Cwan said blankly.

"You prevented Morgan Primus from escaping the ship. That was not your job. It was my job. Mine, and my people. We fumbled it. You recovered it. So I am thanking you because I feel it is the right thing to do." It was rare that Kebron ever uttered that many sentences together, and the significance of it was not lost on Si Cwan.

"No one blames your security force for losing track of Morgan. The ship was going haywire at that moment. It was—"

"Inexcusable. I owe you, Cwan. And I do not forget my debts. So thank you."

"You're welcome," said Si Cwan. "And who knows, Kebron. I've made mistakes in the past, I admit that. I don't pretend to be perfect. Perhaps we've gotten off on the wrong foot, you and I. Perhaps this is the beginning of a new and improved relationship between us. Perhaps we can put aside our differences and genuinely build a basis for a true and lasting friendship." And he stuck out a hand for Kebron to shake.

Kebron stared at the open, outstretched hand, and then he looked Si Cwan squarely in the eyes. "I don't owe you *that* much," he said, and walked away, leaving Si Cwan shaking his head in amusement.

Dr. Selar glanced across sickbay and saw someone unexpected. Mark McHenry was there, talking to Dr. Maxwell and touching his back with a pained expression. Maxwell actually seemed to be smiling as McHenry spoke, then nodded and indicated that McHenry should get up on a med table. McHenry did so and proceeded to remove his shirt while sitting up, as Maxwell stepped over to a rack of instruments. As Selar approached the two of them, while McHenry was sitting with his back to her, she could see that Maxwell had taken the neodermic applicator off the wall. The applicator was designed to create a graft of new skin, and was primarily used for quick and easy repair of abrasions. In short, it was a high-tech Band-Aid.

Maxwell saw her coming and looked at her questioningly. Selar, for her part, was looking at McHenry's back. There were scratches across it, as if he'd been clawed. She casually gestured for Maxwell to hand her the applicator, which he promptly did.

Upon closer inspection, she could see that the cuts raked across his back. There were five of them, each running parallel to one another in a diagonal path. Being a fairly bright woman, it did not take Selar long at all to figure out just exactly how those cuts had come into being. Without a word she began to run the applicator across them. Automatically disinfecting the wounds, it left a trail of pink new skin behind it.

McHenry let out a low sigh. "Ahhhhh . . . that feels good. Magic hands, Doc." Selar said nothing, and McHenry continued, "I have to tell you, that Burgoyne . . . s/he's a wild one."

"Mmm," Selar said noncommitally.

"I shouldn't. I mean, I really shouldn't. I know that. I'm kinda weak-willed when it comes to that department. Guess I don't have to tell you about what that's like, right, Doctor Selar?"

Selar was taken aback. She had been caught off-guard by McHenry's affect of inattention.

"Only problem is," admitted McHenry, "I feel like . . . like I'm taking advantage of hir, you know? Because I'm not what s/he wants, I know it. I'm not who s/he wants. But I think s/he's afraid of how much s/he wants who s/he wants, because s/he's never felt like that about anyone. I wish I were a strong-willed enough man to insist that s/he do what's right for hir, but I'm not 'cause I'm having too much fun. So I go along with it, even though I know that what s/he really wants is to be with . . . someone else. This . . . someone, hell, I figure she'll never admit that she wants to be with Burgoyne as much as Burgoyne wants to be with her. They're going to have a baby, for crying out loud! I mean, I'm a modern sort of guy. It's not as if my mind or morality is stuck in the twenty-second century. But these people have a bond, both emotional and familial. You'd think that would mean something. You'd think they'd want to work together, not be so petrified of intimacy or commitment that they'd give each other a wide berth." He sighed again, but this time it wasn't with pleasure. "I knew Christiano, y'know. We used to hang out. Decent enough guy considering he wound up as just a hand. If I learned anything from that, it's that life is just too short not to go for something that you really want."

Selar had absolutely no idea what to say. She had wanted to have a talk with McHenry, to ask about Burgoyne. She had heard about what had happened in Engineering, heard of Burgoyne's heroics in saving Ensign Beth. The entire experience had been a terrifying one overall, and although Selar was far too stoic to actually be terrified, she still felt a great deal of concern for Burgoyne. She had wanted to go down there, to ask personally if s/he was all right, to say something . . . try to make some sort of connection, even though she wasn't sure what to say and was even less sure whether Burgoyne wanted that connection.

And here she had wound up having a talk with McHenry, or a listen at least. Except she felt as if she were an eavesdropper. Selar was a highly moral individual, and this entire business now seemed sneaky and wrong to her. She stepped back and then saw Dr. Maxwell watching out of the corner of her eye. She gestured for Maxwell to come over, and handed him back the applicator and quickly slipped away. He watched her go, shaking his head, and then leaned over to finish the skin application on McHenry's back. Selar, for her part, retreated to her office.

"Everything okay back there?" asked McHenry.

"Certainly," Selar said. "But Dr. Maxwell will continue your treatment."

"So . . . so what did you talk about?" Maxwell asked, after Selar had left.

"Nothing," McHenry said easily. "Nothing important at all. Trust me, Maxie, it's nothing that you have to know."

"I have to know."

Robin Lefler had entered the brig and was now standing opposite her mother, leaning against a corner of the wall. Morgan wasn't even looking at her, though.

"Mother, did you hear me?"

"Yes, I heard you. You said you have to know."

"Mom . . ." She tried to find the right words. "The other day, when Engineering went haywire . . . we could have died then. All of us. Now, I'm not afraid of dying, Mom. I'm really not. It's not like I'm eager to, you understand. And it's not like, if someone tries to take me down, I won't go kicking and screaming. Believe me, given the choice, I'd rather be dancing on the dirt than lying under it, you know? But I . . . I don't want to die in ignorance. For years I thought that my life was simply unfair and tragic, but at least I was used to that. Now, though, I find that it makes no sense. I don't know why it makes no sense. I don't know why anything anymore. I backed you up when it came to talking to the captain. You have no idea how difficult that was for me. No idea at all. But I did it as a gesture, to show you that I was capable of trusting you. Now . . . now I need you to trust me, Mother. I need you to tell me what's really going on. The truth of everything. Will you do that for me, Mother? Will you please do whatever you can to try and help my life make sense again? I want . . . I want to go back to being the woman I was. I was happy once. I can't be happy, ever again, until I know and understand this. Please. Please do this for me. If you've ever done anything for me in your life. If you've ever really, truly believed you loved me: Be honest with me."

"You won't believe it," Morgan said quietly.

"I will."

"You won't." She looked up at her sadly. "Your father didn't believe. Not at first. At first he thought I was just crazy. And then, when I . . . when I proved it to him . . . he was afraid of me."

"Afraid of you?" Robin couldn't quite believe what she was hearing. "How could he be afraid of you? You were his wife! The mother of his daughter! He adored you, he——"

But Morgan was shaking her head vehemently. "I'm telling you that you will react in exactly the same way, Robin, and I just can't bring myself to risk doing that to you . . . and to me. Not again."

"Mother, I'm in Starfleet. My life is risk. I can handle it. I swear to you I can."

"You won't understand——"

"I'm not a child, dammit!" Lefler fairly howled in frustration. "Don't you get that? Don't you under-stand that——"

And then Morgan was on her feet, and in a cold and deadly voice, she said, "And don't you understand that I'm not who, or what, you think."

"What are you saying, that you're not my mother?"

"No. No, I am. I have been many things over the decades, but you know, the fact that I'm your mother is probably the thing that I take greatest pride in."

"Over the decades. Mother, what are you talking about?"

Morgan took a deep breath. "I am . . . older than you think."

"Okay, fine," Robin said, throwing up her hands in frustration. "Fine, don't tell me. I don't know why I bothered. I don't—"

But then Morgan grabbed Lefler's arm and spun her around to face her, and there was fire in her eyes. "You wanted the truth, little girl?" she said in a voice so dark, so frightening, that it was barely recognizable as that of her own mother. She was speaking with an odd accent, one that Morgan couldn't even begin to place, although it sounded very faintly like a cross between Scot and British. "You wanted it? Here it is, and you will listen to every damned word. I was born centuries ago, reached maturity, and discovered that I did not age any further . . . and did not, *could not,* die."

"That's . . . that's impossible," said Lefler, trying to pull away. "No one can live that long."

"No human, but not no one. While I was raised on Earth by human parents, I soon realized that I was from somewhere else. I was very adept at creating identities for myself, living in them for a time, then faking my death and moving on. I even joined Starfleet for a time, at first hoping to find my people, then thinking that misadventure would do what the years would not.

"But it didn't work. I have an . . . an aura about me that protects me from mortal harm."

"An aura," said Lefler tonelessly.

Morgan nodded. "I tried a phaser at full disintegration; it didn't harm me. I thought of setting a transporter to disperse my molecules through space, but I'm afraid that, somehow, I'll retain consciousness in a demolecularized form, floating like a ghost—an even more terrifying state than my current one."

"I should think so."

And Morgan—Morgan, who did not lose her temper, Morgan who was the epitome of coolness and control—slid into a white hot fury and faced Lefler, shouting, "Stop it! Stop patronizing me!"

The sound of her voice was like a rifleshot as Lefler went down. A security guard was immediately at the door, prepared to go in and stun Morgan for the purpose of hauling Lefler out, but Robin put up a hand. "Stay where you are!" she shouted. "I'm fine!"

"The hell you are, Ches'. The hell you are, you are light-years away from 'fine,'" retorted Morgan. "Don't you get it? I was tired! Tired of watching loved one after loved one die while I went on and on and on! You would think that after centuries of it I'd get used to it, but no. Every single loss was like a knife to my heart. I couldn't take it anymore. I just wanted to end. And my body wouldn't let me . . . except in ways that would be so high risk that I was terrified to try them for fear that they'd leave me worse off than when I started. I wanted something safe, certain. Don't you get that?"

"I get it, I get it," said Robin. She watched her mother from as far away as she was able to get from her. "You're not human. You've been around forever."

Her immediate anger spent, Morgan sagged down onto the bench. "I wandered the galaxy for a time, slowly despairing," she said, sounding as much as if she were talking to herself as to Robin. "Then I returned home, met your father, and fell in love. And after we married, for the first time I knew enough love that I saw a future for myself. I had you. And as I watched you grow, my love, I realized I couldn't stand to watch you get older . . . grow up. I've lost so many people that I loved, but every day I watched you get older, it was . . . it was more than I could take. So I faked my death earlier than I would normally have and left. I left because I was selfish, and determined to find a way to put an end to my miserable existence. Are you happy that you know, now, Robin? Are you happy?"

"Mother," Robin was shaking her head. "Mother, look, I . . . I know what you said about Dad . . . and how he didn't believe . . . but I . . . This is so much to try and handle. This is . . . It's . . ."

"Preposterous?"

"Yes."

"Absurd?"

"Completely. I think . . . I think maybe you should see someone. There are people who can help you."

"Would you like to see something?" she asked.

"Uhm . . . sure. If you want me to."

"All right. I'm going to show you a trick."

She turned around away from Lefler's view, and there was a sound like a snap. When Morgan turned back, she was holding up a knife. The blade, three inches long but extremely sharp, glinted in the light.

"Mother, what—"

And very quickly, very efficiently, in one smooth move, Morgan held out her right wrist and drew the knife down it. She slid it lengthwise down her forearm, opening up the vein, and blood began to well out, thick and red.

"Oh my God!" shrieked Lefler. Immediately she sent an emergency call to sickbay.

"Don't worry," Morgan said calmly. "I've done it before."

"Mom, oh my God, Mom!" Lefler cried out as she leaped toward her mother, clasping her hands frantically around the fountaining forearm. She tried to apply pressure, to stop the bleeding, but the blood was leaking out between her fingers. "Mom, how could you? How could you?!"

"About five seconds," Morgan said calmly. "Four . . . three . . . two . . . one . . . let go. You can let go."

"I can't let go! You'll bleed to death! You'll—"

With an impatient noise, Morgan pushed her daughter aside. She called to the guard, who was still outside as he awaited backup from the sickbay medics. "Do you have a towel on you? A cloth?"

"A . . . a cloth?"

"Never mind," she said, utterly calm. She lifted up the cushion that they were sitting on and used it to wipe away the blood. "Just send for a new one of these, okay? This stuff stains."

"Where's the medical team!?" Lefler fairly shouted. "Where the hell is the—?"

And then Morgan extended her arm, practically under Lefler's nose. Robin looked down . . . and couldn't believe what she was seeing.

The blood flow had completely stopped. Where there had been a vicious cut only moments ago, there was now simply a thin pink line standing out against the tan of her skin. And even that was already disappearing. Lefler looked in stupefaction as the pink skin of the freshly healed wound changed color and matched the tan of the rest of her arm.

At that moment the medical team came charging

up. They saw the blood collected on the floor and staining the mattress, and they looked around in confusion to find the person who was apparently bleeding in such copious quantities.

"Thank you for coming by, gentlemen," Morgan said calmly, "but I'm afraid it was a bit of a false alarm. I was just showing my daughter here a magic trick—a rather sanguinary one, I'm afraid—and the dear guard here overreacted to what he was seeing. I'm terribly sorry to have wasted your time. Although if you gentlemen would be so kind as to send someone to clean that up"—and she pointed at the blood—"I would be most obliged. Robin," she said, taking Robin by the shoulders, "you look somewhat shaken. Perhaps you'd best go on about your business now. Don't you think that would be wise?"

"Yes," Robin said, clearly still in shock. "Yes, that would be . . . be wise."

The guard shut down the forcefield long enough for Lefler to leave and for a cleaning crew to come in and attend to the mess on the floor. And Lefler put as much distance between herself and the brig that was holding her mother as she possibly could. She paused only briefly to glance over her shoulder, and caught a glimpse of her mother, looking rather serene in her cell as if, all of a sudden, she didn't have a care in the world.

XIII.

THEY'RE HERE. . . . THEY'RE HERE. . . .

Her lover cries the warning to her, and she strokes it for the confrontation that is to come.

"There's no one here."

Calhoun rose from the command chair and walked over to Zak Kebron's tactical station as the world of Ahmista turned beneath them. "What do you mean?"

"I mean preliminary sensor sweeps indicate no humanoid life-forms."

"None?" Calhoun asked incredulously. He turned to Soleta, who was already at work at her science station. "Soleta?"

"Scanning. At this point, confirming Mr. Kebron's analysis. Although the ecosystem is capable of supporting life, and there appears to be some minimal animal life, there are no humanoid organisms."

"It's the wrong planet," Shelby suggested.

"But it's right where Si Cwan said it was," McHenry pointed out from the conn.

"Could there have been some sort of . . . of war? They wiped each other out?" Calhoun said.

"There are no traces of lingering radiation, no burned areas, no pollutants from toxins or germ warfare; none of the usual indicators that a war sufficient for the annihilation of all life upon a world has occurred," said Soleta. "Furthermore, Si Cwan described the populace of this world as being fairly low on the technical scale. They very likely would not possess the type of armament necessary to do away with every man, woman, and child on the planet."

"Well, *grozit*, Lieutenant, where are they, then?"

"Unknown at this time, sir."

"Perhaps they're all hiding somewhere and waiting to pop out so they can say 'Surprise,'" Calhoun said humorlessly. "Soleta, I want you to scan every square foot of that planet if necessary. If there's so much as a campfire burning, I want to know about it. Bridge to Si Cwan."

"Si Cwan here," came back the ambassador's voice quickly.

"Mr. Cwan, kindly join us on the bridge. There's a question or two that could use your attention. Calhoun out." Without missing a beat, he turned to Kebron and said, "Have security escort Morgan Primus up here as well."

Robin Lefler turned at her position at Ops. "My mother?" she asked.

"Unless there's another Morgan Primus on the

ship, Lieutenant, yes. Why, is that a problem for you?"

"No," Robin said quickly, suddenly becoming incredibly engrossed in her instruments. "No, that's no problem for me at all."

Moments later, both Si Cwan and Morgan had emerged from the turbolift onto the bridge. Calhoun noticed that Robin was carefully endeavoring not to meet her mother's gaze. Something had happened between the two of them, something since the time that Robin had appeared to be making inroads with her mother. He knew that there had been some sort of odd incident in the brig. The report he had received had been extremely confused and confusing: An attempted suicide, except that, although there was blood everywhere, there was no sign of any sort of wound on either Lefler or Morgan, who had been the only occupants of the cell at the time. It made absolutely no sense at all. It was just one of a number of matters that needed addressing.

"We have a bit of a curiosity," Calhoun said, circling them. "You, Morgan, told us that the trail of the Prometheans indicated that this world was the place where you might be able to connect with them. I notice that you never told us how, precisely, you knew this. Would you be so kind as to enlighten us now?"

"Comments we heard in our investigations. Writings buried in assorted rare texts. A long process that—" Then she saw the way he was looking at her, and for the first time since he'd met her, Morgan actually seemd less than certain of herself. "Ultimately," she admitted, "what it came down to is that Tarella and I . . . we just . . . knew."

"You just knew."

"Yes."

"That's the best you can do. You just knew."

"It's not impossible, Captain," Soleta commented, never taking her eyes away from her scanner. "Remember my experience with the similar disk. There may be some sort of connection to a greater whole."

"You're saying they're like the Borg, but little disks?" Calhoun said skeptically.

"Well, that's certainly less threatening in any event," said Shelby.

"Ambassador," Calhoun turned to face Si Cwan, "do you have an estimate as to the number of people in residence on Ahmista?"

"I couldn't say for sure, no," Si Cwan replied. "Five . . . maybe six billion, I suppose."

"Would you like to know how many there are now?"

"One."

The reply came from Soleta, which naturally captured the immediate attention of everyone else on the bridge. Calhoun crossed quickly to her station. "You found someone?"

"Took a while longer since the population was so sparse—well, sparse being a generous term, I suppose. I have managed to detect a single humanoid lifeform down there."

"A single one?" Si Cwan asked, sounding appalled. "That's . . . that's absurd! Where is the rest of the population?"

"That," Calhoun said, "is what we're going to try and find out. Commander," he turned to Shelby, "I want an away team composed of yourself, Si Cwan, Lieutenant Soleta, and Mr. Kebron to head down there and see just who or what it is we're dealing with. I want everyone armed on this one, because we have no idea what it is you'll be facing."

"Even me?" asked Si Cwan.

Calhoun paused only a moment, and then he nodded. "Even you." He heard a dissatisfied growl from behind him indicating that Zak Kebron was registering a complaint about his captain's decision. He judiciously chose to ignore it.

"What about me, Captain?" Morgan asked.

"What about you?"

"I brought us to this planet," she said. "If anyone is entitled to go down there and see exactly what's going on, it should be me."

"Perhaps in the way you see matters, yes, but that's not the way I see it," replied Calhoun. "I'm afraid I don't have quite enough confidence in you, Morgan, to send you down there while my people have to be watching their backs. For all I know, they may have to watch their backs where you're concerned as well."

"What about the old saying, Captain? Keep your friends close and your enemies closer."

"I'm not altogether sure we're enemies, Morgan. Still, you raise a valid point. I will keep you here, where I can keep an eye on you."

"That's not what I meant."

"Yes, I know, but it's what we're going to do anyway." He nodded to Shelby. "You have your orders."

The named away team headed for the turbolift and, as they left, Morgan calmly walked to Shelby's chair and, with utter confidence, sat in it. Calhoun eyed her coolly. "I did not say you could sit there," he said.

They stared at each other for a moment.

"Would you care to sit there?" he asked.

"I'd be honored. Thank you for the consideration."

"You're welcome," he replied as he returned to his command chair. And he was unable to help but notice how completely comfortable Morgan looked in the position of second in command.

Burgoyne had never felt quite as frustrated as s/he did at that particular moment.

S/he had been going over file after file, experimenting with dozens of scenarios using the computer to plot out the likely outcome of each one. And not only was s/he unable to find any direct reference to having such a creature firmly ensconced in one's warp core, but every single plan s/he designed for the purpose of getting the damn thing out of the engine ended in there being a likelihood that the ship would wind up being destroyed. It wasn't a consistent likelihood. Sometimes it was as high as ninety-nine percent, but other times it was as low as eighty-three percent. Somehow, though, s/he didn't think that even the low-end odds were going to go over too well.

S/he looked at the warp core and could see the thing pulsing slowly within the clear tube of the core. In what could only be termed a desperate measure, s/he stared at it with a very, very angry glare in hope that Sparky would sense the overt hostility and flee in terror.

Sparky did not appear to notice.

"Burgoyne."

Selar walked up to hir, looking as efficient and removed as ever. "Doctor," Burgoyne said neutrally.

"I thought you might wish to know. I have taken several tests and I am most definitely pregnant. I felt it was not wise to rely solely on my inner instinct for such matters."

"Well, that's . . . that's great, Selar. I'm very happy for you."

"I am . . ." She took a deep breath as if plunging into something. "I am . . . happy for us."

It took a moment for the comment to sink in on Burgoyne, since s/he was still rather distracted by Sparky. But slowly it penetrated, and Burgoyne turned and looked at her with clear surprise on hir face. "I'm not sure which I find more surprising, to be honest," noted Burgoyne. "The part about being happy, or the part about us. I was unaware that there was an 'us.'"

"Do you find that thought attractive? Or do you wish to avoid the prospect of an 'us'?"

"I know that you're not interested in an 'us,'" Burgoyne said, sounding rather defensive.

Selar drew herself up. "Do not presume to speak for me, Burgoyne. You do not even know your own mind. Do not think you know mine."

"Know your mind!" Burgoyne said. "I can't even *find* your mind!"

"Oh, now you insult me. How very typical. How very emotional. I should have expected as much."

"Yes!" said Burgoyne, more loudly than s/he would have liked. When s/he realized that others were taking notice of the increasingly loud discussion, s/he started to pull Selar in the direction of hir office while saying in a low tone, "Yes, you should have expected it, because the rest of the galaxy is populated by people who laugh and cry and get really really angry, unlike Vulcans, who think they have a complete handle on emotions simply because they never use them! I—"

Selar had stopped. She was no longer following him. Instead her legs had become practically anchored to the floor and when Burgoyne tried to pull her along, s/he was completely unsuccessful. "Selar?" s/he said in confusion. "Selar, what're you—"

Selar wasn't hearing hir. Instead all of her attention was focused on the warp core. And inside the clear tubing, the energy being—whatever the hell it was—began to stir.

Slowly, one step at a time, Selar began to approach the warp core. "Where do you think you're going?" demanded Burgoyne. Selar didn't respond. Instead she continued toward the core, as if hypnotically pulled. Suddenly Burgoyne began to feel extremely apprehensive for her. "Selar! Listen to me! Back away from that thing, right n—"

S/he grabbed Selar's arm, and Selar stiffened it and shoved hir back. Burgoyne was strong and agile, there was no denying it, but the abruptness and strength of Selar's gesture caught hir completely off guard. Burgoyne hurtled backward, slamming up against a wall array and sagging to the floor, stunned.

And Selar moved unceasingly toward the warp core, beginning to stretch out her hands as she did so.

The first thing that Shelby heard was singing.

The moment that the sound of the transporter beams faded, the lyrical singing floated through the air. It seemed an aimless tune; whoever was singing it appeared to be making it up as they went. Shelby looked around to see that Si Cwan, Kebron, and Soleta heard it as well.

There was a steady breeze blowing that was carrying the singing to them, and it appeared to be just up ahead. They had materialized on a pathway that led up the side of a small mountain, which gave Soleta a bit of stomach cramps considering that she had more than had her fill of mountains recently. But there was no helping it.

"What is that?" asked Shelby.

Soleta listened a moment more and then said, "Offkey."

"Thank you for your opinion, Lieutenant." She gestured for the others to follow and they slowly made their way up the moutainside.

As they got nearer, however, the aimless song—which had seemed lighthearted at first, almost playful—became darker-sounding. The singer went to a voice that sounded more base and—if Shelby were to judge—more ominous.

They came around a curve in the path and suddenly the music stopped. And so did they.

They weren't quite certain that what they were seeing was real: a woman, so skinny that she seemed, more than anything, like a skeleton wearing a skin suit. She might have been someone released from a labor camp, or who had been tortured for a year behind enemy lines before being returned to her loved ones. She appeared to be human, or at least she had been. Her eyes were sunken, her hair somewhat stringy and unkempt. Her clothes, what there were of them, were in tatters.

And she was wrapped around something that

looked rather daunting, her arms and legs clutching it as a drowning woman would a life preserver.

If Shelby had to guess, she would have said it was a weapon of some kind. It was hard to tell, however. It was cylindrical with what could very easily be a muzzle at one end. It appeared to be at least two yards high, and a foot in diameter.

"Is that . . . a weapon?" Si Cwan asked softly.

"If so, it is a big one," replied Shelby.

The weapon pointed straight up. The woman had stopped singing altogether, but she didn't seem to be completely aware that the away team was approaching her. "Hello," Shelby said in as quiet a voice as she could, for something in the air around her made her feel as if a hushed tone was required. Although she was armed, she made sure to keep her hands clear of her phaser. She didn't want to give the impression that she was hostile. Putting aside that she had no desire to frighten the woman, if that thing was indeed a weapon and the woman suddenly aimed it at her and fired, there would be nothing left of Shelby's upper body with the possible exception of a few fond memories. "I'm Commander Shelby, *U.S.S. Excalibur*. This is Lieutenant Soleta, Lieutenant Kebron, and Ambassador Si Cwan."

Si Cwan bowed slightly. "You're looking fit, madam."

Kebron looked at him incredulously. Si Cwan shrugged at him in a sort of *What did you expect me to say?* manner.

"Would you like to tell us your name?" Shelby said.

The woman said nothing. She merely rocked back and forth, ever so slowly, and she looked into midair and appeared to see nothing.

"Would you . . ." Shelby took a few more tentative steps forward, and didn't seem to get any particular reaction out of her. "Would you like to tell us where everyone else went? In case you didn't notice, this planet is fairly deserted. Was it deserted when you came here?"

And she spoke.

It was a frightening voice, a voice that sounded like the lid to a coffin slowly creaking open. It was difficult to determine just exactly how old or young the woman was, but her voice sounded like the voice of one who had been dead for centuries.

"They wanted to take away my lover," she told them.

"Oh," Shelby said sympathetically. "That's . . . that's too bad. Who would 'they' be?"

"Them." She started to hum once more in that odd tone of hers. "All of them. But my lover, it's strong. It protects me. It protects us."

"May I ask who precisely it protected you from, ma'am?" Soleta inquired. "There doesn't seem to be anyone around."

For the first time, the woman seemed to focus on them. She looked at Soleta and there was something approaching demented amusement in her face.

"Not anymore," she said.

They looked at each other, and it was Si Cwan who said, with as much control as he could muster, "Are you saying that . . . your lover . . . got rid of all the people who wanted to separate the two of you?"

"It protects me. That's why it's a good lover."

"Listen," Si Cwan said. "Madam, you know, this would be easier if we knew your name."

"Should I tell them my name?" She was whispering

to the large cylinder, talking to it as if it were a close friend. "Should I—yes. Yes, you're right, of course. It doesn't matter." She looked at them and said, "I am Tarella."

Immediately the name was familiar to Shelby. That was the name of the friend who had accompanied Morgan on her search for the Prometheans.

"Tarella," said Si Cwan. "Tarella, we have a very complicated situation here. But I am certain that we can work it out in such a manner that—" Then he paused. "Why do you say it doesn't matter if we know what your name is?"

"Because," said Tarella, "we're going to kill you now."

"You had to ask," muttered Kebron.

And he unslung his rifle.

Zak Kebron wasn't a big fan of phasers. He generally preferred to rely on his own strength and bulk. However, the captain had ordered that they go armed, and he had obeyed the captain's instructions. Normal-sized phasers, however, were even more problematic for him than they were for the large and hairy hands of Ensign Janos. He could operate a normal phaser, but it wasn't easy for him. So when he went on away missions, he generally preferred to carry a Type III phaser rifle. It was slung across his back and looked fairly impressive hanging there.

Now the phaser was in his hands, leveled at Tarella, and he thumbed it to a high setting as he warned her, "Do not move or take any threatening physical action."

"You want to take my lover," Tarella said, her voice rising. "You want to take it away. But I won't let you. It's mine. I won't let you take it away."

"Tarella," Shelby said urgently, "there's someone back on our ship that you should really see. It's your friend, Morgan."

The name seemed to have an effect on her. Her body trembled slightly and she clutched the weapon more tightly than before. And from her cracked and dry lips hissed out the words, "Morgan is dead. Don't you say her name."

"But—"

"Don't you say her name!!!"

And the weapon erupted.

"Down!" shouted Kebron, knocking the others back with a wave of his huge arm as he fired off a shot from his phaser rifle. The blast from the phaser rifle struck the energy ball disgorged by the weapon, by the lover, and it roared forward but off its intended flight path, deflected ever so slightly by Kebron's phaser blast.

The energy ball roared through the air. It missed them—but just barely—barreled through a clearing, and struck a mountain range.

And destroyed it.

The mountain range exploded on contact. The main brunt of the hit caused the range to be reduced instantly to ashes, but the rest of it erupted skyward, showering the entire area with pulverized debris. It rained down everywhere, including upon the stunned away team who had taken up refuge some feet away behind a wall of rock. Seeing, a half mile away, the complete demolition of a mountain range with one shot of the weapon that Tarella was clutching was enough to make the away team realize that their temporary shelter was going to shelter them from precisely nothing.

Shelby hit her commbadge so hard she wound up leaving a bruise on her chest. "Away team to transporter room! Get us the hell out of here!"

Then they heard Tarella howl, "I don't want you! I don't want Morgan! And I don't want your ship!" And with that pronouncement, she unleashed the power of the weapon straight up.

The shields came on automatically before Boyajian at tactical realized that they were under attack. The computer also sent the *Excalibur* into immediate red alert. "Captain, incoming!" shouted Boyajian. "Some sort of energy plasma! Readings off the scale!"

"McHenry, evasive maneu—" was all that Calhoun was able to get out as the energy ball smashed into the *Excalibur*. For all the good that the shields did, the ship might as well have been protected by plastic wrap. The energy ball slammed amidships into the vessel, and anyone standing throughout the entire ship was thrown to the ground.

Calhoun had been standing and moving toward the command chair when the ball hit. He was sent flying, crashing into Morgan and tumbling to the ground. Morgan clutched the armrests of her chair desperately and managed to maintain her place, but the impact of the ball was the least of the problems.

McHenry's station nearly exploded as a concussive buildup blasted him back and out of his seat. McHenry smashed his head against the upper rampway and went limp, blood trickling from his mouth. The conn station was in complete disarray, flames starting to shoot out. Overhead extinguishing systems were out of commission, and Morgan desperately grabbed an emergency hand extinguisher in a wall compartment, staggering across the bridge to get to the conn and put the flames out.

The bridge filled with smoke. She tried to make out her daughter and saw that she was slumped forward at the Ops station, a huge swelling already appearing on her temple. She was barely conscious and trying to pull herself together. "All stations, report!" she managed to get out. "This is Ops, report status, all stations!"

The ship lurched, and Morgan managed to snag on to a chair and prevent herself from tumbling over. But then she saw the viewscreen, saw the planet lurching toward them . . . No. No, they were spiraling down toward the planet.

Morgan dropped into place at the conn station, tossing aside the extinguisher, and looked at the distressed readouts. If she was at all thrown by the calamitous nature of what she was facing, she gave no hint of it. As if she'd been doing it all her life, she began rerouting controls, trying to restore helm control so that she could pull the ship out of her dive . . . before it was too late.

Burgoyne, for all hir cat-like reflexes, was nonetheless knocked off hir feet as the ship was hit hard.

And Selar stumbled forward and struck squarely the exterior of the warp core.

And deep within the warp core, the entity residing in there—whatever it was—seemed to move down toward Selar. She clutched the warp core tube as it coalesced within around the area that she was touching.

Burgoyne scrambled to hir feet, stumbled over toward Selar, and tried to pull her away. To hir surprise, s/he had absolutely no success at all. It was as if Selar were suction-cupped to the warp core and under no circumstance was she about to let go.

Her eyes were glazed, and her lips seemed to be trying to form a word, or words, but Burgoyne couldn't make any of them out. All s/he knew was that somehow, in some way, Selar was in direct connection with whatever the hell it was in the warp core. Since Burgoyne didn't know precisely what was going on, s/he wasn't sure if it was safe to try and pull her away.

On the other side of the bridge, Calhoun could barely hear himself over the screech of the red alert bell as well as the sounds of exploding equipment all around the bridge. *This is going to take forever to fix,* he thought bleakly, and then he saw that they were heading for a crash landing. He looked toward the conn . . . and was astounded to see Morgan at the controls. He staggered across the bridge, fighting the rolling motion of the floor beneath him, as he shouted, "What are you doing?!"

She looked at him with a cold, fixed, and utterly calm gaze. "Saving your ass," she informed him, her fingers flying over the controls.

And the *Excalibur* suddenly pulled out of her dive before she fully entered the atmosphere, avoiding any further strain on the shields due to reentry.

"Helm restored," called Morgan as the ship arced upward and away from the looming planet surface. The ship moved slowly back into orbit, having barely withstood the assault and not knowing if another was forthcoming.

"Shield status!"

Lefler was rubbing her forehead, trying to see straight. "Shields at eighty percent and holding, sir. Structural integrity is holding; most of what we experienced was purely impact."

"Meaning that if we didn't have shields at all, we'd have been smashed to bits."

"Yes sir. Captain, transporter room reports a call from the away team to be beamed aboard just before the attack."

"We can't bring them up with our shields up, and we don't dare lower shields. Comm system?"

"Just back on line, sir."

"Calhoun to away team." He brushed some debris from his uniform as he helped McHenry to his feet. McHenry clearly looked confused and there were burn marks on his uniform shirt. Chances were that there were burns on his chest to match. For a long moment, Calhoun was convinced that he wasn't going to hear a word from the planet surface.

But then Shelby's rattled voice came back. "Away team, Shelby here."

"Commander! What's going on down there? Our readings didn't indicate any sort of massive weapons array, but somebody shot at us and damn near took us out!"

"It's a woman, sir. A woman with a gun."

Everyone on the bridge, sitting up bruised and battered and trying to staunch bleeding wherever they could, exchanged looks of utter incredulity. "Did you say *a* woman with *a* gun?"

"That would be correct, sir."

Robin Lefler had seen the captain in a variety of moods and reactions. But she couldn't recall having seen him looking quite as stunned as he did at that moment. "How could one woman with a gun almost knock us out of orbit?!"

There was a pause and then, apparently, because she couldn't think of any other way to explain it, she said, "It's a really big gun, sir."

Calhoun didn't know what to say to that aside from, "Oh." McHenry, for his part, was looking in puzzlement at Morgan, who was at his station. Morgan quickly rose and eased him into his seat.

"Furthermore," Shelby said, "it appears to be in the possession of the woman whom Morgan described as her former associate."

"Tarella?" Morgan called over the comm system.

"That's right."

"Captain," Morgan turned to him, "please let me go down there. I'm the only one who can possibly get through to her."

Calhoun did not like the odds of the situation, but he didn't see a lot of choices. "All right. We're going to have to risk this. Mr. McHenry, bring us back to maximum transporter range. Let's try and put as much distance between ourselves and that . . . big gun . . . as possible. Morgan, get down to the transporter room. We'll drop our deflectors for just the length of time it takes to beam you down there, and then we'll bring the shields back on line. Shelby, what's your read on the situation? Shall we bring you back up when we send Morgan down?"

"Negative," Shelby said after a moment's thought. "From our vantage point, it seems as if Tarella is just sitting there now. It's almost as if she's forgotten that we're here. She seems to fade in and out of reality."

"I can relate to that," McHenry said.

"Captain," Lefler suddenly said. She rose to her feet, slightly unsteady but determined. "I would like to accompany Ms. Primus to the planet . . . if that's all right."

Despite the disarray on the bridge, Calhoun managed to force a smile. "Somehow I had a feeling you were going to say that," he said.

XIV.

MORGAN AND ROBIN SHIMMERED into existence on the planet surface a few feet from the away team, which was still crouched behind the shelter as if it provided them with any protection at all. Shelby gestured for them to approach, which they did as quietly as they could. She immediately noticed the banged up condition of the newcomers, but there was no time to discuss it. "I was so worried she'd open fire on the ship while you were coming down," she whispered.

"Do we have a plan, Commander?" asked Robin.

"Yes. It's called 'not getting killed.'"

"Good plan," said Si Cwan. "Is there anything beyond that?"

Slowly Shelby turned in her crouch to face Morgan. An eternity of time seemed to pass between them.

"You really think you can get through to her?" she asked.

Morgan weighed all the possibilities, all the unknowns, and finally admitted, "I don't know. Not for sure, I don't know. At least I can distract her."

"Good. An honest answer. What did you do up there that caused the captain to trust you down here?"

"I saved the ship," Morgan said evenly.

Shelby turned and looked at Robin, who nodded confirmation. "All right, Morgan. Take it slow, take it careful . . . and take it over there," she said, pointing several feet to the right.

As Shelby had indicated she should, she stepped several feet to the right. She took a deep breath that seemed, for a moment, to be a bit unsteady, and Robin realized that her mother was—at the very least—apprehensive. Looking back over her life, she came to the realization that she had never, ever, seen her mother in any way other than completely composed and confident.

But why? If her mother was truly immortal, as she claimed, what was she so nervous about? Then Morgan cast a glance to her, gave her a quick "thumbs up," and Robin realized why she was reacting that way. Morgan was anxious about Robin's safety. She wasn't concerned about getting out of this herself. She was worried that Robin wouldn't make it.

Robin returned the gesture, and then Morgan slowly pushed herself out into the open.

Very, very tentatively, Morgan approached the woman that she had known, in happier times, as Tarella. It was all she could do to suppress the shock of what she was seeing. Tarella was humming softly to herself in a very sing-song manner, an idle and aimless tune. "Tarella?" Morgan softly called her name.

"What did you say, lover?" Tarella wasn't looking at her at all. Her thoughts seemed to be otherwise occupied, and considering the way she seemed to be moving her body up and down against the weapon that she was clutching to her bosom, it was not hard to guess exactly whom she was addressing.

"Tarella, it's me. It's Morgan. Remember? I'm . . . I'm out. I'm back. I'm here to finish what we started." She waved her hand to try and get Tarella's attention. "Tarella, that is a . . . a very impressive piece of hardware you have there. Want to tell me where you got it?"

Tarella seemed to focus on her, but her eyes were dark and fearsome things, and she held the weapon even tighter. "Morgan."

"Yes. Morgan."

"You're dead." She paused and seemed to be read-justing her position slightly. "My lover," she continued, "says we should kill you."

"If I'm dead, then you can't kill me," Morgan pointed out. "Why waste your lover's bounty on a ghost?"

It was a long shot at best, and not for one moment did Morgan expect her to go for it. To her surprise, though, Tarella seemed to be considering the notion very carefully. "I hadn't thought of that," she said, every other word going up in pitch, making her sound like a small child, or an adult cooing to one.

All the while, Morgan was drawing closer and closer

to Tarella, one very careful step at a time. "Tarella," she said as unflappably as if they were at a cocktail party together, "would you mind introducing me to your lover? Does he . . . it . . . have a name?"

"No name. We don't need names, no we don't, do we?" and she stroked the weapon affectionately. And then in that same bizarre sing-song voice, she said with an undercurrent of danger, "You're going to try and take my lover away from me, aren't you? That's what my lover is telling me. My lover wants to kill you, right here, right now. But I'm holding it back. Me. I'm doing that. Because I miss talking to my old friend, Morgan, even if it's just a ghost of Morgan. That makes my lover jealous. But that's okay, isn't it? It's okay to make your lover jealous every so often. Helps the relationship to stay fresh."

"I've always thought so," Morgan agreed. She almost stepped on a place where the footing wasn't as sure, and she very delicately moved her foot around it so that she would be on more solid ground. She had no desire to slip and possibly startle Tarella out of whatever psychosis-induced stupor she had fallen into.

It was difficult for her to believe that this was the same woman who had been her best friend and partner. An adventurer, a person full of joy and life. Virtually unrecognizable now, drained dry of life and love and spirit by a sick relationship with an engine of destruction that had aspirations to sentience.

It took all that she had to keep the revulsion from her voice as she asked, "Where did you meet your lover? How did you two get together?"

"The Prometheans were here," she said. "You

remember them, right? They were here, just like we thought they'd be. It was as if . . . as if they were waiting for us. For me."

"That sounds like them, all right," agreed Morgan. "Master chess players, master manipulators. It was probably like a Möbius strip. They knew we were searching for them, and arranged for us to find them. Our quest created the quarry."

"That's very clever, Morgan. You always were oh-so-very clever. But not clever enough to get off Momidium, were you?"

"No. No, I wasn't."

"I waited for you. Do you have any idea how long I waited for you?" Her voice was starting to rise, her hands trembling, and Morgan was becoming increasingly concerned that she was about to fire. "Do you have any idea how long?! I've been here for three hundred years!!"

Morgan stared at her, shaking her head. "Tarella, it's only been five. Five years. Not three hundred. Five."

And this announcement seemed to surprise Tarella greatly. She ran her fingers through her stringy hair and said in quiet wonderment, "Only five? Are you sure?"

"Yes."

"My God . . . it . . . it seemed so much longer."

Her thoughts were starting to drift, and Morgan knew it was important to control the direction in which they went. "Tarella, your lover. You didn't tell me . . . how did—"

"The Prometheans gave my lover to me," she said. She laughed at the recollection. "They thought it was just a weapon. Silly Prometheans. A weapon that responds instantly to the thoughts of its lover. Whatever I want, it wants. And whatever it wants, I want. We are one. We are together. We are . . ." For just a moment, her mind seemed to flutter, and as if pulling straws from the past, she said, "The Prometheans said they wanted the Ahmistans to have it. So they could better defend themselves against possible enemies. They gave it to me . . . to give to the Ahmistans. But I realized that it was a mistake. That the Ahmistans couldn't possibly handle it. They weren't ready for this kind of technology. They weren't right for it. And they didn't love it. That's the most important thing." Tears were starting to roll down her face, her voice choking. "I knew that I was the only one who could take care of it, who *should* take care of it. The Ahmistans, they came for it. They wanted my lover. They wanted to take my lover away. I couldn't let them do it. I had to stop them. You see that, don't you, Morgan?"

"Of course," Morgan said firmly, even as her soul recoiled at what she was hearing. "If I were in your position, I'd have done the exact same thing. It had to be that way. You did the right thing."

She was close now to Tarella, so close that she felt as if she could reach out and touch her.

"And my lover wanted to stay with me as well. I was protecting it. I didn't want anyone getting near it. My lover didn't want it either. But you . . . you can stay, Morgan. It upsets my lover, but you can stay. Because you're my friend."

"Yes. Yes, I am. We closed out bars together, and made plans together. Did everything together. You're Tarella Lee; you know that, don't you? Your favorite color is blue, your favorite season on Earth is winter."

She was speaking faster and faster, trying to find the woman within this husk of a being. "You like white wine, but not red. You dress mostly in black. When you laugh, it's not a dainty laugh, but a big horsey bellow from your diaphragm. You remember all that, don't you?"

"I remember Tarella Lee," she said with what sounded like wonderment. "Amazing. I haven't thought of her in so long . . ."

"You look so tired, Tarella. You do."

"I am." Her body sagged against the weapon. It seemed as if it was everything she could do to stay conscious. As if all the strain that she had been through, for who knew how long, was catching up with her all at once. "I am so tired."

"Tell you what: That looks so heavy. Let me hold it while you take a rest—"

The moment she said it, Morgan wished she could call the words back to her. For the merest mention of it pulled Tarella forcefully and fiercely out of her distracted state. She clutched the weapon with redoubled fury and howled, "You want to take it away! You're just like all the others!"

Knowing that she couldn't clear the distance between herself and Tarella before Tarella fired, Morgan backed up, trying to recapture the moment of trust. "No, Tarella, see? You're wrong. I'm way over here now, and I'm not at all trying to—"

But Tarella wasn't buying it as she howled, "You're trying to take it away!" It was a fearsome howl as if torn from her soul, and she started to bring the weapon around.

And suddenly Robin was out from behind the rocks, shouting, waving her arms and calling out,

"No! Don't do it!" Morgan couldn't believe it as Robin interposed herself between Tarella and Morgan, continuing to cry out, "Don't do it!"

Morgan tried furiously to shove her out of the way, but Robin wouldn't go. She clung tightly to her mother as she repeatedly shouted, "Don't do it! You don't want to! Leave her alone! Leave her!"

The shouting and commotion seemed to distract Tarella for a moment as the tormented woman blinked in confusion, trying to comprehend what she was seeing. And there was something . . . something in her eyes, in her face, and for a moment—just a moment—Morgan saw a hint of the woman that she had once known peering at her from within those haunted and sunken eyes.

"Morgan, help me." she whispered.

And it was at that moment that Si Cwan leaped in from the other side. Tarella's attention seemed torn, and by the time she was focused on the assault from the Thallonian, it was too late. He slammed into her from behind, and even though she had been wrapped around the weapon, there was no real strength in her arms or legs. The jolt was enough to send the weapon clattering from her grasp. She started screaming frantically, completely out of control, and she lunged for the weapon, which had fallen to the ground. But Si Cwan scooped her up with one arm, and he couldn't believe how light she was. It was literally as if he were lifting nothing at all.

"Let me go!" she howled. "Let me go! Let me go to my lover, it needs me, it's terrified, can't you feel it? Can't you feel it!?"

Shelby, Kebron, and Soleta were emerging from behind their refuge, and Shelby said briskly, "Kebron, get her secured. Cwan, good work. Morgan, you too."

"Don't touch it! It doesn't want you! It wants me! We are one! We . . . we . . ."

And then, slowly . . . ever so slowly . . . something started to fade from her eyes. Something that she hadn't quite realized was there until it began to dissipate. It was as if a cloud were lifting from her, and in a low and confused voice, she said, "Mor . . . gan . . . ?"

"I'm here, Tarella. I'm right here." Morgan took Tarella's face in her arms, and couldn't believe it. Once Tarella had had the softest skin, but now it felt papery, dehydrated. What in God's name had the thing done to her? "Everything's going to be all right now."

"All the people . . ." Her memories seemed to be flooding back to her. "The people . . . there were people here . . . millions . . . ashes . . . ashes to ashes . . . my God . . . Morgan . . ." She began to quiver. Whether it was from fright, or horror, or self-loathing, Morgan couldn't even begin to tell. "Morgan, what . . . what did I do?"

"You didn't do anything."

Kebron had lifted the weapon carefully, wary of any mind games it might start to play with him. "It seems almost hollow," he said in rare wonderment. "How is that possible?"

Tarella wasn't listening. Not to Kebron, nor to Morgan. Instead she heard something else, something only she could detect. "Do you hear them, Morgan? Do you?"

"I don't hear anything," Morgan said.

"The people . . . the people are screaming. . . . I

can hear their voices," and she started to become completely unraveled, the last throes of a slow descent into what would likely be complete and utter insanity. "Hear their voices calling me, begging me to stop, but it won't let me. . . . I don't want it to, good God in heaven, what have I done, all those people, bodies are ashes, floating on the wind, get it off of me . . ."

Shelby tapped her commbadge. *"Excalibur,* this is Shelby. Prepare to beam us directly to sickbay, we have—"

And in a voice filled with more pain than she had ever thought she could feel—filled with more pain than Morgan had ever heard in all her lifetime—Tarella Lee howled with all her heart and soul, with ever fiber of her being: "I WISH I WERE DEAD! I WANT TO DIE!"

The weapon in Kebron's arms responded, one final time, to the impassioned wish of its lover. It almost leaped out of his grip as it belched out a ball of energy plasma that had, only moments before, leveled a mountain range. This ball was smaller, much smaller, but no less devastating. It streaked across the clearing before anyone could make a move . . . not that it would have done any good.

Tarella saw it coming, knew what was about to happen, and she spread wide her arms, threw her head back, and sobbed with the joy of release. "No!" screamed Morgan, but it was too late, as the ball struck home and blew Tarella to ashes. There was a burst of heat that left them feeling almost crispened and then, seconds later, the last remains of Tarella were lifted up onto the winds of Ahmista and carried away to join the final remains of all her victims.

Kebron immediately upended the gun and shoved

the muzzle down straight into the ground. He sank it in a couple of feet and then nodded approvingly.

There was dead silence as the away team tried to take in what they had just seen, and then Morgan lifted a fist and shouted in fury, "Damn you! Damn you, you all-seeing bastards! You think it's funny, don't you? You think it's so damn funny! You're laughing at us, I know it! Come down here! Come down here so you can laugh at me in person and I can push your teeth into the back of your head!"

"Mother, calm down!" Robin urged her. She faced Morgan, hands on either arm, as if she were trying to brace her. "Calm down, for God's sake!"

"Calm down! Calm down!" She was trembling with rage, unable to control herself, but she looked into Robin's eyes, saw the concern there, then slowly, very slowly, she managed to pull herself together. She nodded, as much for herself as for Robin's benefit, and then drew her daughter to her and embraced her tightly. "Okay," she said softly. "Okay, I'm . . . fine now."

"Commander, take a look at this," came Soleta's voice.

Shelby had just been updating the *Excalibur* as to the status of what was happening on the planet surface. She now said, "Stand by, Captain," and walked over to the fallen weapon, which Soleta was examining closely.

"Look here . . . and here," said Soleta, touching different points on the weapon. Shelby knew at that point that she should have been surprised, but by that point in the state of affairs, virtually nothing was surprising her anymore.

Inset into the side of the weapon was a disk,

identical to the one that Morgan had shown them on the ship. And next to the disk were two shallow holes in the metal, each of them looking as if they were designed to accommodate another disk. Soleta tentatively reached into the shallow holes, examining them by touch. "One of these," she said, "has a sunken flame emblem inside it, as if it's designed to fit into the medallion that Morgan possesses. The other," and she felt inside the next one, "is raised. It will most certainly fit mine." And from a pouch in her belt, she removed the disk that she had found on Zondar.

"You brought it with you?"

"It seemed a logical precaution, Commander."

"Captain," Shelby said, tapping her commbadge once more.

"Calhoun here, standing by."

"Captain, there appear to be receptacles for the disks possessed by Soleta and Morgan, inset into the weapon itself. Shall we insert them?"

"Very well. But I'm keeping the transporter on standby. First sign of danger, we beam you right out of there."

"Roger that," said Shelby.

"Commander," rumbled Kebron, "I suggest you allow me to do it—and all of you stand significantly behind me."

"Kebron," began Shelby, but then she realized the wisdom in the suggestion. She turned to Morgan and indicated that she should hand her medallion over to Kebron, which she did . . . albeit with a look of reluctance.

Kebron took the medallion in one hand and Soleta's disk in the other. They both looked tiny in his huge hands as he crouched down next to the weapon.

The others hung back as Shelby said, via her comm-badge, "Captain, about to insert the disks."

"We're standing by and monitoring for any trace of a power surge that would indicate a trap," Calhoun assured her. "We'll have you out of there within a second of any danger signal."

"I appreciate the repeated assurances, Captain, but frankly I wish you'd stop because you're starting to make me nervous."

She could almost see him smiling at that, even though he was in orbit. "Understood."

"Preparing for insertion," Kebron announced. "Three . . . two . . . one . . ."

He clicked them into place.

Sixty seconds later, all hell broke loose.

XV.

THE MED TEAM, LED BY DR. MAXWELL, looked helplessly at Selar as she clung to the side of the warp core. "Heart, respiration are all remaining within Vulcan norms," he announced as he ran the medical tricorder over her. "Brain wave functions remain stable. Whatever's happening, it's not hurting her."

"You don't know that for sure," Burgoyne said angrily as s/he pulled once more on Selar's hand. It did no good. It was as if she'd been fused to the exterior of the structure. "This is insane! What if she never comes out of it? What are we supposed to do? Work around her?"

When he saw Burgoyne's look, Maxwell said in frustration, "I don't know what to tell you, Chief! The Vulcan mindmeld is something I've only read about, never seen. I could bring in instruments, hook her up to them, and send electricity jolting through her. That might disrupt the telepathic connection, tear her loose, but I don't know for certain if it would and I sure as hell don't know if we should! We need to get Soleta up here; she's the only other Vulcan on the ship, and maybe she can—"

And suddenly alarms started to go off all over the ship.

"Perfect," grated Burgoyne. "Just perfect."

At first the insertion of the disks had no effect at all. Kebron was braced for something, but nothing appeared to happen. Shelby turned to Morgan questioningly and said, "All right, Morgan, you're supposed to be the expert on these beings. These Prometheans, as you call them. You said if anyone could help us with our situation, they could. So now what are we supposed to—"

And suddenly a soft humming began to sound from the weapon. Then it began to build in intensity, vibrations spreading from it in all directions, becoming fiercer with every passing moment. Shelby felt her teeth rattling, and she had no idea what was happening.

That was when the planet dissolved around her in a sparkle of color. The next thing she knew, she and the rest of the away team were standing on the transporter platform of the *Excalibur*.

At the controls was transporter chief Polly Watson. She breathed a sigh of relief and then said, "Transporter room to bridge! I have them, Captain, all in one piece."

Shelby nodded in appreciation at Watson's quick work as she and the rest of the away team descended quickly from the platform and headed up to the bridge as fast as they could.

Boyajian had taken over Soleta's science station while she was on the planet, and when he had called out, "Captain, energy spike! Something's happening down there!" Calhoun had not hesitated a nanosecond.

"Transporter room! Get them out of there, now! Boyajian, keep me apprised!"

"Still building, sir. The exact nature of it is hard to tell. I've never seen wave readings like this, but if I had to guess . . ."

"Yes?"

"Sir, I don't think it's going to explode. I don't think it's a destructive force. Best guess is that it's similar to our subspace transmission waves."

"You mean it's sending out some sort of message?"

"Best guess, yes, sir."

Calhoun frowned. "But who are they calling?"

"Captain!"

Calhoun had a sense for danger. Always had. Almost a sort of sixth sense that tipped him off about dangerous situations moments before they occurred. This time, however, there was no chance at all, for even as he suddenly felt that buzz of alarm, it was too late.

Space was beginning to distort all around them, the stars seeming to stretch as if the ship were suddenly kicking into warp speed . . . except the *Excalibur* hadn't budged from its orbit. A massive corona of roaring power was surrounding them, kilometers off in all directions but completely enveloping them like a gargantuan container. It was every color in the visible spectrum, flaring all around them. It was as if someone had plunged them into an ocean of blue, orange, yellow, every color imaginable.

"McHenry, get us out of here!"

McHenry scanned the area, looking for a path, a course to set, but he shook his head in frustration. "There's nowhere *to* go, sir! It's all around us! It's like we're trapped in the middle of a warp bubble! But its readings are totally different; it's like an alternate version of hyperspace, something that's sideways of us, different physical properties altogether."

"Shields up! Red alert!" Even as the klaxon blared, Calhoun moved quickly to McHenry, leaning over the instrumentation as he said, "What if we pick a direction and simply try to ram our way through?"

"Wouldn't do it, sir. Beyond the fact that it's warping space, I'm not getting any sort of a read on it at all. It could tear us to bits the second we come in contact."

The turbolift opened behind him and the erstwhile away team quickly assumed their positions on the bridge. Shelby stepped in next to Calhoun, who said, "Good to have you back. Any thoughts?"

"We're in trouble," she said tightly.

"On the same wavelength as always, Commander. McHenry, I'm not going to have us sit here and wait for the trap to snap completely. Set course one-five-eight mark four, all ahead full. Shields on maximum."

And McHenry was about to do it when suddenly it all became moot.

"Captain!" called Soleta from her station. "Whatever it is . . . it's dropping out of warp!"

"Where?"

*"Every*where!"

She was right. A vessel unlike any that they had ever known was materializing all around them, shimmering into existence out of the inadvertently named "sideways" of space. It did not seem to have any solid sides, no interior or exterior as was understood by the human mind. The ship was huge beyond their ability even to measure it, much less describe it, with shimmering waves of unearthly power radiating in all directions. It was as if a Dyson sphere were materializing around them, but one made of pure force.

This, then, was a Promethean ship.

Its very existence threatened to blast the *Excalibur* out of existence. Everywhere there were energy waves pounding on them from all directions. There was nowhere for the ship to go, no defense that it could mount. Calhoun had never been so frustrated in all his life. There was no enemy to shoot at, no target to train his phasers on. It was as if space itself had come alive and was attacking them. The *Excalibur* shuddered under the pressure of a universe gone mad.

Never before had anyone seen anything like it. Usually in battle, if a missile struck one of the shields, there was a brief flare of energy as the shield absorbed the impact. Not this time. No, the shields were completely lit up along the entire length and width of the ship, wave upon wave of energy rolling over them, giving off light of such intensity that it was almost blinding. The shields were never designed to deal with that sort of punishment, and the energy levels of the shields dropped faster than Lefler was able to call them out. Within seconds there would be no shields in place at all, and the *Excalibur* would be pulverized, ground into bits only moments thereafter.

And there was nothing, absolutely nothing that Calhoun could do about it.

Selar had lost track of time.

She felt as if she had been floating forever, somewhere in a state of infinite comfort and bliss. She was no longer aware of her surroundings. Instead she felt a warmth, a peace such as she had never truly experienced before and—she suspected—would never know again.

There was something just beyond her, something that seemed in touch with a universe that had once seemed unknowable, mysterious, and even just a little bit frightening. But she was reaching out to it now, as it—in its slowly developing intelligence and sophistication—was reaching out to her.

She was unaware of her own physical presence against the warp core, oblivious to the concern of Burgoyne and the others. All she knew was it, was the beautiful entity that she was seeking out . . .

And then she sensed alarm.

It was too overwhelming for her not to notice. The shouts, the alarms, the fear that radiated throughout the ship, the terror of not knowing what was going to happen, the belief that this was, somehow, *it:* All of it began to pour into her consciousness.

She touched the mind, the spirit, of the entity, reaching to it as it had called to her, and she needed to find a concept that it would understand. And she sought out one of the oldest, simplest, most primal urges that any living being had: the instinct of self-preservation.

"Protect yourself," she whispered as her mind

reached out and repeated, *Protect yourself . . . you must . . . protect yourself. . . .*

And that was when Sparky fought back.

"Complete loss of shields," called Lefler, "in three . . . two . . . one—"

At that precise moment the trembling stopped.

Calhoun looked around, confused, as did Shelby. "Ops, did we lose shields or not?"

"Shields are gone, Captain, but there's—" She turned and looked at Calhoun in total confusion. "There's something else. Some sort of . . . of energy barrier that just came into existence around us."

And then Calhoun saw it. Something was indeed surrounding the *Excalibur,* acting as a barricade against the assault that they had been receiving at the hands of the utterly alien Promethean vessel. For a moment, just the briefest of moments, it reminded Calhoun of the great flame bird that they had encountered during the destruction of Thallon, but this didn't seem to have any shape to it. It was simply a massive shield of fire-like power that had surrounded the ship and was staving off any further assault on the vessel.

"Captain," Soleta said. "I'm getting wave readings off the energy force that has surrounded us. They are identical to the wave readings generated by the creature currently housed in the warp core."

"You mean that . . . *thing* in Engineering is protecting us?" asked Shelby.

"That is correct, yes, sir. And it appears to be holding . . . with very little problem, sir."

"Bridge to Engineering," Calhoun called.

"Engineering, Burgoyne here."

"Burgy! Did you find some way to harness the power of that thing you call Sparky? Because right now it's the only thing between us and annihilation."

"No, sir, it's not me. It's Selar. And we could use Soleta down here, because she's the only one who's got a shot at—"

The rest of what Burgoyne was saying was abruptly overwhelmed by a massive rush of noise. It was almost deafening, staggering everyone on the bridge, like a roar of millions of voices all at once in perfect unison.

Although Calhoun sensed it, Morgan was the first to spot it. A wave of energy beginning to coalesce on the bridge itself, taking shape before their very eyes. It was so intense that it almost demanded that Morgan look away, but she did not. For she sensed what it was she was about to see.

For years—for well over a century—she had sought the Prometheans, for her own purposes. In her time, she had witnessed many strange things, encountered many amazing races. She had seen beings of almost god-like ability. She had encountered races of almost pure thought, races who were infinitely grotesque, races who were so beautiful that to look at them moved one to tears. And in all that time, she had tried to imagine what the Prometheans would look like. These most unknowable, most all-knowing of beings; how would they appear? Would they be great, satanic beings with huge, bat-like wings and evil visages? Monstrous, dark and black, spider-like creatures? Would they be angelic, beings of pure light, with expressions of endless peace and serenity on their faces? No matter how much she tried to envision them, she always suspected that whatever she pictured would be wrong. That the Prometheans would be nothing like what she anticipated.

And as the Prometheans materialized aboard the bridge of the *Excalibur,* as Morgan Primus's long quest finally came to its climax and conclusion, she couldn't help but think of just how right she had been. No matter what it was that she had been expecting . . .

It sure as hell hadn't been this.

XVI.

"Hi. How y'all doing. Glad to be here. Really am."

The Promethean was nearly six feet and looked completely human, a man in his late thirties, early forties at most. He was dressed in a fairly tight suit of purest white, much like a southern sheriff from the 1930s. His stomach was taut and flat, his jaw was squared off, and he had a thick head of blond hair.

He took a step down from where he was standing, smiled at Lefler and touched her cheek. "Hi, little darlin'. You doin' okay?" To Calhoun he said, "My pardon if my accent is a little off. I haven't been to Earth in several hundred years."

"I'm . . . fine, thank you," a stunned Lefler said. For no reason that she could discern, she felt an almost primal urge to scream in ecstasy and faint.

The Promethean nodded in approval, then clapped

his hands together and rubbed them briskly. "So, who's the captain of this fine vessel?" he asked.

Calhoun eyed the newcomer warily. "I'm Captain Mackenzie Calhoun, in command of the *U.S.S. Excalibur.*"

"Fine ship you got here, Mac. Can I call you Mac?"

"Under the circumstances, I think I'd prefer 'Captain,' if you don't mind. Particularly considering that this . . . this vessel of yours"—and he indicated the gargantuan sphere of power that still encompassed them—"damn near destroyed this fine ship."

"We wouldn't have let that happen," the Promethean said confidently. "Just wanted to see how much your ship could take. And who's this?" he asked, facing Shelby.

"Commander Shelby, my first officer."

He took her hand and gently kissed the knuckles. "Charmed, ma'am."

"You're . . . the Prometheans?" she asked.

He smiled dazzlingly. "If that's what you want to call us, that's happily a name we'll answer to, ma'am. Yes. We're the Prometheans."

"I appreciate that," Shelby said in mild confusion. "It's a . . . a pleasure to meet you."

"Thank you," he said suavely.

"You're a Promethean?" Calhoun asked.

"That's us," he said, slapping his chest confidently. "I am them, they are me. We have a sort of all-for-one thing going, know what I mean?"

"May I ask a question?" inquired Shelby.

"Ask me anything you want, ma'am," the Promethean said, his hands spread wide.

"How could you, an advanced race, possibly have

made your technology readily available to people who clearly weren't ready for it?"

"We're the Prometheans, darlin'. We are the bringers of knowledge."

"Your bringing of knowledge destroyed an entire race!"

He raised a scolding finger. "We bring gifts, that's all. What people do with 'em . . . that's their business."

He sauntered through the bridge as he spoke, occasionally shaking hands with crewmembers, patting them on the back. It was as if he was working the room. "We go to various worlds, pick likely subjects, and introduce certain knowledge to the world— whether they're ready for it or not. Sometimes it works out. Sometimes it don't. (Pleased to meet you.) Ultimately, it's up to the people and races we choose. And we lay down puzzles and rewards for some really lucky folks. (Hi, how you doin'?) That's how we wound up here, now. We scattered some of our connector disks throughout this sector of space. Kept waiting for someone to bring 'em together and find where they go. (You havin' a good time? That's nice.) Only took a few hundred years. You folks are improving. Y'really are. We're proud of you. Really proud."

"But that's irresponsible!" protested Calhoun. "If you're truly an advanced race, you would know that! Going around, doing whatever you want, without regard for the rightness or wrongness of your actions in terms of how they impact on others. You need to understand boundaries, to be aware of the result of the things that you do. You can't just interfere whenever you want. You can't . . ."

"Do what *you* do?" asked the Promethean.

Calhoun hesitated, looking to Shelby. She shrugged. Clearly the same thing had been going through her mind. Calhoun turned back to the Promethean and said tersely, "It's not the same thing."

"It never is, Cap'n," said the Promethean. "It never is."

He had nearly completed his circuit of the bridge, and then he stopped as he got to Morgan. He stared at her for a long moment, scratching his sideburns thoughtfully. "Do I know you, ma'am?"

She said nothing. Merely regarded him with amusement, her arms folded.

He snapped his fingers as if in recollection. "Alabama. Nineteen thirty-four. Am I right?"

"Maybe," said Morgan, "but unlike you, I've moved on since then."

He pointed to Morgan but addressed Calhoun as he said, "This is a very special lady. She's been looking for us for a long time now. You take good care of her now, hear?"

And suddenly the *Excalibur* was jolted. Then it began to shudder ever so slightly, and it seemed as if they could almost hear the sound of metal being strained.

The Promethean turned to face Calhoun, and he had a wide smile on his face. His teeth were remarkably white. "So let's see if I understand you a'right, Cap'n. You're saying that we should not interfere. That we shouldn't help others with our advanced abilities. Well, you got a creature down there that could bust your ship here to pieces, and is about to, because he's in the process of getting hisself born. Now I could remove him from your ship, no sweat.

Just another example of the Prometheans taking care of business. Or maybe I should just let him burst out, smash your engines to pieces, blow up your whole ship. Kill everyone on board. All in the interest of noninterference, y'understand. Is that what you're saying I should do?"

"No," Calhoun said tightly. "That's not what I'm saying."

"Then I want you to ask me for my help. No, better," and he grinned widely. There suddenly seemed something very dark and frightening hidden behind the "aw-shucks" attitude he displayed. "Beg me . . . just like the captain of the *Grissom* begged you."

There was dead silence on the bridge.

And then Calhoun said, "Soleta, come with me." He pivoted on his heel and headed for the turbolift, Soleta obediently following behind, leaving the Promethean looking rather surprised at the rest of the bridge.

"Now don't that beat all," he said.

Burgoyne looked up as Calhoun and Soleta approached Selar, who was exactly the same way that she had been earlier. "Captain," s/he said formally, "Energy readings are building to an uncontrollable level. I think it may be time to abandon ship."

"Not yet. Soleta, do you think you can get through to her?"

Soleta studied Selar as if she were looking over a statue. "I believe so, yes."

"Is she in communication with the creature?"

"That would be my best guess, yes."

"Put me in communication with it," Calhoun said.

Soleta looked back at Calhoun and there was no hiding the clear surprise on her face. "Captain?" She was obviously not certain she had understood him properly.

"The two of you, working together . . . let me talk to it."

"We've never done anything like that, sir," Soleta said worriedly.

"Well, we're going to do it now."

Soleta looked from Calhoun back to Selar, clearly trying to figure out exactly how to proceed. Then, with grim determination, she said, "All right. Here, then." She pulled Calhoun over to her. "Clear your mind," she told him.

Calhoun did so. He washed away any thoughts of the imminent danger, any concern over what was about to happen. He allowed himself to descend into a place of calm and serenity, where nothing and no one could hurt him.

Soleta was somewhat impressed by Calhoun's powers of concentration and his mental control. *This might just work after all,* she thought to herself as she placed her fingers against his forehead. As she did this, she put her other hand against Selar's forehead. She let go of herself, of her consciousness and identity, and she whispered, "Our minds are merging."

And Calhoun suddenly felt as if he were falling, floating, and flying, all at the same time.

All of space laid itself bare for him, and he felt peace such as he'd never known, such as he'd never thought possible in his lifetime . . .

There was light and warmth all around him, and at first his impulse was to push away, to protect himself,

261

but he surrendered that impulse, surrendered himself to that which was carrying him down, down and along to whatever it was that was beckoning to him. He was drawn to that very light, and part of his mind cried out a warning of what can happen when the unwary come too close to the light, but he did not care, he knew it was there, he knew that was where he had to go.

He felt alien whisperings in his mind, he felt cold and logic and emotion all wrapped up and bubbling within him, and there was Selar and there was Soleta, and there seemed to be a sort of chatter, the details of which he could not discern, but it didn't matter because he felt Selar guiding him then, pushing him in the direction he wanted to go, felt something pure and perfect and frightened brushing up against him . . .

And he saw it: It was void and without shape, but it *was* nevertheless. It was having a full sense of itself, and it was afraid, so very afraid. For all its power, for all its energy, it recoiled as Calhoun drew nearer.

No time, a voice called to him, and he didn't know if it was Selar's or Soleta's, or Burgoyne's own warning filtering through from some still tenuous link to the real world. All was blackness around him except for the light that the being gave off. *No time, hurry.*

You have to leave, he told it. **You have to leave. You'll destroy us otherwise.**

It couldn't communicate in words. It didn't have the knowledge or understanding yet. It was a premature birth, a confused and disoriented being.

Instead every emotion it was feeling washed over

Calhoun, and he drew in the sense of it and the comprehension of it . . . and he realized that the creature wasn't simply trying to be born, it was resisting its own birth throes, clinging scared and uncertain to the *Excalibur,* seeing her as the last link to its "mother," the great energy being that had deposited it there, almost by accident.

It did not know itself. It did not know its mother. It only knew fear. When it lashed out earlier, it was the actions of a terrified infant.

Feel this, know this . . . and Calhoun fed into the creature images of its parent. The massive flaming bird, glorious and powerful, enveloping all, spanning star systems, hurtling off into the void, truly one of the most amazing things that Calhoun had ever seen.

And it felt pride. Pride and eagerness, and joy at comprehending its own origins. Selar had not been able to project her own visions of the gigantic creature, for her mind had been fairly overwhelmed by the desires and needs of the being within the warp core, but three minds combined as one were able to handle it, to punch through the overwhelming need and give it what it truly did need.

You can leave here, he told it. *You can leave here without hurting us. Your continued presence will destroy us. Leave us now. Leave us in peace and go in search of your mother. Leave us.*

And the creature, emboldened, newly confident, gathered itself. Inspired by the images that it had seen, it drew itself up, up and out . . .

Selar gasped, taken aback, her hands slipping off the warp core. She staggered, her legs giving way, and Burgoyne caught her before she fell. Moments later, Soleta and Calhoun came out of their meld as well,

Calhoun leaning against the core to brace himself, trying to pull himself back to the real world like a waking man trying to toss off the last vestiges of a powerful dream.

The creature coalesced all around the *Excalibur,* all of its being coming together at last, and then it tore loose of the starship, whirling above it, and it screeched in a voice that was heard in the voices of everyone in the ship. It had no wings yet, it had no complete sense of itself beyond the fact that it existed, but that was more than enough. It stretched out its essence, feeling the joy of deep space, feeling the full truth breadth of life.

Then, with a howl and an outraged scream of confusion . . . it vanished.

As did the Promethean ship.

Burgoyne's scans only confirmed what s/he already knew. "It's gone, Captain. Sparky's gone. Away from the engines, away from the ship."

Calhoun had sagged into a chair, still endeavoring to pull himself together. Nearby Selar was breathing deeply as Soleta stood over her, steadying her. "Our shield status?" he asked.

"Shields are gone, sir. At least three solar hours to effect repairs and bring them back up to full power."

"But we're still here," Calhoun said slowly, hauling himself to his feet. "Guess they found out how much our little ship could take."

Suddenly there was, once more, a burst of choral voices and a flash of light. A moment later the Promethean was standing there, looking cool and confident. "Thank you, Captain."

"Thank you for what?" asked Calhoun.

"Why, for our latest acquisition, Cap'n. That creature you had growing in there. Let itself go, let itself get born. And now part of our gestalt being."

"Let it go," Calhoun said angrily. "It's a free being, and deserves its freedom."

"Freedom?" laughed the Promethean. "Cap'n, you just don't get it. It's ours now."

Calhoun felt a deep, burning rage building in him. He'd felt the creature's fear laid bare, felt that—to some degree—it had even trusted him. "I said let it go."

"You got the stones to make me?" challenged the Promethean.

He was still laughing when Calhoun flattened him. His feet went out from under him and the Promethean hit the floor, never having even seen the fist that smashed into his chin. He lay there for a moment, clearly stunned and surprised. "Son, that was not a real bright move," he said slowly, rubbing his chin.

"Let it go," Calhoun said again.

The Promethean did not bother to get up. Instead he sat on the floor, looking up at Calhoun, shaking his head in wonderment. "You got a fire in your belly, son. I like that. I do. The fact that I like it is the only reason you're still breathing. But a fire can burn pretty bad. You took a major chance with me, just for the sake of something, until real recently, you were concerned would destroy you all?"

"It deserves protection. All beings do. Especially those that are alone in the universe."

"Well that all is a real nice sentiment, son. Just bring a tear to m'eye, but now you tell me this and tell me true: Let's say we let it go. Wave our hands and, *poof,* it's gone. And if I told you that, once we release it, it will seek out the nearest heavily populated planet and devour the inhabitants? Make a mighty big snack of 'em. What would you say then? 'Cause I'll tell you right now, that's what it's gonna do. Is that what you want? You get to choose, son. The creature . . . or a planetful of living beings? Decide."

All eyes were on Calhoun and, slowly, the captain realized that he had absolutely no choice in the matter. "All right," he sighed. "Keep it with you. But do it no harm."

"Cap'n! We are an advanced race, son. We don't hurt nobody 'less we have to." He rose, dusted himself off and, in a very offhand manner, added, "Oh, and Cap'n, just so you know. The nearest heavily populated planet is called Tulaan IV. Bunch of fairly nasty folks who call themselves the Redeemers live there. Had you continued to insist I release the creature I would have done it, and it would have blown 'em away for you. As it is, they are going to be coming after you in force before very much longer with the intention of turning you into space dust. Funny how there are no easy answers, huh?"

"Yeah. Funny," Calhoun said with absolutely no trace of amusement.

And with that, the Promethean tossed off a salute . . . and vanished.

"Soleta . . . Selar . . . you okay?" asked Calhoun. He received nods from both of them, although Selar looked a bit more haggard than usual. Then he tapped his commbadge and said, "Calhoun to bridge. Stand down from red alert. All stations at normal status. It would appear that the danger is past."

XVII.

THERE WAS NO WIND BLOWING on the surface of Ahmista. It was almost as if the entire world was waiting for something to happen.

Morgan stood there, contemplating the weapon. Nearby was Robin, and standing close were Kebron and Calhoun. Calhoun had been determined to see this superweapon for himself, and he shook his head in wonderment at something relatively compact, which, nonetheless, had nearly demolished his ship.

Morgan crouched down in front of the barrel, stroking the surface.

"Go ahead, Mother. Do what you have to do," Robin said softly.

Morgan looked up at her, her expression unreadable. "What do you mean?"

"I'm not stupid," Robin told her. "I figured it out. The reason you were seeking out the Prometheans. You wanted a weapon that could put an end to you. That would enable you to die, for certain. And now you've found it. You found what you've been searching for all this time. This has more than just fire power. You heard Tarella. It'll do whatever you want it to do. If you want to die, it'll do it for you. So, go ahead. Bond with it or whatever you have to do, and put an end to it. You know it's what you want."

Her gaze flickered to Calhoun. He nodded. "Robin told me what you are . . . what you want. Who am I to interfere in a quest of this magnitude? If this is your wish we'll honor it."

She looked at the gun then . . . *really* looked at it. Then she looked to her daughter, who was—with effort—keeping her face neutral and determined. Her jaw was proudly set, her dark eyes free of tears.

An eternity of time passed. An eternity almost as long as Morgan's life.

She turned to Kebron and said, "May I borrow your rifle for a moment?"

Kebron looked questioningly at Calhoun, who nodded. He unstrapped his phaser rifle and handed it over to her. She cradled it, feeling its weight, and then with an impressive display of strength she braced it against her shoulder, took aim, and fired.

It took more than a dozen shots, but eventually Morgan succeeded in blasting the weapon into free-floating atoms.

Robin gaped at her, not quite believing what she had seen. And as Morgan handed the rifle back to

Kebron she said, "When Tarella looked like she was going to shoot me, you got in the way. Even though there was no point to it, your instinct was still to try and save me. You were willing to die for me. The least I can do is be willing to live for you."

And Robin trembled, trying to suppress her sobs, but she was only partly successful as she half walked, half ran into her mother's embrace.

"What is with them?" muttered Kebron.

"That's what I like about you, Kebron," Calhoun said. "Your sentimental side."

Shelby let the warmth of the shower flow over her. As she did so, she mused about how things had turned out. They had come upon a tragic situation and made the best of it, but there were no easy or clean answers to this one. Sometimes there just couldn't be any.

At least the one upside to it all was that Mac had had thrown into his face a being who was the incarnation of Mac's philosophies, taken to their logical extremes. The Prometheans followed a sort of anti–Prime Directive, moving capriciously as they saw fit, an entire race governed by what felt right at the moment. And she had a feeling that Mac had seen something of himself in that. Perhaps he had come to some hard realizations about himself. Perhaps, thought Shelby, just perhaps, he was growing up a bit.

A few hours later, in the corridor, Zak Kebron approached her, looking puzzled.

"What's on your mind?" she asked him.

"Commander," he began, "the Promethean mentioned the *Grissom,* and you could have heard a pin drop on the bridge."

"Spit it out," Shelby said, although she had a good idea where the large security chief was going.

"So I was wondering, what happened on the *Grissom?* To the captain, I mean."

"I'm not at liberty to say," Shelby replied.

"And I take it you advise against asking the captain directly?"

"That's not a story the captain is ready to tell."

"And if I asked him about it. . . ."

"You might find yourself guarding the interior of waste extraction for the next six months."

"Thank you, Commander."

"You're welcome. That's what I'm here for."

In sickbay, Mark McHenry was having some of the bruises he'd sustained attended to by Selar. "You are becoming something of a regular customer here, Mr. McHenry," observed Selar.

"Wasn't my intention. Things just keep happening to me. Speaking of things happening . . . congratulations are in order, I hear."

"Thank you, Mr. McHenry. And I . . . ." She cleared her throat. "I must thank you, I believe . . . for your ability to handle with such equanimity the rather odd relationship that has developed between myself and Burgoyne. I am, frankly, not sure if we are together or not together. It is very confusing, and—"

"Doctor," McHenry said confidently, "don't worry about it. Whatever happens, happens, and I'll be fine with it no matter what. There's very little that—"

At that point, Burgoyne entered and seeing McHenry and Selar together, headed over to them. "Burgy," said McHenry, "I was just telling the good doctor here that whatever ends up happening with you two s'fine by me. There's nothing that I can't take in stride."

"Well, that's good to hear, considering I've got some interesting news. Affects both of you, in a way."

"Oh, really? What?" asks McHenry.

"Well, Selar, it appears that your child is going to have a sister or brother."

"What?" She shook her head, not comprehending. "I do not understand, Burgoyne. I am not having twins. And if you are under the impression that we will be making a second child at some point in the future—"

"No, no. Actually, I guess I should have said half-brother or half-sister. You see . . ." Burgoyne cleared hir throat. "I'm a little surprised about this, I'm the first one to admit it. But, well . . . it appears that I'm pregnant. Congratulations, Mark. You're going to be a father."

And Mark McHenry passed out. Slumped right back onto the med table unconscious.

"Well, well. Guess that proves there's some things he can't take in stride," observed Burgoyne.

Selar shook her head scoldingly as she reached for a spray hypo to bring McHenry out of it. "That was not funny, Burgoyne," she said as she prepped the hypo. "Making up something like that just to prove you could get a reaction out of him." Then she stopped, the hypo poised in midair as she said warily, "Burgoyne, you . . . you *were* making that up, were you not?"

Burgoyne smiled cryptically.

**Be here for the next Adventure in the
New Frontier . . .**

**Star Trek® New Frontier
Captain's Table Book Five
ONCE BURNED
The story of Captain Calhoun
on the *U.S.S. Grissom***

By Peter David

Look for STAR TREK Fiction from Pocket Books

Star Trek®: The Original Series

Star Trek: The Next Generation®

Star Trek: Deep Space Nine®

Star Trek®: Voyager™

Flashback • Diane Carey
Mosaic • Jeri Taylor

#1 *Caretaker* • L. A. Graf
#2 *The Escape* • Dean W. Smith & Kristine K. Rusch
#3 *Ragnarok* • Nathan Archer
#4 *Violations* • Susan Wright
#5 *Incident at Arbuk* • John Greggory Betancourt
#6 *The Murdered Sun* • Christie Golden
#7 *Ghost of a Chance* • Mark A. Garland & Charles G. McGraw
#8 *Cybersong* • S. N. Lewitt
#9 *Invasion #4: The Final Fury* • Dafydd ab Hugh
#10 *Bless the Beasts* • Karen Haber
#11 *The Garden* • Melissa Scott
#12 *Chrysalis* • David Niall Wilson
#13 *The Black Shore* • Greg Cox
#14 *Marooned* • Christie Golden
#15 *Echoes* • Dean Wesley Smith & Kristin Kathryn Rusch

Star Trek®: New Frontier

#1 *House of Cards* • Peter David
#2 *Into the Void* • Peter David
#3 *The Two-Front War* • Peter David
#4 *End Game* • Peter David
#5 *Martyr* • Peter David
#6 *Fire on High* • Peter David

Star Trek®: Day of Honor

Book One: Ancient Blood • Diane Carey
Book Two: Armageddon Sky • L. A. Graf
Book Three: Her Klingon Soul • Michael Jan Friedman
Book Four: Treaty's Law • Dean W. Smith & Kristin K. Rusch

New Frontier *Star Trek* Exclusive

Captain Calhoun Action Figure

T he Official *Star Trek Communicator* magazine celebrates the latest addition to the *Star Trek* family with our most exciting offer ever: the never-before-available action figure of Captain Mackenzie Calhoun from the Pocket Books best selling novel series, *Star Trek: New Frontier!* This is the first time that Playmates Toys has created an action figure based upon a character that appears in Pocket Books' best-selling *Star Trek* fiction line. It is now available exclusively through the *Star Trek Communicator* for pre-order ONLY!

Each Captain Calhoun action figure is fully articulated and comes with the sword he used while leading the rebellion on Xenex along with a figure base. Highly detailed right down to his purple eyes and scar on his cheek, this is a must-have for any *Star Trek* collector!

Pre-orders are now being taken for shipping in September 1998. The Captain Calhoun action figure is very limited and may sell out at any time. This figure will not be available anywhere else. Order this unique *Star Trek* collectible before September 30th and receive two dollars off the price of subscription to the Official *Star Trek Communicator* magazine. Join Captain Calhoun and the crew of the *U.S.S. Excalibur* by ordering your exclusive figure today! ☝

ORDER TODAY!

To order with your
Visa/Mastercard call:
1-888-303-1813
Monday thru Friday
6:00 AM to 10:00 PM MST

or send check/money order to:
Captain Calhoun Action Figure
c/o *Star Trek Communicator*
PO Box 111000
Aurora, Colorado 80042 USA

☐ STF20 _____ (quantity)
Captain Calhoun Action Figure(s): $9.00
U.S. each (plus $1.50 shipping charge per
figure)

☐ T117 Special Subscription Price to
the *Star Trek Communicator*: $17.95 (reg-
ularly $19.95) with purchase of action
figure.

TAF

TOTAL ENCLOSED: [   ]